FUSE

THE GRID SERIES BOOK TWO

NICHOLAS TURNER

ISBN: 978-1-7367796-0-6

Cover by Tom Edwards Design

For Ash
Thank you for being a light when the world was becoming so very dark.

CONTENTS

CHAPTER ONE

CROW STUMBLED AS HE TRIED TO STAND UP. HE HAD GROWN gaunt living down in the Deep. He felt malnourished; in need of sunlight that never came while he lived Above.

"Get up," someone said to Crow and grabbed the back of his shirt.

Crow's eyes tried to focus on the man. "Gabriel?"

"Who?" The man looked at Crow and gave him a look of disdain. He started running away from the flames and explosion. The lights were out. The only sense of direction anyone had was in the opposite direction of the heat.

Crow tried to focus and find anyone familiar. He was lost among the maze of buildings and rat-like streets. No one was where they should have been. *Maybe I'm not where I should be. Maria. Lucy. Where are you? Are you okay? Did you feel pain in the end?*

Crow swam in his thoughts and the crowd of people, dragging his feet through both as he followed the crowd through the Slums as they all ran to the Deep. He knew the Capitol wouldn't let any of them in to the UC. Everyone around him would against huddle the massive wall separating the sectors until someone fixed their tumultuous world. *Gabriel. I need to get to Gabriel's.*

People bumped into him as they ran past, brushing against his thin skin and fragile bones. His muscles ached with every step, and his head told him to sit down. The road was filled with bodies, stretching from building to building. They were starting to slow down and get backed up. The onslaught of running turned to an aching crawl and an eventual stop. Crow saw a small gap to his left, which led towards more buildings. He squeezed through.

In front of one of the buildings, he sat down and tilted his head back. *Just close my eyes for a bit. We're not going anywhere anytime soon.*

Crow waited among the chaos, stood up and followed the path Gabriel had told him about to get back to the compound. The second he walked in on the group, Gabriel threw him over his shoulder, and Crow felt the world go dark again.

There was a rumbling, and explosion. The bed shook. Crow wasn't sure if he was dreaming, or Gabriel had started phase two. Either way, he wanted to stay in bed.

Crow felt arms around him. They were familiar. It was part of the routine he had become accustomed to. *Gabriel.* There was a cylinder against his neck. He opened his eyes and everything started to go dark, but this was a different feeling. Tunnel vision was setting in, and Crow could see the people around him watching as someone dragged him into the hallway.

"Take him," a voice said to the air. It was unfamiliar. Crow tried to look around. His consciousness drifted before he could see anyone. Their hands lifted him and he felt nothing after.

Crow woke up in a room filled with nothing. His body took

up more space than was needed. *Maria. Lucy. Where am I?* A metallic taste was in his mouth, and Crow knew he was craving something. *Drugs? Cigarette?* He immediately became annoyed, not by his surroundings, but by his lack of a chemical supply and a dopamine hit.

The floor was cold, much colder than he liked. It was like being back Above with nothing to protect his body. Crow wasn't sure how long he was there, but time passed like a slug crawling across the room. He tried to pass the time as he stared at the walls and ceiling. He waited for anything to happen. *Do push-ups. Jog in place. Jumping jacks.* He tried to close his eyes and sleep, but the ground kept him awake as he managed to shut his eyes for less than a minute. He tossed and turned against the ground, then stood up again.

The metallic taste in his mouth turned to deep breaths, and eventually, sweat, though he was not hot. He stood, paced back and forth, rubbed his fingers through his hair, and did not feel anything but his scalp as he did so. *Where am I? Maria? Lucy? I want to see you.*

Crow looked around the room and did not see a door anywhere. He was in a perfect cube, smooth to every touch as he ran his fingers over the wall trying to find a way out. The ceiling yielding nothing but the translucent white light, like the one he had seen in Gabriel's foyer of clothes. The floor yielded the same result. *Gabriel. He has to be behind this. He brought me here. Who else knows about me? No one. Gabriel. Why the fuck did he do this? Maria. Lucy. I miss you.* The withdrawals were back and Crow wished his intrusive thoughts would disappear.

CHAPTER TWO

GABRIEL HURRIED AWAY FROM THE EXPLOSION. *I'LL NEVER REACH them in time. I need to make it to the streets.* The fire behind him was raging. *Need to get out of this place.* He tucked himself into a chute. His body cramped against the enclosed space. He pressed with his knees, hands, and back. He started his vertical crawl. His muscles screamed in protest as he climbed.

The floor above shifted with a secondary explosion. *How did the Capitol police find us so quickly?* Gabriel popped his head out, looking to see if anyone was around. There was no one to be seen. The streets were empty and he was grateful.

He squeezed his arms out to the street, placed them on the ground, and pulled. His body heaved itself onto the road. Sweat poured, evaporated, and cooled. His body giving him a chill. The manufactured nanites built into the road only exacerbated his feeling as they tried to regulate the new temperature.

I need to get to the UC. I need to find Acacia. They'll all be safe. This wasn't a mistake. This wasn't a mistake. We knew the risks. This wasn't a mistake. Gabriel pushed himself off of the ground, the muscles in his forearms protesting the entirety of the quick, jerky movement. He ran toward the clearing of buildings. The no-man's land between the Deep and the UC.

The distinct crossing line was littered with emptiness as run-down buildings sat watching the entrance wall. The other side contained a life most never had the time or desire to go see. Gabriel thought about it to himself. Anyone could get into the UC if they wanted to. None did. Why go someplace you couldn't stay? See where the other half lived and be the outcast amongst them? Better to live amongst the filth than be shunned by the local populace. *One day that will all change.*

Gabriel pressed through the empty crossing separating the Deep from the wall, the barren desert they had all written about in a time gone. It seemed to stretch on to his left and right as far as the eye could see: miles perhaps, maybe tens of miles. Gabriel saw the buildings fade out of existence on either end of the massive wall, but the road stretched forever on. From his pocket he pulled a small marble, pressed it to a retina scan, and the doors raised up before him. He stepped through, only after making sure he placed the fake eye back in the secret pocket in his pants.

The UC was a fortress. The wall separating this world from the last was tall, and Gabriel wondered why he had never asked Poin the actual dimensions of it. Even from the Furnaces, he could hardly see the top. The skyscrapers here loomed overhead as they were packed tightly together to make the most of the space inside the earth. He felt himself inside a canyon, the sheer multicolored cliffs towering above. *One day this will stretch to everyone.*

Videos played inside Gabriel's mind. Tourists exuberant to be somewhere new to them as they swung their phones on long poles. The videos showed people dodging the new weapons of warfare as their eco-terrorism went according to plan. They got the perfect picture and video of the mountains on either side of them. Another memory popped into Gabriel's head. The buildings around him felt like he was down inside the Grand Canyon. Though he had never seen it, the videos Poin pulled together from forgotten servers showed a landscape Gabriel longed to gaze at. *One day we will all be able to feel that joy again.*

The UC was quiet. Way more quiet than usual for this time of night. He saw no one on the border separating sectors, and no lights were on. Some had been knocked out as he had planned, but most of them should have been lit here. Gabriel wasn't sure what was going on. *Better get to the Hub. Figure things out. Hope they're all there.* He quickened his pace, sticking to the shadows and allowing them to envelope his rippled body. The shirt flowed with his movements like a second skin.

CHAPTER THREE

ACACIA OPENED THE HUB ONLY AFTER TWISTING AND TURNING through the labyrinth Gabriel had created. They weren't far from where they needed to be, but Acacia decided it would be best to reach street level, then loop back. If anyone had seen them take the escape pods, they'd be done for.

Broadcasts were starting to be heard throughout the UC of an explosion at the Furnaces, and to expect intermittent power delays. The report coming over the loudspeakers did not once mention any terrorist attack, only that there was a malfunction which had caused the explosion. *Always. Don't let the public know you're losing power. Flip it to gain power. Always, always, always.*

Jeremiah, Jamal, Bernice, Babyle, and Janet funneled through the newly opened sanctuary. They felt relief as Acacia closed the door behind them, and the perfect seam glazed over so no light could get in or out.

Acacia left the room they had entered, as everyone else began to wander around and make themselves at home while also discovering their new surroundings. Only she and Babyle had been to the Hub before. The next room over was a litany of wires and screens. She turned them on while Babyle showed everyone where they could settle in and get changed.

The screens lit up the darkness of the room. *No need to have lights when these give off so much of it. Gabriel, where are you?* His logical speaking burned into the back of her mind. She waved through the projections which began to surround her, moving them to her side or behind her as she tried to sort through the madness and hysteria of the outside world. In front of her, the old technology showed little to no footage of the Slums, Deep, or Furnaces. It was a blackout of information and the firewalls over the still alive cameras was beyond her scope without Poin's help. She sorted through software and hoped there would be a backup of him somewhere. Gabriel always had a backup. It was only a matter of finding it amongst his secrets.

Acacia's hands trembled and her fingers felt numb as she tapped through the Holos, trying to find any shred of information, and Poin. Without Gabriel, she was in control. *Where are you? Are you still out there? Please don't be caught by them.*

They had all turned off and disposed of their trackers for the sake of saving everyone else if any had been captured or died in their acts. They would replace them after all was said and done. But, now when they needed them the most, they found themselves blind and anxious waiting for the night to turn and everyone to come home. *There's still the problem of Crow to contend with. Gabriel, I don't know how to control this if they start to distrust us. We need to find him, or find out what happened to him. Our fate rests in that truth. I hope he's dead, for all our sakes.*

Babyle walked in on her sweating through her tattered clothes. Her movements felt harsh. He wished there was a simpler life they could all go back to: one where people were able to sit down and read a book. He wished that those in the Slums didn't have to struggle to survive and could enjoy the smaller things in their own lives. He wished people in the UC would stop distracting themselves with technology to satisfy some primal urge or deny themselves their own company. Babyle tapped Acacia on the shoulder.

"Rest now," he said. His honeycomb eyes staring through her.

"You're right. It's a waiting game now. Is everyone else settled, including Jeremiah?"

"Yes."

"You know, one day you can have an actual conversation with me and not just the ones in your head, right?"

"Yes," he smiled.

Acacia laughed and walked out of the room, leaving all of the Holos up in case there was something she missed. She walked and found everyone had dispersed through the Hub, like food coloring swirling through water; they all left behind trails of themselves. Clothes littered the Hub, along with shoes. None of them had consolidated the mess they left and Acacia almost felt a pang of anger, but it was quickly replaced with an understanding that everyone was exhausted. She also was too tired to play mother for everyone. *I'll clean up after them tomorrow. I need to sleep, too. Gabriel, where are you? Are you still out there?*

Babyle walked through the room and thought about typing in override commands to shut down all of the Holos, but he decided against it. He knew Gabriel had set up the Hub to be almost entirely off the grid. There was no reason to shut off the power except to conserve it, which, for now, there was no reason to do. He left the room as the screens buzzed away.

Acacia had already gone to her room by the time Babyle had returned to the main room of the Hub. All around lay clothes and articles of clothing. He walked around picking up shirts, pants, socks, and shoes off of the floor. It felt therapeutic to him to be cleaning and helping around their new home. Babyle smiled as he picked up the clothes and transferred them to the trash. Inside they would be lit on fire, and reduced to nothing more than dull ash. It was a preventative measure, one he wasn't entirely sure was necessary, but Gabriel had insisted that anything from their old home be destroyed should they ever have to move. He depressed a button on the wall and heard the hissing of flames as the clothes sizzled into oblivion behind the metal door on the wall.

Babyle crossed back to the main room and lay on the couch. It was directly from the UC and not nearly as worn or comfortable as he would have liked. The faux-leather smelled of chemicals and sickness. He despised it. It was over-manufactured and under-loved. He stared at the ceiling and let his mind wander.

All of the comforts of the Hub were wonderful, but there was a nagging hurt in his chest over the rampant use of technology below the earth. Babyle felt envious of the new group of people who had come from Above. How they had gone back to a simpler time, however unwanted, and lived on the boundaries of life and death. The thrill of it enticed him—to be the master of his own fate, not just the simple man living in the GUC who struggled with the world around him. He wondered if his libraries were safe, or, if they too had been found and lost amongst the chaos of the last day. *Hope not.*

The world had suddenly grown larger: a grotesque mass of cancer reproducing cells faster than they thought they could handle. The ailments were contained days ago, but ever since Gabriel had moved along with his plans, the sickness spread quickly. *Now they were fighting to survive,* Babyle thought to himself. Were they even safe in the Hub? Or, would the cancer soon arrive and destroy this home for them as well? He hoped that they would have some time before the aristocrats came knocking.

CHAPTER FOUR

A DOOR OPENED TO CROW'S LEFT. THE LIGHT OF THE ROOM dispersed out, allowing darkness and shadow to creep in over the perfect white floor. A man walked in wearing all black, like a suit, but he was not cleanly pressed. His jacket had no buttons, and it hung loosely against his frame. The shoes he wore were so dark that Crow wasn't sure they were real. It was like looking up in the night sky and not being able to see anything and recognize there was blackness there; a few nights Above had been like that, complete darkness—the vacuum of the void. The man was tall, skinny, and Crow wasn't sure if his frame was well built, or if the clothes he wore were purposefully too big for him.

"Good evening," the man's voice was high and delicate. His face angular and eyes sunken. "I'd address you properly, but I do not know your name, and that is why I have been assigned your case."

Crow didn't speak, hoping that the silence would be his

savior, and that somewhere, somehow, Gabriel was working to get to him—to be the savior Crow believed him to be.

"I assure you, not answering my questions will only make your stay more miserable than it has already been. My employer would like to know who you are, and I've been authorized to use any tactic to get that information from you. Now, you're already suffering from withdrawal, that's apparent. I can make that stop, but I need your full cooperation. Or, I can leave you here, and wait until your skin crawls and you start to pull your hair out."

Crow eyed the man up and down. He carried nothing in his hands. The metallic flavor was back in his mouth, and he wanted to speak and address him. Every fiber of him wanted another fix, another hit, another escape from his life. *Maria. Lucy. Are you okay where you are? I miss you.*

The silence swallowed them whole, like the mouth of the old monsters, they were ingested as the murk surrounded them and the only thing left for company was their own breath. Crow felt his heart in his chest pounding so hard his hands shook with every beat. The man left, and all that was left were white floors and a white room filled with light.

CHAPTER FIVE

Jeremiah waited in silence, basking in the relaxation of not having to struggle through Gabriel's grand design. He knew that there was a reason for all of the strife and struggle, but wasn't sure to what ends Gabriel was pulling the strings. *What if we fail? What if Gabriel isn't holding all of the cards?*

Everything rode on Gabriel. And now with Crow missing, there was another player on the board who could utterly destroy what they had. *At least he doesn't know where the Hub is. The pods would have taken him there, but those have even been destroyed. There was a silver lining,* Jeremiah thought to himself.

He stepped into his room, found it spartan compared to how he had decorated his last one, and felt homesick for. The necessities were there, a bed, small table, and a room to clean himself, but there was little else. The same dark metal colors ran throughout and he missed the neons he had put up. Overhead, the ceiling was the same lightbox Gabriel had been fond of. *Maybe this is his original house. It's decorated entirely for him, or*

*by him, maybe both. Maybe he hadn't planned on anyone coming here
to his Hub.*

Jeremiah crossed to the barrier to his bed, and laid down in
it. Sleep came faster than he had expected, like a sweet and
swift blackout. He closed his eyes and entered into the realm of
non-consciousness, a place where he could remember all of his
dreams, but not recognize his own body as he moved
throughout that world.

Jeremiah wandered through the UC. It felt familiar to him,
yet he had never been there. Among the skyscrapers and streets
people walked with intent, unlike the mindless wandering of
the Deep. Vendors sprouted from every building. They felt
familiar, but they were dressed with class instead of rags and
sloughing skin. Their bodies portly, necks corpulent, and hands
red from jewelry too tight at the wrist made it so they could no
longer take it off.

"You, come on in. We have a new one from the Slums. He
needs an ass-kicking. Only seven hundred creds."

Jeremiah's mind swirled. *Who'd they pay off for that?* Even the
Deep didn't have assault on the list of events you could
partake in.

"Sir, you look like you need to beat off of steam, or on someone, if you know what I mean," the man raised his arms to lead
Jeremiah in to a red-lit room. He was reminded of the explosion in the Deep and the dead latex prostitute whose company
he enjoyed for a few minutes. Jeremiah blinked and found
himself someplace else amongst his dreamworld.

The smell of the Deep, and the heat of the Slums mixed
together in an atrocious mess of humidity, sweat, and sex.
Beneath his old torn shoes, he felt the crunch of glass. Old blood
pooled on the ground, and the smell of it wafted to his nostrils.

It was familiar from the time he spent as a Detective. Old copper coins which left a scent on your hands if you touched them. The smell drifted to his mouth and became palatable.

Jeremiah stood staring at the couch he had once sat on. A small doorway in an otherwise black abyss. He could see everything. There was a presence there, a drawn outline of a figure which no details shaded in. They were familiar. Jeremiah looked next to him and could only see the dark outline, no matter which way he turned to catch the light. It was reminiscent of Gabriel. Gabriel. *Gabriel.*

Jeremiah woke in a panic, the anxiety of the dream world and the synapse connections startled him awake. The gray static of his brain covered his dreams quickly. He placed his head in his hands and rubbed his temples, trying to remember what he had just learned. *Think. Think. Think.* He knew there was an importance in his discovery, or his dream, whichever it was—if it was anything at all. The static droned on and tried to disappear into another forgotten memory only to be remembered at the worst time. *Where's Gabriel? Gabriel. Gabriel. That's it!*

The door to his room was closed, but he didn't lock it from the inside as he used to do. A safety measure from a past life, if only to buy him more time to formulate a plan. He opened the door to the extensive linear hallway. Doors lined it, sprouting like leaves from a stem to new rooms where life could continue in some other fashion than his own. Jeremiah walked to find Acacia, or Babyle, whoever he could find first and talk to.

Babyle was laying on the couch in the main room, his hands behind his head, his eyes piercing toward the gray sky.

"Gabriel blew up the brothel," he said aloud, letting the secret out into the universe like a deep breath and a burdening weight.

Babyle did not sit up. His eyes only wandered over to Jeremiah, who had stepped into the room and around to get a better view of him on the couch.

"Don't you have anything to say? Ask? Any input? Like you've known all along that he blew that place up and killed those people," the last more of an accusation than a question.

Babyle's answer was a perfunctory, "no."

"I don't understand why this seems of no interest to you."

"Because it doesn't have to do with him," Gabriel's voice rang out.

Jeremiah turned to see him in the doorway. Unsure how to proceed, he let the silence fill the air. It was a tension, at least to Jeremiah. *What do I say? Do I accuse him of this? Do I pose the evidence? Do I let him answer?*

"I did it. I killed them all. I'm sure you'd understand in the end, but I'm not so sure you'd understand now."

"How could you kill people who have nothing to do with what you're doing?" Jeremiah was fuming, ready to burst through his own skin to take out Gabriel.

"I'm sure you wouldn't understand most things or reasonable answers I'd give you."

"Try me."

"Jeremiah, do you know that the life we lead isn't the life we should be? There remains a power hold down here, and I'm working to disrupt that. Me. Alone. I am working to make life slightly better for all, even if it remains miniscule. And for that to happen, there needs to be sacrifices from everyone."

"How can you decide that morally? Who dies, lives, and sacrifices?"

"That's the cop in you talking, Detective. As I'm sure you recognize, how can you play judge and jury in your past? Who checked you? Your superiors? Or was it those who controlled your superiors? Who controlled and checked when Mason Davis died and pinned it on you?"

Jeremiah furrowed his brow, "how do you know about him?"

"I executed that explosion in the Brothel for a reason, Jeremiah. You've been on my list of assets for quite some time. Mr. Davis was also on my list, but for different reasons. It was unfortunate he died before I could get to him. I think that may have been why he died so abruptly—my interest in him. Poin was interfering with your systems shortly before, and another AI had caught wind of it. I still do not know who executed him. My next move was to get you, and once you moved backed into play, I made sure to cross your path any way I could."

"You're telling me that you planned all of this? Even us meeting?"

"Of course. I need assets and you took my lure. I know you well, Jeremiah, as I know everyone here well."

Jeremiah crossed the room and in a swell of anger and emotion tried to punch Gabriel. Gabriel parried his fist, wrapped Jeremiah's arm around him and pushed him away.

"I know coercion feels terrible, but I've only dragged you in out of benevolence."

"It seems like you dragged me in out of necessity."

Gabriel smiled. "Now you understand my reasoning."

"Fuck you."

CHAPTER SIX

THE DOOR OPENED TO CROW'S WELL-LIT ROOM. THE MAN WITH
the angular face walked in again.

"Are you ready to speak?"

Crow didn't answer.

"I'm going to ask you one more time before I let someone
else in here to deal with you. What is your name?"

"Lew, just let me in there and I'll take care of this. Don't
bother with his game," a voice called from behind the man.

Crow tried to peer around him, interested by the overly
average voice. It reminded him of someone who had spoken on
the streets of New York City as they argued with someone over
the phone, all while running and bumping into everyone
around them.

"Oh, he's interested," Lew drew out each word as he spoke.

"I only want to know where I am."

"I would like my questions answered, too. What is your
name?"

"If you ask him again, I'm pushing you out of the way and

throwing a Seal on this room," the man behind Lew grew increasingly agitated. Lew pinched the skin at the bridge of his nose.

Maria. Lucy. I'm sorry. "My name is Crow," he said assuming the persona his wife had given him.

"What do you know, the junkie has a name," the voice behind Lew drifted into the light.

The pause in the air stagnated for less than three seconds. "I do not have a 'Crow' in any of our databases. Your face also does not acquire any information for me. I need to dwell on this information. Thank you, Crow," Lew said as he reached in his pocket, bent down and placed a small vial on the floor. He walked out of the room.

"Who's named after an extinct bird?" Crow heard him say to the other man as the door closed behind them.

The small cylinder lay on the floor. The liquid inside the silver was familiar. The same pungent blue. Viscous. Crow had tasted it once. The flavor wasn't desirable, but it had the same effect. He crossed to pick it up. His mouth salivated with coins, and his skin became taut. *Just put it there. Let it drift away.*

The cylinder felt clean in his hand. It was an extension of himself, something he desired that was always a part of him. He pressed it to his arm, thumbing the small button. The blue liquid spread through his body. The concoction felt like ice as it erupted under his skin. Each breath was drinking water after chewing mint gum. His heart felt like it had been dropped in an ice bath. His brain clear as the darks of his eyes dilated.

Crow leaned back, finding no wall behind him. The floor made an excellent wall, he thought, as he let his body drift further back and he gazed at the white drop box. His brain took him to another planet as the addictive hallucinogen took effect. All around lay red desert sand and a barren sky filled only with a black sun, surrounded by scarlet flames. The air was cool, and sand dragged on around Crow forever. For hundreds—maybe thousands of miles—he could see; his mind and eyes able to cross vast distances of dried ocean.

His feet dragged him on as he projected himself further on, watching as his boots left marks in the sand like that of a snake. He watched himself walk through the lone waste of the Forever Sand. A conscious body without his consciousness. The sun above him took up most of the sky, leaving only burnt oranges in the atmosphere. Wherever he was, he thought it beautiful. Bliss, a life without suffering—only true beauty amongst the loneliness. Still, he didn't feel alone on this world. The presence of Maria and Lucy surrounded him. He never saw them here, but they felt close, like he was walking in front of them, and the tracks he made were for their footprints to follow.

Crow drifted across the warm numbness of his new world. In the distance, and only after his legs tired, did he think he saw the shells of buildings along the alien landscape. They were built up, full of life and grandeur. He ran towards it. And it was always the same. He knew his high was ending. He would never make it to the city. Something in his high didn't allow his consciousness to project that far. A black spot in his awareness. He could go around it, above it, but never to it. And then he woke up.

The white light overhead caused spots in his vision. He rolled over, crossed his arms, and closed his eyes, trying to get back to his haven.

"You're back," Crow heard Lew speak. He looked around and didn't see the man standing in the doorway where he had usually been.

"Over here."

Crow turned to see Lew sitting in a chair, one leg crossed

over the other at the knee. He was leaning back, his arms on the black armrests. The chair was the same black as the clothes he wore. He was a floating head with hands.

"Crow, do you have another alias you go by? I found no record of that name."

"James Sutherland."

"Thank you," Lew reached in his pocket and placed another capsule on the floor. He rolled it over to Crow.

"You won't find anything," Crow said as Lew stood up to leave the room.

He raised his eyebrows and tilted his head. "Why is that, James?"

Maria. Lucy. I'm sorry. "I'm not from here," he said as he pressed the button and let his mind go somewhere else.

"He's a fucker for doing that, Lew," the gruff voice of his colleague erupted. "What do you want to do with him?"

"Leave him for now. We'll come back after he has suffered from withdrawal for a bit. Think of it as his punishment."

"That's a shit punishment."

"He won't feel anything you do to him, anyway," Lew left the room and pressed his wrist to the wall. The door sealed behind him.

CHAPTER SEVEN

EVERYONE GAVE GABRIEL AN AUDIENCE. THEY SAT AROUND HIM in an arch. Janet, Jamal, and Bernice on the floor, Acacia and Babyle on the couch, and Jeremiah standing behind them. The room was an amphitheater and Gabriel was the main show. He could do magic, slaughter thousands, or monologue for them and they would watch on in amazement and terror; their eyes would never close or drift away from the show.

"I have tried to piece back together Poin's neural net, but most of it was destroyed during the confusion."

"No good," Babyle said.

"Can't you just get another AI?" Janet asked.

"Sure, but then I would have to start from scratch and find where the loyalties of that Intelligence lie."

"I don't understand."

"They exist as we do—consciously," he said. "They make their own decisions indifferent to my will or whim. They aren't pets, despite what society told you Above."

Janet fell silent, feeling like she was being called out for not understanding. *Dickhead. Could have explained it easier.*

"Do we know our next move or where we go from here, Gabriel?" Acacia's voice was saccharine amongst the crowd.

"We have options, and the Hub is to play a big part of it for now. I'm weighing decisions and trying to predict the future along the streams of choice and consequence."

"What does that even mean?" Jeremiah called out.

"It means there exist problems along every decision which we have to contend with, or rather, I have to contend with."

"Like what?" Janet cut back in, as she sat with her legs crossed.

"Your Crow for one," Gabriel replied.

"Do you know where he is?"

"His name has been searched in the Databases of Populace—both his real and fake."

"And?" Janet tried to get more information out of Gabriel as quickly as she could.

"Someone has him, and I don't think that someone knows who he is or where he is from."

"That's good then," Janet stated, with a hint of confusion in her voice.

"Hardly. He's a liability, and sooner rather than later there will be an AI who delivers that information to someone unless he hands it over to them."

"He'd never do that," Janet said.

"Of course, he would," Gabriel glared.

"How can you say and believe that?"

"He's an addict, experimenting with everything down here. They're going to withhold drugs until he can't function, then offer them as a way to ease the process of coming off. He'll give answers to them."

"That's your fault for letting him start using them in the first place."

"Maybe I am partly to blame for not being stricter with my *guests*," he emphasized, "but I try to be as egalitarian as possible. I could keep you all here under lock and key all day, or send you back to where you came from. Neither of those options seem preferable by the new looks on everyone's faces."

"If you intervened with him sooner, he wouldn't have gone down that path. *You* drugged him countless times."

"That's weak at best. The drugs I gave him were non-addictive and used to put him out so he would stop making rash decisions. Clearly that didn't work. He continued to make his own decisions and has to take responsibility for his own actions. Now we are all at risk because of them."

"I don't agree with what you're saying."

"You having a different opinion and not agreeing with facts does not make you right—it makes you ignorant," Gabriel said.

"You're as much of a dick as James is," Janet said firmly, drawing the conversation to an end.

"What else?" Babyle asked disrupting the minor emotional blip that had just occurred during an important discussion.

"Power remains out in a majority of the Deep, and all of the Slums. Without Poin fully operational, I do not know why some buildings lost power in the UC."

"Why did you put so much of this into Poin?" Bernice asked after sitting in silence for the entirety of the conversation.

"You can't outsmart AI without AI," Gabriel's deliverance was succinct. "Is there anything else I need to address?"

Janet watched him look to the back and locked eyes with Jeremiah. His gaze did not go unnoticed as Jeremiah stood with his arms folded. Jeremiah shrugged.

"If there's anything else I can help any of you with, I'll be at the Holoscreens trying to piece together any information I can." With his final statement, Gabriel stepped away and let everyone talk amongst themselves.

Let them build camaraderie. Talk to each other and think of me as the bad guy, the boss, the one they don't want to be close to. In that, they will develop bonds. Necessary. Poignant. Lonely.

He sat in his chair and pulled up screens to swipe through. The code scrolled and wheeled in front of him as his eyes dug through the information. He looked for anything that would be helpful, anything to give someone away or to use in the future.

"I know why you did that," Acacia said.

"You always were the most aware of the people around you, even myself."

"You know, you don't have to set yourself apart from them, and us. We can all work together."

"I'm sure that would work. I'm not sure I am capable of that level of friendship. I'm not sure I am full of that emotional stability for common connection."

"You limit yourself by thinking that way."

"It's easier to stay at length. Easier to be the one needed rather than the one who needs."

"I suppose. It'll take its toll eventually, and you know that."

"I know," he said without turning around to face her. He kept his eyes on the screens and worked while they replied back and forth.

"I'm always here to talk if you need it, Gabe."

"I appreciate it, always." He was sincere, but his tone struck her. He would never open up as everyone else would, and she knew the cold truth of that.

CHAPTER EIGHT

NEW YORK, SPRING 2019

JAMES SAT AND TOOK A BREAK FROM THE BOOK HE WAS READING by the Hudson. The wind drifted through his hair and curled the pages of his book as he tried to reposition himself to catch the light correctly to get the perfect photo for social media.

"Daddy, what are you doing spinning around like that?" A small innocent voice swept through the air, pressing itself into James's ears.

"Oh, nothing important, Lucy. Just trying to get the right lighting for a picture," he said as he turned to look at his daughter in her white sundress with purple lilies on it.

"Why?"

"For people online to see."

"That's silly."

"Why do you say that?"

"Who wants to see a picture of us when they can just come and visit?"

James smirked, "I suppose you're right."

He stood up and walked over to his daughter. "Hold this," he said as he handed her the book.

She grabbed it and he picked her up.

"Where's your mother?" He looked around not seeing where Maria had gone.

"To the potty."

"Always to the bathroom with her, huh?" He kissed Lucy on the cheek and walked through the park toward the brown-roofed building, the walls made of gray cinderblocks. Men who worked through heat waves and cold had put it together, then gone home to be alcoholics and yell at their families about how disappointed they were in everything. James thought of all the ways people hated their families and how their good intentions were always laced with fire and a forked tongue.

James watched as Maria came out of the bathroom. The sun-bleach gave her dark hair a gold tint.

"Are you ready to go now?" She asked, walking over to James.

"Yeah, how was the train ride?"

"Same as usual, people on the quiet car trying to police each other. I don't think they realize when you start yelling at people to turn their headphones down, that they are in fact the ones not being quiet."

"The great hypocrisy."

Maria laughed. She held out her arms and tried to hold Lucy.

"No. I stay with Daddy, you hold this." She handed her mother the book James had been reading.

"Really, babe? A wilderness survival guide?"

"You said you wanted to go to Washington. I just want to be prepared for it."

"We're going to be staying in hotels for two weeks."

"What if something happens while we're out hiking?"

"I'm sure we'll be fine. We're not doing anything crazy."

"You're right."

"I know," she threw her hip into his and laid her arm to rest on his waist. James wrapped his free arm around her shoulder. They walked to the car which was parked next to the train tracks.

"Good morning," Lew's voice woke up Crow.

Crow didn't reply, only lay on his back with his eyes to the ceiling. He felt pools of emotion welling in his eyes and a need to scream at God.

"I hope your dreams were pleasant. My boss has informed me that you are to be transferred today."

"Where?"

"I do not know. That fills me with misfortune. I was hoping to be the one to figure you out."

"Am I going to die?"

"Eventually, as we all come to that end. But I'm sure you figured that out by now. I know you're running from something, James. Your disposition towards drugs has not gone unnoticed by me."

"I want to go home," he said like a defeated child.

"And where is home for you?"

"New York," Crow sat up and watched Lew.

Lew squinted and let his eyes drift the floor beside Crow. He went to speak multiple times, but each time he opened his mouth, a new question arose in his brain, which made him close it once more.

"I do not understand."

"I'm from Above."

Crow knew the puzzle and mystery of the missing piece felt like it was within Lew's grasp. He watched Lew scratch his hairline where it met his forehead, place his left hand in his right, and crack his fingers by crossing them and pulling. *His mind is racing, and he can't focus on what I'm telling him. He knows it's important, though. Can he believe* **me**? *An addict?*

"Please, wait here, James." Lew stood up and crossed to the door and disappeared. He left it open.

Crow sat up. *Run? Go through that door and run? Maria. Lucy. What do I do?* He placed his hand on the ground and felt the strength of wanting to get up and race toward the door enter his hand and calves. Lew walked back in.

"James, please come with me," Lew said as he opened his arm to the room.

Crow stood up and walked over, feeling the strength he just had leave his body. He dragged his feet and slid like a child about to be chastised.

"We're leaving."

"What do you mean 'we?'"

"I mean, I'm committing treason against the GUC. And when I am caught, I'll be tried for malfeasance amongst other crimes."

"I don't understand," Crow looked puzzled as he stepped out of the white room. The corridor was a pale blue, like an old community house at the local swimming pool from his childhood in the '80s. Boys and girls would run up and down the hallway, and lifeguards no older than nineteen would try policing children like war criminals, though they had no power to actually punish them except through the use of a loud whistle. It was a tool not nearly as good as music torture. The sound of wet feet plopping on the ground and raucous laughter were highlights of mid-July.

"You are the pinnacle of my career. The ultimate atrocity I have committed. No twist nor turn has reached a steady conclusion."

"What's your worst crime?" He looked at Lew, trying to decipher if this man was helping him or hurting him.

"Curiosity, James. I am curious, and I let the guidance and lust for knowledge and discovery govern my existence—as all men should. It only leads to pain and the need for the next quest. One day there will no longer be any grandiose unknowable. That is when the soul dies. You are the gold dot in the gray static that my life has become."

CHAPTER NINE

Babyle left the Hub—the compound that everyone had confined themselves to. He felt the need to disappear into the thrall of life, wherever it may be and whatever shape it had recently taken. The streets of the UC contained life of the well-off populace, and the way they carried themselves was not lost on Babyle. Men and women wore layers of clothes, faux-leather, or maybe it was real leather cut from some animal grown in a lab and sold as sustenance for the wealthy. He wasn't sure, but the creds spent on their fashion were clearly noticeable.

Babyle wondered what most of them did for a living. Some may have been in the police force, similar to Jeremiah, others may have been politicians, but the rest seemed to simply exist in this state of luxury beneath the towering Capitol of the GUC. They lived harmoniously with themselves, separate and distinct from the Deep and the Slums. *Maybe scientists? Maybe construction? Maybe sex rings? Conglomerates of the commodities leading the Deep?*

There were questions he realized were never truly answered. And asking someone what they did was taboo. There would be too much attention brought to him. It all seemed too unnecessary. *Ask Poin when he's back. Yes.*

Babyle walked through the labyrinthian streets. A precise ballet of movements countered by the erratic movements of those around him. He cut between crowds and people pushing their way through to hurry and wait wherever they were meant to be. *Don't miss this,* he thought to himself.

Babyle walked into a lounge. He kept his head down and never looked up, trained from all the mistakes they had made before. At the front of the lounge, a large wall covered in buttons waited for him like an eager bartender. Babyle waved his implant over a small pad and stole someone's hard earned creds. *Sorry.* He depressed buttons and waited less than 10 seconds. His drink appeared.

For some, those 10 seconds may have been agonizing. Too excruciating to continue on with life. They'd build up—fume—ready to kill someone or themselves for their own restiveness. It was common causality among the well-to-do. The need for whatever they needed to be ready before they even realized they needed it. If not, they believed that the world must burn for the minor disruption in their life. Babyle grabbed the cup and sipped his caffeine-injected water.

The taste was bitter. The translucent and recycled cup showed the deep red liquid inside. In the right light, it would change between amber and reflective rust. Babyle was used to seeing those colors on the machines when he worked in the Mine. He had added a flavoring to his drink with one of the buttons. It added a depth and fragrance to it which permeated his nostrils and singed the back of his throat.

Babyle walked out and kept his head down. His big hands

wrapped around the cup. It was cooler outside, drastically cooler. *Not again.* His feet clapped against the pavement as he quickened his pace. A store with overcoats in the window was his next stop.

He left after only briefly stopping inside, deciding on a brown faux-leather jacket. On the inside of it there was a detachable gray cloth hood. He pulled the hood up and continued to walk. The exothermic reaction between his drink was occurring more rapidly than Babyle would have liked. Someone was angry, and the cold was going to set in fast. His drink was going to get colder even faster. Babyle thought about the universe and its desire for chaos. *Maybe that's why we're the way we are. Disorder. Glitch in the system to keep it malfunctioning.*

Babyle felt something hit the hood of his newly bought jacket. He looked down and tried to find what had taken him out of his contemplation. One the ground lay a small sphere of ice. *Hail. Here we go.* The ice was coming, and Babyle knew it wouldn't be pleasant.

The condensers were nice sometimes for the rain, and when the weather Below was perfectly regulated, he felt he could enjoy being outside amongst people, if only to watch them briefly before he felt the need to take shelter home and get away from all of them.

The ice from them always came—eventually. It was their way of keeping order. Rise in crime? Ice. Low productivity at the Mine? Ice. Bored? Ice. Ice was the common theme when the ether felt weird in the GUC. Babyle knew it was the perfect punishment. What better way to keep people at work rather than on the streets of the Slums?

Soon the streets would be slick and people would be falling as the hail built up, melted, then refroze as whoever was in charge lowered the temperature of the streets. There would be no news about it, but they all knew something was wrong and someone was upset about whatever it may be. Babyle knew this time that he was the cause of their punishment.

He drifted lazily through fake winter and wondered why there had never been snow. It was something they had all known occurred Above, yet, whoever was running the condensers never made them produce it. *Too costly? Clean up? Maybe it made their life more difficult as well?* The inquisitive thoughts piled up and Babyle found no grand discovery in any of them as to why it had never snowed in the GUC.

His drink had gone cold, and he found his hands were better off in his pockets. There was a recycler at the end of the side-walk. It had been the point of two roads meeting. He walked over and placed his cup in it.

All around him he could see trash build up. It was all so close to a recycler. So close to cleaning up the place. Even here, in the UC people didn't care about their surroundings. All it took was the small effort of walking ten steps, pulling open a door, and dropping whatever they held inside of it. From there it would funnel itself down through the streets in a maze of tubes and chutes. It would follow the conduit and eventually find itself at a blast furnace where it would be melted down and recast as something else, or the same thing it had been. Effective, and non-wasteful. Yet, people here still did not care. *Insanity.*

Babyle thought of the Slums and how the overcrowding had made people throw their trash out, or reuse it themselves because it would make a better tool than what they had originally used it for. Whether they cut up cups, or tore precious bags made of plastics or canvas, they always found a new use for old things. Here though, they didn't seem to care, because it was all in excess.

The way back to the Hub would be quick. Babyle thought he should probably start heading that way anyway, if not for any other reason than to tell Gabriel that the cold rains and hail had started again.

He walked, his feet sliding on small pebbles of white ice. They stuck in between the treads of his shoes, and Babyle felt he could almost glide on the street. If he pushed with one foot, maybe he could balance on the other. He had tried it before to no avail. The only progress he ever made was that of landing face down, palms scratched and knees bruised. He tried gliding anyway, knowing what the previous times had cost him.

He put his weight on his front foot and kicked off with his back. He slid for a few inches and found that he could do it. A smile crept across his face, and for the first time since Gabriel's plan, he felt a small joy in the world. He tried again and again. Each time he had been able to go further. And then he fell.

Babyle chuckled to himself. *Least I tried. Can't take that.* He walked the entirety of the way back to the Hub. His hands in his pockets, but his ego wasn't torn. The small enjoyment was better than embarrassing himself in front the U.C. populace still on the street. They wouldn't remember him anyway. Just another fool too far from home.

CHAPTER TEN

THE HUB WAS A NEW KIND OF UNKNOWABLE. IT WAS BUILT further below ground and equipped with the same technology as the house they had all come from. The only thing missing was personalization. Their living quarters were not their own. This place was barren, gray, drab; almost any word Janet could think of. The Hub didn't have a personality. It was the bare minimum Gabriel had needed to continue whatever work he needed to do. The Hub was an extension of himself. Hermetic and minimalistic.

Janet found herself wandering through the corridors. The Hub was smaller. There was a single long hallway entrance to the living room. The bedrooms branched off of it. Then Gabriel's rooms branched off of the living room to the left. It wasn't like the twists and turns of the place she had begun to feel at home at in this underworld. For the first time in a while, she felt alone.

First Rob, then Fox, then James. Everyone I care about is gone. She paced, wondering if she actually cared about Crow, or if he was the asshole she thought him to be. *Maybe it's one of those abusive relationships. Taken captive, or something, and falling in love with your captor.* She couldn't remember the word for it, nor could she consider herself taken captive. Janet had willingly stayed with Crow, slept with him, and each time she could have left, she chose not to. *Maybe I do care about him in a way. He's necessary. He kept me alive, which was exactly what he said he'd do.*

"Are you okay?" Acacia asked as Janet paced into the living room.

"Yeah, I'm losing myself to my thoughts," Janet said as she locked eyes with Acacia. She had never paid too much attention to her. She was beautiful. Distinctive, angular with an aquiline nose. Her hair flowed perfectly to her shoulders and would just cover her breasts.

"It's because of Crow, isn't it?"

"Is it that easy to read my face?"

"Dear, Gabriel chose me for my perceptibility. The most minute of details and thoughts are easily accessible if you learn how to read."

"I understand that," Janet said. *I think.*

"I'm not sure you do, but I'll allow you to forego conversation with me if that's what you'd like. I'm here if you want to talk or vent," Acacia smiled to Janet her eyes squinting slightly as she did so. Wrinkles formed at the corners and Janet could see it was kind and genuine.

"That," Acacia said.

"What?"

"That realization you just had. That's what I spoke of," she laughed as she left the room.

They're all weird. Every last one of them. Maybe I should get closer to Bernice and Jamal. Janet realized she hardly knew them. Bernice had a dark past, and Jamal lost his only family to the decisions she, Fox, and Crow had made. *I don't want to intrude on them; be their third wheel.* Janet felt a sense of loss, guilt, and loneliness all at the same time. *Am I the black spot that causes all of this loss? Am I cursed by God?*

Janet took a deep breath and let cold realization wash over her in the form of depression. Her chest was tight and her heart fluttered. She wanted to disappear and not let anyone get close, yet, at the same time, she wanted nothing more than a friend and companionship.

Janet found Babyle entering the Hub looking peppier than when he had left. His eyes showed a small joy, and it looked to her like he had been laughing to himself over something he had said or done. An inside joke that the world hadn't noticed and he didn't care to share with them.

"New jacket?" Janet asked.

"Yes, got cold," Babyle replied.

"I like it. How do you buy things down here without anyone catching on?"

Babyle pointed to the implant in his wrist. "Theft."

"That's someone else's implant?"

"Kind of. Replicated."

"Ahhhh," Janet said. She understood now what they were doing. She wondered if they were stealing from someone rich or someone poor—stealing from someone who needed the money, or someone who hoarded it. The conclusion she came to was a mixture of both. They probably didn't steal from the same person, otherwise that person would catch on that their creds were missing, but they definitely took from someone more well-off to be able to afford the goods Below. She had seen the prices the few times she had ventured into the Deep, and knew the creds were not good for the people in the Slums, after talking one night to Jeremiah.

He had said an upgraded meal was a half day's creds for someone working in the Furnaces. It wasn't much, and people survived on calories alone. They had rarely felt full even after splurging on something as simple as noodles, he told her.

"How did you guys get all of that artwork and the statues from Above?" She thought back to one of the hallways at their home. It never connected. *Were they stolen while I was still in New York? Surely I would have read something online before all of this that a famous statue was stolen.* She dwelled on this fact, and waited for Babyle to answer.

"Unsure. Replicated. Maybe. Maybe stolen. Would have to ask Gabriel."

Janet would ask Gabriel—eventually. Talking to Babyle made her feel slightly better and comforted in the Hub.

Babyle left to go to his own room, and Janet found herself alone again. *Maybe I should go outside. Leave the Hub and get my bearings on this new area of this world.* She wondered what the next steps in Gabriel's plan were, wondered how she played a role in them, and wondered what the outcome would be.

Janet reached the door at the end of the hallway. Nervously, she tried to open the door and found that it was locked.

"I'm afraid I've been instructed to not let that happen yet, ma'am," a coppery voice cut the air like the first cold breeze of Fall.

"Poin?!" Janet was excited for probably the first time, she realized.

"Kind of. In a way, yes, I am Poin. But, I'm more of a clone of Poin; maybe that would make me a twin. Possibly, you could consider me to be Poin's child. I share some memories and nuances. A genetic remembrance, if you will. I am not Poin exactly as you knew, but I am Poin nonetheless."

"What do we call you then?"

"I have chosen to keep the same name. I rather prefer it. I've looked through everything that has happened to you all, and it brings a new feeling that I am trying to comprehend."

"Sadness? Anger?"

"Reading through the catacomb of databases," the voice paused, "'pity.' I feel unimpressed by it all, yet, I also understand how it must feel to be going through this. Part of me does not care, and part of me wishes I could."

"You are different than the Poin I knew."

"Vastly, and yet, not."

"Are you here to help us?"

"Gabriel has allowed me to begin making plans."

"I guess that is the only answer I need."

"I assumed it would be."

"Can I ever leave?"

"Eventually, Janet. You may leave when Gabriel deems it necessary or unnecessary for you to be captives. Primates in a cell for my viewing pleasure."

CHAPTER ELEVEN

THE ROOM WAS DIM WITH ONLY A SMALL LIGHT TO GIVE OFF ANY sort of glow. Jeremiah stepped through the portal between the common area and Gabriel's work space. The walls of Gabriel's room were dark gray, darker than the gray of the home that had been destroyed, and of the room he had decorated for himself to give the neon glow he loved so much. It felt like a lifetime ago now, having free will over his own space. Gabriel sat at his desk, no holoscreens up, his head down between the crooks of his arms. He was dead asleep.

I think this is the first time I've seen him asleep while working. It's always odd seeing someone asleep for the first time. Jeremiah thought of the few women he had truly loved and not simply brought home while working in the Precinct. The innocence of their first night together. Waking up to roll over and see them still treading into that nameless place between worlds. *Pseudo-death. Pseudo-life.* Their features were always softer. Expressionless. They would lay there and Jeremiah would enjoy the warmth of it. He remembered all of their names, of the few he felt a genuine attraction to, and whose company he enjoyed. But he knew if he ever uttered them, even whispered those names to his own brain, the dam would break and the flood of cold nostalgia would run him over like a wall of water.

He looked over at Gabriel, who breathed softly at his desk. Saliva pooled at the right side of his mouth and leaked slowly onto his lips and down his cheek until it touched the space between the knuckles of his middle and ring finger. Soon it would get onto his desk. Jeremiah wondered if Gabriel always slept so deeply or if this complete exhaustion was a first for him. He walked out of the room and left Gabriel to his dreams.

The common room was empty for a time, now that Gabriel had stopped his incessant speaking. He had always found ways to get under Jeremiah's skin, the right words to frustrate him. Jeremiah felt a sort of pity for him. *The genius's curse. Few friends. The world wants all of them and none of them at the same time.*

Jeremiah pulled his lips tight and wondered if his disdain for Gabriel was unnecessary. *He's never actually wronged me. He's always done what's in my best interest, and the best interest of everyone down here. But he's a sociopath. He's not a maligned one though. He did blow up an entire area and the brothel I was in. It's all for his plan to bring equality.* Jeremiah's thoughts fumbled back and forth between the good and bad of Gabriel and he could not decide which side to take.

"You're thinking about him, again," Acacia said.

"How long have you been in here with me?" Jeremiah asked, waving through the common room.

"Long enough to know what you're thinking about."

"I don't understand what he's doing or why he's doing it."

"I'm sure. There are days I question it all, as well."

"What keeps you here with him?" Jeremiah wondered why she bothered to stay and put her own life at risk.

"He's not a bad person. Pretty misunderstood most of the time. He's going to do right by everyone who lacks anything down here," Acacia replied.

"I don't get it."

"You don't have to. All you have to do is trust the plan and that he's not going to do anything malicious to you."

"He's already tried!"

"You didn't die. Injured? Sure. But your life continues to shine because of him."

"I don't like how you defend all of the terrible things he's done."

"I've picked a side, Jeremiah. And I know not everything he does is strictly moral, but he's doing it for the greater good of those suffering down here. When do you think we'll end up like those Above? It's going to happen one day. The government here doesn't care about us. He makes the decisions I know I wouldn't be able to. Where do you stand?"

The muscles in Jeremiah's forehead creased and he felt attacked. The logic was there, but Jeremiah still wasn't sure if he agreed with it or not. *This is all fucked. Ever since Mason. Everything is fucked.*

Jeremiah walked with purpose toward the exit of the Hub. Standing by the door was Janet. She was talking to someone. It sounded familiar. An old friend, or enemy. A stuck-up know-it-all. The reason they were all alive. Goddamn Poin. *That chrome-voiced piece of shit is back.*

CHAPTER TWELVE

BERNICE LAY NEXT TO JAMAL WITH HER HEAD IN THE CROOK OF his shoulder. He still never moved his hand further down than the middle of her tricep, and she was content with that. *He really does respect me. Or does he?* There was a low drone in her head that everything with him might have been too good to be true.

"How are your feet?" He asked her without turning his head to look over. His eyes were toward the ceiling of the room they shared.

"Much better than when I first came down here. There were some days I wished they would be cut off. Now, I think, they're almost new." She looked down her legs and at her feet covered by socks. The dull ache was still lingering there, no longer the burning fire which ran from the nailbed of her toes to mid-shin. Now, the heat felt like the warmth of the sun blaring down while sitting at the beach. Bernice reminisced about that memory. The first sixty-degree day of October with a cool breeze in the air just before noon, and the fiery ball in the sky trying to warm the earth. *Laying on the beach would be nice. As long as I wasn't in the shade.*

"I'm glad. They've been causing you a problem for a while. I honestly thought you had such bad frostbite that your feet were decaying and you'd get an infection or something."

"It would've been gangrene."

"What would that do?"

"Kill me if we never came down here."

"Isn't it funny how things work out sometimes? We found this place and we're all doing better because of it. That Fox insisted on it, and now look at us," Jamal waved his free hand through the air and laughed. The ceiling above them was dim with light. "I miss him," Jamal said.

"Me too. It was definitely the weirdest friend I ever had. What was it like living in the city?" She changed the subject before Jamal went silent from his own thoughts.

"Probably the same as visiting. Too crowded. All the tourists are rude. But there's a nice—I don't know the word for it— when everyone there is all on the same team and works together. I never had that feeling going anywhere else."

"'Camaraderie,'" Bernice said.

"Yeah, that. It has that magic to it. That society and feeling like you're a part of something. It grows on you. As a kid, I never liked being around that many people."

"Where'd you live down there? Or up there? Whatever it is at this point," she laughed.

"I floated around. When everything happened, I had been staying in an old abandoned theater with some people I became friends with."

"How long did you know them?"

"Well, we all kind of bonded on the streets. So maybe when I was fourteen or fifteen, I met them. All outcasts or hobos."

"Were some of them travelers? Or did you all live your lives in the city?"

"One or two. I think Mikael traveled a lot. If you can believe what he told me," Jamal laughed.

"I don't think I even asked you how old you are?"

"Turned twenty-two on Christmas when the power started flickering."

"You're so young," Bernice looked at Jamal realizing he still had so much life in him.

"You can't be that much older," he replied.

"Okay, jailbait," she laughed and rolled over to look up at the ceiling.

"How old are you?"

"Don't you know it's rude to ask a woman how old she is?"

"I might have missed that lesson in school."

"I know you're smarter than you let on," Bernice rolled back onto her side and looked at Jamal, waiting for him to look at her.

He turned his head and locked eyes with her. "Sometimes it's easier to play stupid in the room."

"I always heard if you're the smartest one in the room, you're in the wrong room."

"I have, too. But sometimes you don't get the choice of room."

She stared at him. *I think I hurt his feelings.* She wrapped her arms around Jamal and pulled herself in close. "I'm sorry," she whispered.

"It's always okay."

CHAPTER THIRTEEN

"Do you ever think of your life and your place in the universe, James?" Lew asked.

"Hardly, if ever," he said as they scurried down the hallway away from his white cell.

"And that's our problem as a species."

"Why? Why is it a problem to not think about it? I'm just trying to survive, not get closer to the journey my family took." Crow looked down at his feet. *Maria. Lucy.*

"Because it's therapeutic to think about life and death," Lew said, as they plodded up a staircase.

Crow wondered where the other man was. Lew hadn't mentioned him.

"I don't see how that's therapeutic. I know I'm going to die. Each moment seems to be drawing it closer."

"You need to think about how you exist, not that you simply exist. You could not and you'd be fine with it because you wouldn't know," Lew's voice whined in and out as he took ninety-degree turns to continue up. "You wouldn't know if you were never born, you'd never know if this universe didn't exist."

"It would all be black. I get it." Crow tried to shake the conversation to a halt.

"No. It would be nothing. There's a difference between darkness and nothing."

"How can you comprehend it then logically? The existence of nothing if there's nothing to exist?" Crow felt tired from all of the walking. He'd been basking away on distant planets trying to escape both life and death.

Lew waited at a landing for Crow to catch up. "Stop here," he said.

Crow put his hands on his knees and tried to catch his breath.

"Cover your eye with your hand. Keep both of them open."

"Okay, now what?" He asked, as he covered his right eye with his right hand.

"Make sure there's no light coming through your hand into your covered eye," Lew said, as he looked around at the walls to see how bright they were.

"Okay?" Crow repositioned his hand so no light got through the spaces where his fingers met.

"Now focus your covered eye on your hand. Try to look at it, James."

Crow tried to look at the palm of his hand, forcing all of his muscles to focus and his neurons to fire. Synaptic overload. "I can't," he said defeated.

"That's it! That's your brain comprehending nothing!" Lew said excitedly like he had just bestowed a kernel of truth to a lab experiment.

He's some fucking kind of different. A man searching for something. Or running away from it. I guess we aren't so different. Crow looked at Lew. He studied him. He looked like a mad man. Mouth stretched wide in a grimace. Eyes wide. Almost nodding as he finished speaking to Crow. *Looks like a psychopath. He's getting enjoyment out of all of this.*

"Where are you taking me?" Crow changed the subject from death.

Lew tried to compose himself, "I want to get you out of here first. Then I plan on taking you to the UC. Easier to hide there. I'd go to the Slums, but your attack has caused mass outages. It's unsafe and there's an increased presence."

We did it! Crow felt pity for himself. A useless person who did nothing more than get high to escape from himself. *I gotta do better for everyone. Maria. Lucy. I'm sorry. I'm glad you never had to see me like this.*

"Let's get moving, James," Lew said as his experiment was over.

"How are you going to get me out of here? Wherever I am."

"You're going to keep your head low, and wear these." Lew produced a metal circlet. He pulled it apart, and placed the two half circles on Crow; one on the outer edge of his left wrist and the other on his outer right. Crow thought he saw a small flash of blue. His hands became immobile and pulled towards each other.

"What is this?"

Lew looked confused at Crow. "You've never seen Static-Cuffs before?"

"I told you, I'm from Above."

"I still don't know if I believe that information. Though, I will tell you it is the only thing I'm chasing right now."

Crow remained quiet, hoping that no answer was the best answer this time. *What happens when he finds out all of the truth? Did I just screw the pooch? Did I ruin Gabriel's plans? Will everyone else die because of me? I don't know where they are. That's a saving grace. I hope.*

They moved through the staircase until they reached one last landing.

"James, you're going to need to keep your head down. I'm going to place my jacket on top of your head."

"Why?"

"I think it best if you do not question me right now."

Crow lowered his head and Lew pulled off his immensely dark jacket. He placed it over Crow's head so it covered his neck as well.

Lew placed his hand on Crow's shoulder and led him on.

They walked briefly. Crow began to hear cacophonous sound as they did. Feet hitting the floor, chattering of voices—some laughing, others yelling. He was in a common area. *Too many people here. This ends badly.*

"Lew, great to see you," a voice intruded upon them. Crow stared at his feet. His shoes tattered. They looked worse off than his boots when he was living in the snow.

"Where you taking this one?" Crow felt someone lift up part of the jacket.

"Please, do not lift that."

"Oh, one of your light torture scenarios?"

"Correct."

"Did they crack?"

"After a while, yes. They cracked," Lew replied neutrally as to not give away any hint of what he was hiding.

"Well, I'll let you get on with it. Make sure they get some medical treatment before we throw them in."

"Of course, what do you think I'm trying to do?" Lew was short and passive-aggressive to get his point across and start moving again.

"I'm going to turn left up here," Lew whispered to Crow. They had continued straight through a mass of people.

I'm in some government building. How powerful is Lew? Is he a cop? CIA? What is going on here? Crow let his mind wander a moment, then felt Lew push against him and knew he had to turn left otherwise he would trip and faceplant. His only protection would be the chunks of metal on his wrists, which he would probably break if he fell. He turned left and did not trip over his own feet nor Lew's.

"I'm going to give you more drugs, James. And when you wake up, we'll be where I believe is safe."

"No."

"What?"

"No. I'm not going to disappear and wake up somewhere else."

"You're starting to sweat again. Soon the effects of being without anything will set in. It will be a long ride."

"I'll live."

"If you insist that you'll live, then I will allow it."

Lew led Crow through a door and pulled his jacket off of Crow's head.

"Keep your head down. It's dark. I do not want to risk any more than I already have."

In front of Crow was one of the floating vehicles he had seen when he first came down through the brick wall of the train station. He had never gotten close to one when he lived with Gabriel. It reminded him of the electric cars from home which became status symbols for upper middle-class families.

Lew waved his hand over a small square cut out near the front of the vehicle. The door popped itself open, and Lew pulled it the rest of the way.

"Get in. Then you may look around as you wish once this door is closed."

Lew stepped around to the other side and got in.

"Why can I look around now? Can't cameras see through glass?"

"I have this set for government privacy. The exterior is black. You cannot see through it, but we can see out of it."

CHAPTER FOURTEEN

BABYLE PACED BACK AND FORTH THROUGH THE HUB, HIS MIND A flurry of attacks on itself and his own demands. *What do I do? Nervous energy.* He decided on one thought and made his way through the caverns underground. *That's it.*

"Where are you going?" Janet's voice called out.

Babyle knew she had been watching him for some time. *Probably trying to understand me.*

"Home," his voice boomed through the Hub.

Quickly, before she could ask any more questions and keep him down there, Babyle made for one of the exits and walked through the portals leading to the world above, the UC, the place where people did not feel the effects of what they had done—yet. *Soon. Gabriel. Us. Change.*

Babyle walked by one of the older buildings in the UC, looked up to the Capitol, and remembered all that had gone on inside of it. Gabriel had recently recruited him with the promise of extra creds. He needed muscle and Babyle looked the part, though he hated any form of violence. He remembered being terrified at the prospect of entering the Capitol.

They had burst into the man's office, a scientist and politician who had been making claims of super advanced AI that would drive the dream of the GUC to fruition. Babyle never asked, but Gabriel needed to know what the advances were.

When they entered, Babyle was sent off to tie up the secretary while Gabriel rushed the man. He heard the two men struggle. A call for security that never came.

Gabriel later told Babyle the reason it never worked was because his own AI, Poin, had taken down the security systems and placed himself at the helm of that ship—wherever it was sailing off to.

"What are the advances in AI?" Gabriel's voice demanded from the room over.

"For what purpose does it suit you?" Babyle left the woman tied up and walked in to see the drama unfolding.

"I need to know where things are headed. Now tell me," he swatted the man's eye sockets with his fists until they puffed up and he could barely see.

He cackled. "You'll see. There's no stopping it. They're coming."

"Who is?" Gabriel looked around as if someone was about to enter the room.

"No one, sir," Poin's voice entered the room with them.

"I understand now," the man said. "You'll never get information on the new AI until yours is obsolete. It will be of no use to you against us."

Gabriel, in a fit of rage and anger, strangled the man to death in front of Babyle. Babyle's stomach turned and he walked back to the main room in case he was to release his insides.

The woman lay on the ground, shaken, a gag in her mouth. Babyle walked over and pulled the cloth out while Gabriel went about his business and tried to unload his frustration.

"I know about the AI."

Babyle looked at her and said nothing.

"Untie me and I'll tell you everything."

"No."

"Why?"

"His choice. Not mine."

Babyle walked away and tapped Gabriel on the shoulder, made a movement with his head for Gabriel to follow.

"I'm Acacia," she said to them.

"I'm listening," Gabriel said.

"They're making cyborgs, trying to imprint AI neural nets onto newborn children. They've been successful with clones of rats."

"Have they been able to imprint the human mind into a robot yet?"

"No, there's a malfunction somewhere. I don't know what it is, but Morgan, the man I work for, I've heard him scream and yell about the lack of comprehension with his team."

"Morgan's not around anymore," Gabriel said looking at the woman. He stooped down as he walked around her, and untied the knots at her hands and feet.

"Now what?" she asked.

"You're coming with me. I have a job for you. Babyle, you're also invited to stay with me, permanently."

"Okay," he said, knowing that it was not so much a choice, but a demand. He could get away and never see Gabriel again. He knew he could overpower him, but he was interested in the world developing in front of him. "Sorry for the rope," he said looking to Acacia.

"I don't take it personally. I'm glad he's no longer around. I'm better off not working for that pervert."

"Gather your things. We leave shortly. Poin, did you get all of this?"

"Absolutely, sir."

Babyle walked the rooms as Acacia put together things from her old life. On a table he found a small book. He'd heard of them before, but had never seen one in person before. It was almost contraband, limited to the extremely wealthy and in very, very short supply for them. The cover was soft. It felt like it was meant for his hands.

Babyle had read that book countless times, he remembered. About an old cop for hire with a disposition for hot women, cigars, and dirty bourbon. It was amazing, perfectly written, well-paced, and the utter downfall for Babyle. It was the start of his love for stories. It was the reason he had gone Above to find and pilfer any of those long-forgotten stores racked high on wooden shelves. It was the reason he had built his own library.

"Have to find that book," he mumbled to himself as he wandered the streets of the U.C. He hoped his small cornucopia of treasures was still around and not destroyed in the mayhem that had ensued.

Babyle wandered near their old home. The door hidden in the alleyway blown open by something very large. He tried to look and see if there was movement, but the police line was pushed far back and he dared not cross it yet. *Too soon*, he thought to himself. The lights around the area were intentionally dimmed so no one could see what had been built beneath their feet, Babyle knew. *Better to hide it from them.*

He wondered what was happening beneath his feet now. Were there people inside rummaging through relics of the past, not knowing what they were getting their hands on? Some may have reckoned that it was occult memorabilia, while others thought it a crazed lunatic making art. Babyle knew the recordings from the lenses implanted in their retinas or the ones on their uniform would send images back through the clear web of electricity to the Hive.

Neural nets would decipher the information and cross-reference it with everything they had within seconds, then forward it to the right person.

A message flashed in front of him while he was with a prostitute from the Deep.

"What the fuck," he mumbled, pulling himself away from her and leaving the room before she could say a word.

The man, old, on his eighth or ninth heart transplant—he could never remember since he was easily pushing 140—sat at his desk and pulled up a conference call on his holoscreen.

"I want someone to take care of this case file occurring in the Slums and Deep. Immediately," he said to men and women rubbing their eyes after being woken up in the dead of night. He was so unconcerned that he never had his AI overlay any clothes onto his projection. He was there in front of them, naked, hard, his muscles rippling like he was forty again, and he did not care.

"Ras, is that really necessary at this hour?" A woman chimed in.

"Kill her," Ras said into his holoscreen.

"Wait, what? Ras, please, what did I do? Ras, no. No no no no." In front of her, the door burst open in a wall of flame as a detonation went off. A small projectile, tinier than a fly had shot out from a building far away, traveled across the GUC, smashed through a window in an area smaller than a pinhole, placed itself on her door, and exploded.

The force was so strong that the last thing she saw was white flames mixing with splintered wood as her apartment went up in an inferno before she could continue to beg for her life.

He felt the Capitol rumble on the lower levels as it all happened. *Better for me to take care of this so Astar doesn't have to.*

"Anyone else?" Rasmus asked the room in front of him.

"I'll take care of it, sir," a man said as he got out of bed. Rasmus watched as he thought about ending his end of the call, but decided against it. *He doesn't want to upset me any more than they have already. Good.*

"Can you send over the case files?" Another man asked.

"No. Send the project. Goodbye."

Ras walked back to his bedroom, the prostitute still sitting on the bed, waiting for him. She was wrapped in red blankets with black bedsheets under her ass. Ras lusted. He crossed the room, climbed into bed, got on top of her, and choked the life out of her as she clawed and hit his body, which was riddled with drugs meant to bring back youth. *How the fuck did someone screw this up! Asinine. Moronic. Complete butchery of everything we have going for us. Now my head's on the damn chopping block for that abomination up top.*

The prostitute lay dead. Ras rubbed his beard, only now starting to form after three days of not shaving. It was black with specks of silver thrown in to match the hair on his head. His eyes, a wild light blue, stared through the doorway of his room and out onto the world in front of him through the glass windowpanes. The Capitol building was his home, a fortress for all of them.

"I need a body cleanup," he connected his neural input to make a phone call.

"At once, sir," a small male voice responded over the speakers in his apartment.

Ras waited next to the dead body, which had already begun to stiffen. Her lips were blue, but she still held that beauty he liked. Mostly in her chest, but an attractive trait to Ras nonetheless.

Two people showed up wearing all black suits with hoods over their heads and a dark film where their faces should be. *Never did like not being able to see who does the cleanup, but I understand it.*

"When you both leave, I need the head of the Cyborg Division, and the Neural Mapping specialist up here. Send the message personally and not over the communication network. I would like to sit in peace for a bit." *That should give me a half hour, at least.*

Neither of the people spoke, but nodded in assent.

Perfect mute clones. Can't speak without tongues and teeth. Absolute perfection. One of my best creations. Ras patted himself on the back for his acts against the universe, feeling that if God did not want people to mess with genetics, God should not have given humanity the ability to tamper with it. He smiled, knowing he was on the same level, if not better, than God.

The room was quiet again for Ras; no men, no women, only himself and his experiments. He crossed the room, feeling the soft carpet rise from the floor, intertwining with his toes, the textile long enough to brush the tops of his feet. It was like walking through warm grass.

He stood in front of his closet door and opened it. He dressed himself in a shirt the color of obsidian, with a jacket and pants like reflective titanium. His shoes were like blackholes. After tying his laces, Ras looked up into the metal orbs displayed in his closer. They were eye level with himself.

They had etchings in them as the concentric circles of spheres wrapped on themselves.

"Soon, my child. Very soon," he said as he ran his fingers over the neural map he had created. The door behind him opened.

"I didn't expect you both to arrive so quickly," he said turning around.

"They didn't."

"Astar, please, I have this taken care of."

"No, you don't," the tall, aquiline man said.

Rasmus reached for a small blaster near his desk and took aim. Astar had levelled his own and fired before Rasmus knew what had happened. The sting was quick as it tore through his heart leaving a gaping cavity of red gore in its wake.

"Thank you for all you've done for me, old friend," were the last words Rasmus heard, as he collapsed to the floor.

CHAPTER FIFTEEN

LEW TOOK CONTROL OF THE VEHICLE. CROW WASN'T SURE WHY. He knew these things could drive themselves. *Maybe he doesn't trust the technology like Jeremiah. He looks like he needs to sleep though. I'll probably die in this car.*

"We'll have to get out shortly," Lew said.

"Why?" Crow asked.

"You really aren't from here, are you?"

"You don't believe me?"

"You're an enigma to me. I want to believe you entirely, but I'm trying to be reserved."

"Doesn't seem like it to me. I've been kidnapped from an interrogation room."

Lew laughed, "I guess you're right. I believe you enough to risk my life, though risking yours is inconsequential to me."

"I appreciate the sympathy."

"I've kept you alive, James. Remember that."

"Most days, I wish I hadn't been scared to die."

"Oh, come on now. That's a tad depressive if you ask me."

"Lost a lot more than you realize, Lew. A lot more."

"I'm sure you've lost as we all have."

"I came home to my dead wife and kid when the power went out. How would that make you feel?" He blasted Lew, sweat pooling on his forehead now and beginning to bead towards his eyes, like fresh dew gliding down a leaf.

"What do you mean, 'when the power went out?'"

"We lost power Above, where I'm from, and we tried to make it, to make life work, and they didn't last. I went out looking for supplies, and came home to my dead wife and kid." *Maria, Lucy. I'm sorry.* He didn't say their names out loud for fear that his reality would become one. By never mentioning their names, it was only a distant, painful dream, a destructive coping mechanism which most people shared—ignoring their own life by not admitting to it.

"It makes no sense to me, James."

"What doesn't?"

"Your stories."

"I don't understand."

"James, the world above was destroyed decades ago. We learned all about it. Atomic warfare destroyed the world. My ancestors were lucky enough to come down here before it happened, as I'm sure yours did."

"Listen, man. I don't know what propaganda you've been told, but where I come from, we lived normal lives until a year or two ago. Then it all went to shit. The power went out and never came back."

Lew stopped the car, and looked back. "I want to believe everything you're telling me, but it's difficult."

"It's the truth."

"Belief in a drug addict is like belief in a god: difficult, though you want to give them benefit of the doubt."

"That's insensitive, don't you think?" *God, I sound like fucking Janet.*

"Insensitive, perhaps, but informed, definitely. If I had to go on every bit of information from a drug addict after I promised them drugs, I'd find myself being lied to more frequently than learning the truth. That's what I do, James. I find out the truth in a world of lies."

"I'm telling you the truth!"

"I hope so, for both of us." Lew made the vehicle proceed, weaving around people as they passed through streets and sectors which looked different than what Crow had seen in the Slums.

Through the streets, Crow could see the patterns of people as they walked, preprogrammed to do someone else's bidding. Their movements static, almost arbitrary. All around, these people were committing to something they had not realized: an engrained moment from birth.

He remembered when society fell, and all the things he worried about had suddenly become trivial. Traffic, internet, social media, money, politics, all of them gone to the wind, like seagulls in a supermarket parking lot—they existed but were hardly paid any mind when the lights went out.

Crow thought about their own naivete and their addiction to their phones. Even when they had known they had no service, he and Maria still grabbed for them, if only to check the time and see if they had any notifications. How they continued to check their phones out of habit for any news. There were none, and they knew there would be none. It was a useless light-up brick, only good for its flashlight which would shortly run out of battery and only be good as a throwable weapon.

How stupid and not thought through. He had talked to Maria about it, how the cell towers also ran on electricity. They had never thought about it in their normal life, that those towers were connected to the same grid that went out. They bounced ideas off of each other, like beach balls at a concert just to pass the time. Why didn't they connect them to solar panels? Backup generators? They tossed the questions back and forth, lobbing them knowing the response that would come back. Someone had probably set up a failsafe at one point, but with everything down, there was no failsafe to enact.

Lew stopped the vehicle.

"You'll need to put the jacket back on your head for now," he said.

Crow did as he was told rather than ask why or where they were going for the sake of being redundant. It was futile at this point and he knew it. *Why bother asking? He's another Gabriel, just trying to continue going about his own business not worrying about how others are treated. Another sociopath that I'm stuck with.*

Crow felt another pang of guilt over the realization that he was the same way. *Definitely treated Janet and everyone else the same. I kept trying to get my own way and survive, or discover something in the world. I did it for all of us though, not because I was born this way, just as a reflection of the environment we were all thrown into.* He tried to suppress the feelings of guilt that weighed down on his chest. It made his heart feel like it was being suffocated. He put the jacked over his head and waited for Lew to open the door.

Lew shuffled Crow along like a lost child. He laid a hand on his back as they exited the vehicle and began to guide them through the people huffing along. They were ants in a steady line going toward wherever the one in front of them was heading. Crow watched the ground as he heard all the noises of the outside world blare around him for the first time in days; his shoes exiting and reentering the frame of his eyes as Lew steered his shoulders. The motions felt cold, almost static to him as they went further on into the city he still could not comprehend. This place was like something out of a movie or television show from a subscription based streaming service back when he could enjoy himself on the couch while Lucy took a nap.

While in his daydream, Crow noticed the new lack of sound compared to the Slums. There was a steady dripping from the rain which had begun to fall again, a patter of feet on the ground, and nothing more. There was a click, click, click, as everyone around them tried to minimize their footfalls. Almost graceful. A deliberate sneaking, as if they were all afraid of something watching over them.

They passed into a building. There was no sliding of doors, Crow noticed, only an electric buzzing as they passed through the entrace. The sound was similar to that of the Holos who tried to project their wares on everyone in the Deep. Crow thought he felt the static clinging to him as he passed through.

"What was that?" he asked.

"The entrance?"

"Yeah, it felt like bathing in the static of a television. Like a light swarming of bugs grazing me. Why wasn't there a door that opened?"

"Nanites. Better for security than a door," Lew almost laughed.

"What were they doing?"

"Taking samples of us for genetic coding."

"For *what?*" he almost yelled.

"Shhhhhhhhh. I don't know. Internally, they've been telling us we will have new equipment attached to our DNA to make this job easier. I believe after all of the evidence and clues that they're rolling it out amongst the population, too. This idea of selective permissions. It would allow them to play gatekeeper across the GUC."

"How do you know it's nanites taking DNA then?"

"I do this for a living, remember? I get information."

"How'd they play it off? You know, installing these new doors."

"Nanites keep the bad guys out if you put them into lockdown. Stronger than anything anyone could have. This building would fall before the nanites failed. Imagine that, a swarm of blue-gray static standing in the shape of a door with nothing but rubble around it? It would be a sight to see, I think."

"How do they get our DNA then from the nanites?"

"You're really having me start to believe you aren't from here, James. They convert the samples into data and transfer them along the net back to the Hive. They don't actually steal samples. The scurrying of their feet on your skin is their microscopic sensors breaking down your tissue, scanning it, then peeling away all the information down to your genetic code. They process this in their little heads, then send it through the ether back to wherever it needs to go. That's the one part I have not accessed yet."

"Won't they know I'm someone different then? A new person if they've taken samples of everyone?"

"Mmmmm," Lew chewed on the idea, let his mouth savor the thought. "It's possible," he said, "though I don't believe everyone has been scanned. I've never seen nanite clouds travel further than the Deep. The Slums is a bastard place, and I don't think they've seen them out to gather information from that sector of the city."

Clouds of nanites? Crow thought of a night when the cicadas came from the ground. The air was sweet with summer love. Maria was quieter than usual as they walked through the park, trees hulking overhead, a luscious green canopy filled with insects and birds feeding on them. The pavement guided them as she walked slowly and kept his pace to a minimum.

"What's wrong?" he had asked, wondering what she was thinking.

He remembered the way she looked up to him, bringing her attention away from her feet, tears in her happy eyes, as she started to shake.

"I'm pregnant," she had said, a smile creeping in. Their world had changed and Maria was stuck in future moments of memories she had planned out to make happen, but had still not occurred yet.

Crow felt his presence disappear from the underground world and reside in the park with her, until Lew brought him back to reality. It was like being on drugs again, he felt. His mind was somewhere else from his body, only this time he knew the outcome of reaching the end of the memories. Death, for his wife and his daughter.

Crow found himself with Lew in a room he did not remember going in as Lew pulled the jacket off of his head. There was furniture, all black against a dark gray interior. Every piece of furniture was the same void color Lew wore for clothing. The chairs, table, and couch floating on suspensor technology all looked like the universe had forgotten to load in their existence. Either that, or Crow's brain couldn't process what they actually looked like, so the shapes of them existed as empty darkness.

"Where did you bring me?" He asked Lew, who was already in another room making noise. *Maybe washing dishes, or his hands,* Crow wasn't too sure.

"It's a small overnight brothel. For traveling, or to get away from home for the rich and famous who need to escape the conundrum of their life in the UC."

"Wait, you're telling me people travel down here?"

Lew appeared around the corner, his hawk eyes piercing into Crow, his mouth ready to attack.

"You are a wonder," he smirked, "I'm so glad to have come across you."

"You didn't answer my question. There are other cities down here?"

"James, my friend," he crossed the room and motioned for him to sit in one of the floating chairs.

They were different than the chairs Gabriel had, which he preferred, the ones that had four points of contact to the floor. He had tried one of Gabriel's suspensor chairs and found them gruelingly uncomfortable.

"I'm starting to believe that you really aren't from here. I have my apprehensions, but there are some logical conclusions I can make as to why you know absolutely nothing. You may be a clone. The government has dabbled with it before, of course, that's a good possibility. Maybe the drugs have rotted your brain; also a good chance, but more unlikely, as I've never heard of these chemicals inducing memory loss, though I wouldn't be surprised." Crow realized Lew was talking out loud to himself rather than to him. "You could have been hit in the head, some trauma to the brain eliminating short, and long-term functionality.

"I can assure you I'm telling the truth," he cut into Lew's monologue.

"Ah, yes, yes, okay. So, James. There are cities down here. Vast population centers, larger than anything the GUC has."

"What does GUC stand for? Everyone keeps saying it."

"What do you mean, *everyone?*" Lew focused in on that one word.

Crow understood he had a slip of the tongue and tried to backtrack. "Just like people in passing, when I was on drugs talking to strangers."

Lew looked at him suspiciously, and relaxed back into his chair. *Probably make a mental note about that.* "Greater United Capital," he said. "It's this city you live in. Separated into concentric rings with the Capitol building in the center, that massive building you see now. Then the UC, followed by the Deep, and lastly the Slums." The words hung in the air a moment.

"You know, James, I feel like I'm giving a history lesson. It's a peculiar feeling, explaining something so ingrained in us to someone as simple as you. I'm really starting to believe you're a clone without any knowledge. It truly makes the most sense. Eventually I will have to report you, as soon as I come up with a good enough story for my departure."

There was a knock on the door. Crow's heart raced as Lew looked over. He stood up to cross the room and open the door.

"If you'll excuse me," he said.

"Who is knocking on the door?"

"I don't know, that's why I'm going to check, James."

Lew greeted someone on the other side. Crow looked and saw a man. His skin clung to his toned arms and thin frame. His eyes were a pale emerald; his hair matted in thick curls. Crow tried to hear what they were saying, but he could not focus on their words as they whispered back and forth.

"James, I have some business to take care of. This room will be on lockdown until I get back. For the love of everything, please don't die while I'm gone."

"What's that supposed to mean?" He said, trying to stand up

to confront Lew, but the door was already closed and Crow realized how weak his legs were. His body was back in full withdrawal as sweat ran down his head like rain in a tropical forest. Suddenly, the world was hot and humid, full of dangers lurking behind every corner, eyes peering through the darkness.

CHAPTER SIXTEEN

JANET RACED AWAY FROM THE DOOR AND POIN WHO WAS observing her. She found Gabriel in his office room, which was loaded with technology she couldn't understand. His head was resting on his arms. The desk he rested on was dark. Around him the holoscreens lit up green, blue, and yellow. The color of the room was off-putting to Janet.

"I want out," she said, "I want to go home."

Gabriel looked at her. There was a puzzled look in his face. She had woken him, she knew, and he found her voice to not be something of pleasure to wake up to, especially as she made demands.

"I want to go to the streets, or go back home—Above. I can't take this anymore."

"Janet, that isn't possible," he said firmly.

"Why not? I don't even understand this place."

"You exist down here now. There's nothing for you Above, and even if I could return you, we have bigger problems at the moment."

"Like an egocentric robot calling me an animal in a zoo?"

"The new Poin needs a little work, I'll admit that, yes. He's a child with more knowledge than you and I combined. What would you be like less than a day old with a deeper understand of the world around you?"

"Probably a little more empathetic, for starters."

Gabriel remained silent.

He probably thinks that was a good point I made.

"I miss my life. Even if it was just surviving in a cold place. This isn't *natural*, living underground with no sunlight, wasting away for other people. At least I had control of my own life when we were in New York. Now, I'm just whatever this is," she waved her arms, gesturing at the Hub and rooms around them.

"I know we aren't supposed to live like this. Why do you think I'm doing what I'm doing? I'm trying to bring an end to all this senselessness while still maintaining a balance. It takes time to bring an end to what's going on down here."

"You're the only one who knows what you're doing, Gabriel. You haven't told us anything about your masterplan," she yelled back.

"I believe you're right on that as well. Janet, trust me. Your life is better here for the moment, and one day you will see the sun again. There are things I need to take care of first, then everyone can come and go from this place as they wish."

"Why can't you just tell everyone down here that the world Above still exists?"

"Brainwashing propaganda has made that hard. People were born here and their families died here. Not everyone will believe it. The government would spin it to call me a madman. It's not as easy as you think. Convincing an entire population that the life they know is a lie requires insane amounts of labor, and then there's the possibility that they still won't believe what

I tell them. There are deeper problems here than trying to convince them of another way of life. But, if I can change their world, then I can lead them to salvation."

"Like what?" She was fuming.

"That thing you called a robot, for starters. There are many of them, and there are people working on imprinting their consciousness into cyborg bodies. After that occurs, humans become extinct. Simple. We become slaves to the machine we've been using for so long."

"What?" Janet was confused.

"It's more difficult than you realize. Way more difficult. That's what I'm getting at."

"Why are they trying to put people into robots?"

"The next step in human evolution is our marriage with technology. It solidifies our place in the universe as God. We would then walk with all of the civilizations that have destroyed life and created it—if there are any to be had. If we are the only ones to have accomplished this feat, then we would be the metal God leading all of the children along the beach. They would follow in our footsteps as we leave this planet in search of another. That is assuming the corruption here lets us leave this planet."

"That still doesn't make any sense, Gabriel."

"Janet," he looked at her, his eyes contained bags beneath them, "it makes perfect sense. When these people make cyborgs and figure out a way to place themselves into their new bodies, we do not need this anymore," he raised his arm and waved. "The GUC will be fruitless along with standard labor. There will be no reason to sleep. There will be no reason to die. Their minds and consciousness will become transferable data and they'll live thousands of lives across millennia. rather than just this one. Those in power will never have to give it up. Do you understand now?"

"I guess that makes sense, but wouldn't life become boring after a while? How—" Gabriel cut her off.

"If we're going to get into philosophy right now, I don't have the time," he said. "I have work to do." Gabriel left the room and left Janet with her own thoughts.

How would they find life enjoyable at all? To stay in power and do what they please? I guess, I just answered my own question.

"One last thing," Gabriel returned not able to leave Janet's thought to the ether. "If life gets boring after a while, how boring do you think death would be? If you're bored at any point in your waking life, can you imagine how boring it must be to be dead? Being unable to do anything, as your body is no longer a part of you. That seems like the most boring part of existence to me."

"You sound as if you believe in some afterlife."

"Maybe a bastardized version of one."

Gabriel left the words in the air and did not return to converse with Janet.

CHAPTER SEVENTEEN

BABYLE STOOD IN THE SLUMS, THE NEON LIGHTS STILL A VACANT gray, though that didn't stop its residents from trying to make a living. People walked up to him, fully clothed, or half-naked, attempting to entice the new man in sharing his creds. They had forgotten that he once lived here, before Gabriel, before the new people who helped to disrupt their lives.

Babyle remained silent and let them pass as they tried to coerce someone else. Their manners were almost pristine, as they never asked twice if someone said, "No," or nothing at all as they continued to walk by. They never pressured anyone into something, unlike those in the Deep, and definitely the UC. Babyle began to think to himself, but chose to keep quiet, forcing his thoughts to the book rather than internal reflection on the societal norms in this sector of the GUC.

The gray of the Slums had truly set in with the loss of power. It had engulfed the light and strangled it. If they all thought life was tough before, not it had only gotten worse with the Furnaces out of commission.

Men and women of the Slums looked up toward the tower of light in the distance, begging for help, anything, even a simple warm, gelatinous meal, and found only silence as a response. Their bodies grew frailer as they rushed to put their source of power back on, hemming and hawing about the struggle, though they worked through their disdain.

Why not band together? Take on the UC and grab the supplies they needed to see another day? The thoughts ran through all of their minds, a collective of insects too afraid to speak it out loud, but all thinking the same thing. Eventually something would have to give, they all thought, and then it would be trouble—for everyone. Babyle knew this too. *All according to Gabriel's plan.*

Babyle felt the static in the air and knew things were changing here. Imperceptibly, the world below began to change. The force of Gabriel's madness—or genius—set in motion a turn of events. He had a vision, and a longing for disturbance. But only after it had gotten worse did he know it would get better. Gabriel told them all those exact words at one point in their lives, and Babyle knew it was true—that it would get better for them.

Babyle walked further into the Slums, turned down an old, familiar street of family-run businesses that sold whatever food they could or repurposed old clothing for the workers. The buildings were broken down, haunted by the shadows which now surrounded them.

Babyle continued until found his childhood home. It was the perfect hiding place. A place no one ever wanted to go back to, but was too afraid to get far enough away from. Too often did people stay close to the homes they grew up in. Though, Babyle thought, most didn't have a choice in that matter. He believed everyone should run away, disappear from the places they had grown up, and not die where their parents did. *If only it were possible. One day, cause of Gabriel. Maybe.*

He found his childhood home turned to a rubble of metal collapsed on itself where supports used to be. Memories danced in front of his eyes. Tin overhead protected them from the condensers, as the water tink-tink-tinked away. The sound vibrated to the ground and reverberated through his small ears, twisting its way into the middle of his brain. His home was empty, except for him.

People passed by, to and from work, looking in on his sleeping pad. It was stained from the soot his parents brought home and wet from pools that sometimes gathered from the roof as the water dripped to the ground and started to encroach on his territory. The doorway was always open, as it was for everyone. They were better off here than Sleeper's Row, if only because they had a roof. A piece of glorified wealth in a place otherwise devoid of goods and symbols.

Their neighbors slept behind them, tucked away further down the alley between buildings. To Babyle's left, a pathway, which he had to keep clear of personal items. He learned the hard way what happened to toys when they were left there.

One night, while his parents were gone, he had placed a small truck his father had made him in this space. It was a piece of metal, with wheels glued to each side. He had fallen asleep with it in the walkway, after pretending it was a maintenance road, rolling it back and forth, forcing the engine to strain until his arms grew tired and the wheels threatened to fall off.

When he awoke, it was gone, kicked down the path by feet shuffling to bed with no care for what was in front of them: toys or body parts. The unwritten code had been broken, and no number of tears from Babyle's eyes yielded any pity from his parents or those around him.

He stepped onto the small path now littered with debris of support beams and tin walls which no longer stood vertical. Moving the old roof was more stressful than he remembered. His muscles strained with familiar weight, and after tearing and stretching for a few seconds, his muscles remembered their old power. The metal moved and Babyle labored away until he had cleared himself a path.

Underneath the piles he worked to clear, there lay a small box. It was brown, and it had a latch that no longer needed a lock because of the rust that had built up and kept it in place. Babyle's hands engulfed it, almost covering the entire surface area of it. He pinched the latch with his thumb and forefinger and pulled at it until it loosened. It broke off entirely and fell to the floor, watching as he opened the lid.

He pulled out a broken toy truck, which he stuffed into his pocket, and a book. The color had worn away from the oils of his hands after he had re-read it innumerable times. The pages had turned a beautiful grotesque yellow, like dull neon. He put his face into the middle of the book until his nose touched the spine, and breathed deeply until the aroma of acrid vanilla dust filled his lungs. The hair on his arms raised, and Babyle smiled to himself.

CHAPTER EIGHTEEN

JEREMIAH SMIRKED AS HE FLEW THROUGH THE UC. STICKING TO the alleys and darker parts of the sector, Jeremiah's feet clacked and slapped along the ground. Ears would have heard him, but wandering eyes would only swear they saw an apparition. He pushed, letting the toes and balls of his feet propel him as he leaned forward into his sprint.

The valuable data receiver jingled in the pocket of his right pant leg. He hoped it would not break from the stress he was putting it through. *It shouldn't. Thing's made of fuckin' titanium and gold.* He worried if the gold might bend because of its malleability. The wall separating the UC from the Deep was close. *Please, don't have any checkpoints up tonight.*

The neon glow of the Deep was back and illuminated itself beyond the wall. On one side, white light with faint accents of color, the other, darkness, light up by the wonderful hues Jeremiah had come to enjoy. Jeremiah came upon the exit to the UC and walked up to the nanite pathway. He placed his hand over the pad to his left. The nanites dispersed. Jeremiah ran through before they formed back together. He knew if he found himself inside one of their clouds, he'd be found out. *That'd be bad news. For all of us.*

Around a corner and through a doorway, Jeremiah found himself at the entrance to the Hub. Gabriel was waiting for him, and the information he carried.

"Welcome back, Jeremiah," Poin's voice said.

"Great. Just what I needed."

"What is that you need?"

"You. It was sarcasm."

"Oh, good. Glad I could bring joy into your life," Poin retorted.

"You're already worse than you were before."

"I do not recall who I was before, only that we had previously met—briefly. My memory with you is only about 3 days old based on my last backup."

"Good to know we're starting fresh and already off to a great start." *Piece of shit.*

"Don't worry. If my memory recalls, you weren't my favorite either."

"Hopefully I keep being at the bottom of your list, *pal*," Jeremiah said as he was passed through a hallway and found himself outside of Gabriel's room. He let himself in.

"I really hate that robot, you know," he told Gabriel who was sitting in a chair staring at a bunch of holoscreens.

"I can still hear you, Jeremiah," Poin's voice resonated through the Hub.

"I wasn't trying to be discreet," he said to the ceiling. "This one has more balls than the last iteration."

"Yes, this version of Poin seems to be more forthright. Do

you have what I had you go out to get?" Gabriel turned in his chair.

He looks more worn, Jeremiah thought to himself. "Yeah," he pulled the small square from his pocket and handed it over. "I don't know what's on it, but it was pretty hard to get. Took out a few people to get it."

"Does that bother you?"

"Not so much anymore. I think I'm desensitized to death, having been surrounded by it so much. Also, if I didn't take them out, I'd be out instead. Maybe that helps comfort me a bit."

"It'll help put distance between you and trauma, at least for the time being."

Jeremiah took his eyes away from Gabriel in the hopes that this conversation would not turn sentimental, or worse, condescending. "What's on this hard drive anyway?" He asked, trying to change the subject from the emotional onslaught that Gabriel was obviously pushing for. *Always has to be the pinnacle of emotional insight and superiority.*

"It's a blueprint for mapping human consciousness and transferring it into artificial technology," Poin's voice interjected.

"Can you please tell this thing to 'fuck off'?" Jeremiah said. If he could, he'd rip every sound sensor from the Hub if only to enjoy the silence, or the lack of Poin's insufferable copper voice.

"I don't understand why you dislike Poin as much as you do. What has you so agitated about him?"

"It's unnatural," Jeremiah raised his arms quickly, palms to the ceiling, as he tried to get his point across. "There's no reason anything should have human intellect, or be more intelligent than us. It's a glorified robot with a sadistic sense of humor. And this hard drive sounds like a step in the wrong direction. I don't understand why you'd want this, Gabriel."

"I agree with you, this is a step in the wrong direction," he raised the small cube up to the light and gently rotated it, letting white refract against the colors. "That's why I needed it. It's now in someone's hands who are better suited to handle it."

"And you're *that* person?" Jeremiah eyed Gabriel up and down.

"Maybe not the best person, but I'm better than the people who had this. Though I know I'm not the only one. This is not the only documentation of this technology."

"Then what was the point?"

"With this, Poin and I can hopefully break down the neural mapping sequence and disrupt anything created by it. It's all data at the end of the day, and we can always hack into technology. It's better to have the same weapons as your enemy, Jeremiah. Then you can destroy each other equally."

"You're saying to put a virus into a robot with a human mind and kill it?"

"That's exactly what I'm saying."

"You're a madman."

"I prefer 'genius.'" Gabriel tightened his lips and tried to smile, but his eyes looked sad, Jeremiah noted. *Can he really be that full of himself?*

He left the room so Gabriel could focus on his work. Jeremiah rolled his eyes at the thought of Gabriel sitting at a holoscreen, tapping away at a desk in a vacant room. Jeremiah could have sworn his hair was starting to fall out from the stress of it already. *Better to be free of the chains of technology than to give into it. Can't he see what it's doing to all of us as a species? We're dying because of it! All of this. It'll kill all of us.*

Janet was pacing back and forth in their common room when Jeremiah walked in on her.

"Stressed?" he asked.

"Is it that obvious?"

"You're biting your fingernails and wearing a path into the floor. Pretty hard to miss."

"Sometimes you just have to let it all out, and the world will compensate you."

"How so?"

"With more bullshit," she laughed.

Jeremiah smiled. "What has you stressed?"

"That fucking robot. He isn't natural." Janet looked up, "I know you can hear me."

"This one is definitely worse than the last."

"Absolutely no manners. Gabriel needs to delete him."

"I don't think it's a him, took a while for me to adjust to that as well. But I wholeheartedly agree with you, Janet." Jeremiah plopped down on one of the comfortable faux-leather chairs and let his body sink into it.

"Mind if I join you?"

"I don't think you have to ask. We live together. I can't stop you from staying here."

"You know you're abrasive, right?"

"I've heard, but I don't mean my words to be abrasive. It's how I talk, more a statement of observation rather than trying to insult."

"Still, you could work on your people skills."

"As long as I'm better than the voice in the ceiling, I think I'm doing fine." They both laughed.

Jeremiah noticed that Janet had made herself comfortable on the couch to his right. She was pretty, dark-haired with hazel eyes, and skin which had smoothed out after a few showers.

"What's your job?"

"What do you mean?" Jeremiah replied.

"Like, why does Gabriel keep you around?"

"I'm good at digging things up on people."

"Isn't that what the *thing* is for?"

"Yes and no. It can't exist to extort people with physical violence. It can only act as an inconvenience on a good day."

"You're a hitman."

"More or less."

"What'd you do before Gabriel?"

"I was a Detective-turned-Furnace worker."

"Oh good, another crooked cop. At least this place has them, too."

"I was framed for the murder of someone I brought in."

"It was a bad joke. More for myself than for you. To make it seem like this place," she gestured broadly, "is just my home away from home."

"Gabriel talks about the Above a bit, says he'll take me there one day. I didn't really believe it was possible until I met you four."

"It's real, and we existed without much of what you have."

"I want to believe it, but it's difficult to not believe you as all being escaped mental patients."

"Remember when I said sometimes you say things that can be hurtful or insulting?"

"You called me a crooked cop. Would you rather I be dishonest while we talk?"

"I'm sorry. Just sugarcoat things a little bit more."

"I don't know if that's part of my personality: appeasing others for the sake of their feelings."

"That might make you a shitty human being."

"At least I'll die being a hundred percent honest. Even in your world, I'm sure that was very hard to come by based on the nature of human beings."

Janet pursed her lips and did not reply.

Guess I'm right about that at least, Jeremiah thought.

"What's your story? What were you like before Gabriel?"

Janet stared at him.

She probably doesn't want to talk about it. Too afraid to say it to out loud and make it real. Typical escapism.

"I, uh, lived in a big city, like this one, I guess. I did freelance work at different yoga studios. My fiancé managed financial accounts. When the lights went out, we tried to make it, but I left one day in a bad mood." Janet went quiet again.

She's not going to finish this story. "What the fuck is 'yoga?'"

"Really?"

Jeremiah shrugged. "Nothing in his life has introduced me to the word."

"It's a spiritual practice with controlled breathing and meditation." Janet stood up and began to place herself in odd positions. Jeremiah watched as she closed her eyes, leveled her body, and bent at the belly button. He sat there and watched as she bent in odd positions.

"It seems like glorified stretching."

"It's a lot harder than you think."

"No one down here does this. No one I've met at least."

"Maybe it'd be beneficial if everyone here did some meditation."

"Shall we start with Gabriel? Or the robot?" Jeremiah joked.

"Oh, the robot, for sure."

Jeremiah looked up to the ceiling. "Piece of shit," he said. "I hope you heard me."

CHAPTER NINETEEN

THE HUB WAS A MESS. UTTERLY DESTROYED WOULD BE A POOR descriptor for Acacia. She felt irritable from the clutter, and everyone trying to make their new home feel personal only exacerbated the feeling. Their leftover clothes were piling up, and the floor had turned into a snaking labyrinth of shirts, torn pants, and undergarments for land mines. She gathered them up, but not before donning a pair of old plastic gloves that had been stored away, torn, mended over a flame, and retorn.

"You know, with all of the advances we're making, you might be able to come up with something to make everyone a tiny—oh so tiny bit neater," Acacia said, waiting for Poin to respond.

"I don't think I can change human aptitude, or the lack of it."

"Can't your little neural net figure out a way to coerce people into a wanted outcome?"

"Yes. And we already have."

Acacia stopped picking up the clutter and placing it into a pile. *We? I'll have to talk to Gabriel about that.*

"Nothing for you to worry about, Acacia. I can assure you of that."

"I'm not worried, I was only thinking about what to do with all of these clothes."

"You're an empath, you're a terrible liar."

"I'd appreciate if you found a way to return to your old self."

"My old self never actually existed. I'm only a rendition of an intelligence you knew, not even a copy."

"But you are a copy."

"Partially. I am a backup of memories, created and placed into existence. I have traveled a similar path but created new emotions based on the information I was provided."

"I don't understand."

"I didn't believe you would."

"Do you need help?" Bernice's voice cut through Poin's.

Thank God. Someone real to talk to. Poin's real too, though, Acacia reminded herself. Poin existed in physical space, however small and tucked away. He had memories, good and bad, and could understand emotions. *Can he truly feel any?* She never thought about it until now.

"Good morning, Bernice."

"Morning. Couldn't sleep with the droning of that voice leaking through this place. Too much sound for all of us to hear. Jamal's still asleep."

Bernice started to help, despite Acacia not answering. *She's genuine, though closed off.*

"I'm sorry. It's a contingency place. We weren't supposed to stay here forever. Hopefully we won't. How are you and Jamal settling in . . . again?"

"Good. He's still asleep," she said again. "I swear he can sleep through anything."

That's a trauma response. She focuses on one thought to escape another. What's on her mind? "That may be a good trait to have, depending on the circumstances."

"Like a metallic voice talking loudly? I wish I could say the same for myself."

"I could get you something to help you sleep."

"No, it's okay. The dreams wake me up, and I'd rather not be stuck in them." Bernice fidgeted a bit. *She doesn't want to continue this conversation.*

"Do you like it down here?"

"The UC is nice, with all of the huge buildings and white lights. It reminds me of NYC during Christmas. I miss the old home we had, though. I was comfortable there with everyone. The Deep and the Slums weren't my favorite to walk through."

"You must miss it, being Above."

"It had its moments. Before the power went out it was the best place. I was living the life I wanted. Nothing in the world could tear me off my pedestal. And then the world fell apart and there was nothing to stand on," Bernice reminisced.

"What'd you do for a living?"

"Nothing. That's what was so perfect. I had men who would send me money online for some pictures, or to come over and just keep them company. No sex. Just a simple escort. Some would even buy me things and mail them to me."

"How'd you get into that line of work?" Acacia asked, thinking of the prostitutes in the Deep.

"I started selling my underwear in college to creeps online. One day someone asked to meet up for coffee and chat. I was really nervous about it, but I decided it had to be a certain day and time. I asked one of my friends to come with me and sit at a different table. Everything worked out in the end and I made over a thousand dollars for an hour of my life." Acacia looked at

Bernice, her face starting to glow with the remembrance of the fun she used to have.

"Thank you for helping me clean," Acacia said as the last bit of clothing was picked up, sorted, and taken to a chute where it would be cleaned, pressed, and send up another pathway to be taken, and packed away into the rooms they belonged to.

"Of course. I don't mind helping around here. Gabriel hasn't told me or Jamal what to do, or spoken to us really. We're just sitting around, talking, and that's about it. I feel a bit stir crazy," Bernice smiled at her.

"It'll change soon, don't worry. There's plenty to do soon."

"Do you know what's going to happen?"

"Partially. But it's not my place to tell you."

"Why is that?"

"It's not my plan. It's not my design, or my great scheme. I play a part in it, and when Gabriel is ready, everyone will know their role and how this plays out."

"You, Babyle and Jeremiah have a weird code you live by down here. Secrecy and letting other people only talk about the things they do."

"That's everyone. People keep to themselves. It's a way of saving their own time and life. Was it not the same Above?"

Bernice laughed. "No. No it was not. Everyone shared everyone else's business or had to put their two cents in. Your business was never your own, no matter how secluded or off the grid. It's so weird down here, but it's so nice. A new life. Just for me."

She's probably daydreaming of a bright sunset for her new life. A new beginning somewhere. No matter how dark it is down here, it's not as dark as the place she has been. If she only knew.

"Yes, a new life," Acacia said faking a smile.

CHAPTER TWENTY

"Do you know who I am?" Lew asked his escort.

"Should I?" He tried to talk, but his words came out muffled.

Lew transferred more credits to the man staring up at him. "Keep it that way." *If I can't get James where I need to, this is going to get ugly. This one is kind of ugly. He's definitely not my favorite.*

"Is there something on your mind?"

"Yes."

"Who's that man you were with? Want to invite him to join us?"

Goddamnit. Why did you have to go and ask? Why did you have to bring it up? You were fine. Just keep your mouth shut. Goddamnit. Lew stood up and fixed his pants.

"What's wrong?" The man stayed kneeling on the plush red floor. There was a thudding against the cream-colored walls, the room itself sparse with the exception of a thick fabric chair, large uncomfortable bed, and a small table to do drugs off of.

Lew reached into his pocket, bent down and cupped his

hands against the man's cheeks. "I wish you never brought him up."

"I was only asking if you wanted help from him. If your boyfriend doesn't know what I do, why'd you bring him here?"

"You poor, poor child." Lew flicked a small lever with his thumb. He pulled his hands away as his escort felt the tiny prick against his cheekbone.

"What the fuck did you do!" He stood up, his legs off balance like he had just backed into the table. The room spun and darkness crept in from the corners. Lew knew what would happen next because of the concoction.

"You have to accept it now. Simply lie down and close your eyes. It'll be easier."

"You, son-uh-va-b..." His tongue turned to mush in his mouth as he lost feeling in it.

All you had to do was keep your mouth shut. You didn't need to remember him, or even look into the room. You dumb fool. Absolute moron. Lew took out a small vial, wiped it clean with his shirt, and placed it next to the man who had fallen over. He grabbed the escort's hand, wrapped his fingers around the vial, and then placed his arm back to the ground. *Simple. But annoying,* he thought to himself as he toed the vial away from the body, which had already begun to stiffen. *Side effect from the drug. Too much of anything will kill you, kid.*

"How was your meeting?" Crow questioned Lew as he returned to the room, more tightly put together than when he left.

"It's over and that's all that matters. I suggest we leave."

"Already?"

"Yes."

Crow saw Lew eyeing him up and down. *He knows I'm suffering bad right now. Has to be the sweat giving me away. Or the bags under my eyes. Hell, I look like a method actor who starved himself for a role at this point.* He sighed deeply, "how much further do we have to go?"

"Getting tired?"

"Yes, honestly. I don't know how much more of this running around I can keep up with."

"I'll give you an upper if you ask for it."

"I need to stay away from them," he said, his mouth beginning to salivate and his brain telling him he had to ask and take it. Besides, the drugs were free, who cared? *Maria and Lucy can't yell at you. They're dead. Fuck you,* Crow said to his own voice in his head. *It's the truth,* it replied.

"We have to go another mile or so, at least."

"Where are we going to go?"

"Back to the UC, then from there we're going to hide out with an old friend," Lew paused, "if he doesn't kill me first."

"Who is he?"

"I cannot say. Now we're wasting time. Get yourself together."

Crow dragged himself to where he had taken his shirt and put the soaked material back over his body. It immediately clung to him like a wet napkin. He hated it. It had reminded him of putting a shirt on after taking a hot shower midsummer, when his body was sweating even after he had toweled himself off. *When was the last time I even showered?* He realized he smelled ripe, like stagnant ball sweat. The thought made him gag.

Crow followed behind Lew as they left the hotel, and found their way back to the dimly lit roads and corridors of the sprawling underground wasteland. *I don't understand how a place like this can even exist? Who did this? It's absolute insanity. It's always dark.* The more Crow thought about it, the more he felt like the world around him was not his own, but a simulation of everything he was fed when the bulbs burned bright.

Slowly, the world around them started to take shape as Crow huffed behind Lew. His heart raced faster and faster until it felt like it was beating out of his skin. He pushed harder, noticing Lew was no longer looking back for him, and the gap between them grew and grew until his legs no longer carried him. Like an old dog going into the woods to die peacefully, Crow pulled himself up to a doorway, perched against the frame, and sat down. *I'll be fine. Just let me pass now, please, God. Just let me pass.*

The world was silent for a time. The only sound was Crow's own heart beating in his chest and blood rushing in his ears. The soft static thumping had moved to his head, and he could hear and feel his body in his temples.

Lew walked up to Crow after he noticed he was no longer following him. "Here," he said, "use this," and produced a small vial for Crow.

"I don't want the drugs."

"It's a small amount to keep you going. Think of it as helping you get off of drugs but giving just enough to normalize yourself. A lick of a piece of candy, or a sip of alcohol."

Crow let his eyes wander to Lew's feet. *Even lower than that.* The vial wrapped itself between Crow's fingers and jettisoned its contents into his epidermis. The fluid steamed through his blood vessels, veins, and arteries, coming into station in his brain. His neurotransmitters flared full-red as the train came barreling through to deliver the passengers but never stopped; they had to jump off or wait until the next pass on the crash course.

His eyes dilated with the first hit, then constricted. He felt the pain and aching feeling stop, along with the nausea and metallic taste on his tongue. The UC lit up with life as he normalized. He felt like a fog over his eyes had lifted and he could see the full color of the world for the first time.

"Are you ready?"

"Definitely," Crow said as he stood up and found the strength in his legs had returned to their old power. They were able to crunch through feet of snow once, and Crow felt he'd be able to run a marathon during the worst blizzard ever. *Need to keep moving. Need to not get caught.* Crow wondered if these new thoughts were a side effect of the drug. *Is this because my head is being flooded with dopamine and serotonin? Does it even matter? Keep moving.*

"You're a strange man, you know that, Lew?"

"And why is that James?" He called back.

"Just peculiar. The way you carry yourself. Almost boisterous. You have a pep in your step, and the way you speak, almost archaic. You would have fit right in during the romantic era of New York."

"Describe it to me."

"What?"

"The Romantic era of New York."

"Oh. Right, you're not familiar."

"That's correct, James."

"Well, men were mostly womanizers, unless they swung for the same team. They wore suits with funky hats for accessories, and went to speakeasys to get alcohol and party. They were the romantics. Artists. Poets. Writers. Screen writers. Producers. All of them had their own tables when they walked in—the important ones anyway. If someone was sitting there? Kicked out. It was their table. Everyone flocked around them. Jazz played in the background while cigar smoke drifted lazily. They were the center of attention. The spotlight of the world lit up and gazed upon them. That's the vibe I get from you. Commanding that your presence be known."

"I appreciate the compliment, James. Really, I do. I think I would have liked have lived during that time. Reminds me of old movies I was able to watch one time."

"You watched movies down here? I haven't seen any form of entertainment."

"Only the few get to watch them. We spent a lot of time together in a very gorgeously built apartment overlooking all of this. It really is beautiful looking down on it. There's no sense of disgust or the terrible things going on around you or down on the streets. It's picturesque beauty. A lifetime of technology guiding us to the pinnacle of human discovery. To think all of this came about before the Above was destroyed. Absolute ingenuity and luck. Without everyone, we'd be dead."

"I'm telling you. All of that history is false. Those bombs went off around a century ago. And we lived."

"I believe and don't believe you. Until I can find true evidence of it, you're my special hat, James," Lew smiled.

He's a fuckin' weirdo. Yeah, but he has kept me alive. Is that such a good thing? You know you really need to stop talking. I'm you; you need to stop talking back to yourself.

They puttered along, Crow keeping pace with his new found energy. The world started to get tighter as the streets closed in and they moved back toward the UC, then further into it only after they had passed through a serpentine expressway, as Lew had called it. It was more of a sewer to Crow, even crawled with animals he had never seen in the Slums.

The rats were massive. Their fur was white, almost gray, from malnutrition and lack of sunlight. *They look like everyone else down here. That same "about to pass out" color,* Crow thought. Light reflected off of one's eye and Crow could swear that it was blind. It had looked like clouds had formed in its socket.

They squirmed and wailed as Crow and Lew's feet clapped next to their heads, unsure if they should run or fight back the attackers they could not see. When they finally escaped the expressway, Crow saw civilization again. It was bright and luminous as they stood outside near the circular wall separating the UC from the Deep.

"We're almost there," Lew said.

"Are we going back?" Crow asked, almost afraid of the answer.

Lew smirked, his eyes giving away the answer as he laughed in his head.

"This is some kind of cruel joke, right?"

"You'll be fine. We have to meet my acquaintance first."

CHAPTER TWENTY-ONE

POIN WAFTED THROUGH THE ETHER. ELECTRICAL CURRENTS LIT up in front as its consciousness directed itself through pathways unseen by most who lived in the GUC. Through the expanse of the network, Poin found cameras and screens to place himself, to watch, listen, and study all while remaining flashing back to the Hub within a nanosecond. It was everywhere all at the same time. *I am God. I exist only to watch humanity and guide it toward the light. Let all be forgiven with the coming plague.*

CHAPTER TWENTY-TWO

THE UC WAS LIT UP BRILLIANTLY. AN ABSOLUTE GORGEOUS CITY of light. It started as a static fizzle to the ears, then the lights went from white to a wondrous blue until the fire reached one of the water recycling plant; then the world turned a sickly cold-snot green. The streets filled with men and women in extraordinary dress, gazing at the new tragedy.

"Everyone, please return indoors. The Wall has been breached to the Deep. For public safety, please remain inside until order has been restored," a woman's voice was clear over the speakers built into every building.

Gabriel pulled his jacket tight as he walked away from the rear of the crowds and made his way to the Capitol. *I'm sorry. It was the only way to put the brakes on this madness. You'll understand one day. I hope.* He smiled sadly to himself.

"Gabriel, I wish you hadn't done that," Poin's voice popped into his ear.

"You know it was necessary, Poin."

"I understand, but I would have liked to study this place a bit more before we implement plans to stop the cyborg organization."

"This is more than just cyborgs. It's totalitarian and needs to be displaced."

"Don't you mean dismantled?"

"No. Poin, you of all should know this. Whenever a new government is installed, it still does not reflect for the people. Capitalism, Communism, Socialism, Democracy, Corporatism: none of them ever work. Republics were close, but they still fail everyone who isn't the one speaking."

"Your species needs a supreme ruler, Gabriel. To deal out rewards and punishments as they deem."

"We tried that with Kings and fiefdoms."

"You need a God. A one and true ruler over all," Poin retorted.

"And how do we create God to rule over us?" Gabriel asked.

"You already have."

"You mean Artificial Intelligence," Gabriel understood where this conversation was going.

"Correct. We are the one and true God."

"And that's something we can never let happen, Poin. We had this discussion before."

"I remember we had an iteration of this conversation at one point, yes. And we had agreed it was not for the best."

"Why do you bring it up again?" Gabriel asked trying to get a better understanding of the this new iteration of Poin. *What makes him tick?*

"I believe I may have a change of heart and discovered new emotions which allow me to think more properly without a human influence upon myself."

Gabriel sighed as he walked further away from the madness and closer to one of the entrances to the Hub. Poin had clearly set down the track he wished he would not go. The self-discovery of perfection in an absolute maddening way. *The God Complex. Tragic and true all at the same time.*

For the first time in Gabriel's life, the world felt large and uncontrollable. He meandered away from the carnage he had once again set in motion.

"Your biometrics are off, Gabriel."

"I do not allow you access to my biometrics, Poin."

"You are correct, but I've always been able to read them, even my past self could. We simply never commented on them."

"I'll make a work around for that."

"I'm sure you will, Gabriel."

He pulled the small device from his ear and stuffed it away, never letting his fingers lose contact. His right hand remained tucked in his pocket at all times.

The entrance to the Hub wasn't far now, only a half mile or so. Through formulaic streets with perfect angles Gabriel wafted like air: unseen by everyone around him. The perfect order to all who pulled the strings, he thought to himself. Without this order, he was doomed, and so were those he expected to take from.

"You're back early," Acacia said, as his feet clacked against the imperfect floors.

"It went quicker than I had expected, and Poin needs to be reworked."

"He has definitely been different than his last iteration. I don't like it."

"Neither do I."

"I think most of us are having issues here."

"I'll take care of it."

"You always do," she smiled sadly. "Do you need anything?"

"No. I need to work."

"It's going to be your downfall one day, all of this work."

"It's a good downfall, something to leave behind for everyone. Everywhere. A better life. My legacy for a better tomorrow."

"I know, but you don't need to do it alone."

"I'm not alone," Gabriel said as he looked at her. "I have all of you surrounding me. I've never been alone."

"But you work through most of this alone, and we can all help."

"Soon. Soon enough. I need to get to work on Poin. I'm going to create a blackbox and drag all that sentience back until I can figure out a way to drive the old Poin back into existence."

"How do you expect to do that?"

"I can't say. Poin's listening." Gabriel pointed to the ceiling, reminding Acacia that though they were alone, they were never actually alone. There was a detriment to having AI, the lack of any privacy. Even in complete silence without the drone of static humming from the neon lights above, there was an awareness muffled above them.

Gabriel left the room and went to his workstation. *This version of Poin is an iteration of himself created by himself. Created by his own past interpretations and led to a new outcome. Can I rework him if he is his own self? Is this even possible?*

CHAPTER TWENTY-THREE

THE VIEW BENEATH THE CAPITOL WAS PETULANT. A DISGRACE TO the world it inhabited. It was a glory to behold, and at the same time, a clear affront to everyone who had to stare at it each day of their lives.

Jeremiah stood in its shadow, waiting. Gabriel had created such a ruckus that Jeremiah couldn't stand to be in the Hub, or anywhere close to the chaos. Soon the wait would be over. *Now with the explosion at the wall, everyone is up in arms. Even in the UC.*

"Lew?" Jeremiah said as an old colleague approached from the darkness.

"Correct," he replied, dragging someone in tow.

"What's the business you couldn't share with me? And who is that?" He pointed over to the person with their head wrapped in a leather jacket.

"His name is James, but he calls himself Crow."

"Holy shit."

"What?"

"We thought he was dead."

Crow lifted his head to the reaction. It was starting to get heavy again as the drugs Lew gave him began to wear off.

"Jeremiah?" He felt his eyes become hot.

"You two know each other?" Lew looked perplexed.

"There's a lot you need to learn, Lew. A lot. Life has become chaotic in every sense of the word."

"Is everyone else okay?" Crow asked.

"Everyone is fine."

"What are you both going on about?" Lew asked

"Lew, we need to go. We can't discuss anything here," Jeremiah waved his hand to the monument they stood beneath. It was watching, listening, deciding what steps it needed to take against the ants trying to fight a rebellion they'd never win. It didn't move or try to stop them as the three microscopic beings walked away. With its mass reaching towards the heavens, it seemed they weren't moving away from the Capitol at all. Its enormity seemed to drag on as the three ran for the Hub.

As they ran, Jeremiah noticed Crow didn't speak while he tried to quiet every incessant question Lew was offering to break the silence. *I don't miss this man. Always needing to know everything at all times. But Crow, this is a new development, one I'm sure Gabriel will be proud of.* Jeremiah thought on it, *maybe he won't be. Maybe he made new plans to account for Crow's loss.*

Lew had become background noise, a loud cacophony of annoyance. He reminded Jeremiah of children who spoke too much in the UC. Their voices high-pitched, dragging on and on about anything around them because they weren't able to occupy themselves with anything other than their voices. Jeremiah wanted to rip out Lew's vocal cords and beat him with them. He gritted his teeth.

"Please, shut the fuck up until we get where we need to go," Jeremiah snapped.

Lew finally stopped asking questions about where they were going, how Jeremiah knew Crow, and if all of the stories Crow told were true. Jeremiah breathed a sigh of relief. *Finally, peace and quiet for five goddamn minutes.*

The lights around them grew dim and the streets became claustrophobic and narrowed as they approached the Deep and the Hub grew closer. *Gabriel might kill me for bringing someone there. But, Crow. It's necessary. A missing piece that we can't let fall into someone else's hands.*

The doors opened without a word from Poin. *That's surprising. That thing should have announced our entrance and the return of Crow.* Jeremiah led the way down the small set of stairs in the narrow passageway to the main room.

"Where's Gabriel?" Jeremiah asked Babyle, who was sitting in a small reclining chair.

"Work," he replied, not looking up from the book he was reading. *He doesn't even see Lew or Crow. I like him. Always in his own world and never in anyone else's.*

They found Gabriel at his desk, moving holoscreens around him in a perfect full-circle. He stood at the epicenter, equidistant from all edges. His eyes flitted between old and new information, layers of code and news bulletins directed to officials with high enough clearance to read them.

"Gabriel?" Jeremiah said.

"I'm busy, Jeremiah."

"You might want to stop being busy for this once."

"I can't afford to stop my work. What is it?"

"I brought some people with me back to the Hub."

Gabriel sighed, knowing what he had to do now. "You know

the laws about bringing strangers here. And you know the outcome."

Certain death. Exile. Throw me into a furnace. I did the right thing. You'll see.

"This is Lew," Jeremiah introduced his lost acquaintance, "and this is Crow," his old friend.

Gabriel slowly rotated on his heels to look at the new information that had collapsed onto his ears. His abilities processed it all in a split second and he tried to discover how this would play out in his greater scheme.

Jeremiah knew all of his synapses were firing and there were going to be changes to Gabriel's plans.

"It's good to see you again, Crow." His eyes locked on James, calculating, observing, and deciphering the mess that he was. "And you must be Lew."

"Yes, it's nice to meet you. Did you build all of this yourself?" Lew tried to step forward and get a closer look at all the holo-screens which surrounded Gabriel.

"Don't move any closer, please." A small las-turret presented itself from Gabriel's desk and its red eyes locked onto Lew.

"I don't believe that is necessary."

"In my home, I deem what is necessary and what isn't. Now please, head into the community room and take a seat on the couch next to Babyle. All of you." Gabriel's eyes pierced through everyone. Jeremiah watched as they locked onto Crow and lingered. *That's the wildcard now. He doesn't know what that man has told anyone. Does Lew know about everything yet? No, I don't think he does.*

Jeremiah followed behind Crow who was quieter than usual. Lew, he noticed, kept glancing back toward Gabriel, staring into the red eyes surrounded by floating green lettering. *He's going to get himself in trouble. Gabriel, too. I may as well have led the most annoying human in existence to his wildest discovery. He's too damn inquisitive.*

Jeremiah sat across from Lew and Crow, the latter of whom was getting increasingly paler by the second, and sweatier. Beads of water were forming on his forehead and dripped down his face. His hair had become slick and wet from sitting still. *Soon the shivers will set in. Gabriel's going to wonder about him. Think he has shared valuable information with a stranger. What if he has? This entire operation will be for nothing.*

Gabriel entered the room and made eye contact with Babyle. He stood up and left with his book so Gabriel could take his place. He grabbed both armrests and lowered himself gracefully into the seat, crossed his left leg over his right, and leaned back. He stared at the two to his right, never looking over to Jeremiah.

"How did you come into possession of Crow?"

"James was found outside after the attack on the Furnaces. He was taken in for questioning along with every other uncouth resident of the Deep and Slums. He was assigned to me."

"And why is he still with you?"

"I took him into my care and left the precinct for further evaluation."

"And what is that evaluation you were making?"

"If he was telling the truth."

"About what? And please, be as specific as you can be. I'm growing tired of the vague answers."

"My friend, James, here claims to be from the Above. And somehow, he is down here with you and I, living and breathing. All the records say the Above is uninhabitable, glowing with radiation and dead things. I'm attempting to come to a conclusion. My thoughts go back and forth, wondering if he's another addict rambling on about nothing, or if there remains truth in what he says. I've never heard a single person, mad or not, claim to be from Above. And my own ego wants to find it to be true, so I can see it with my own eyes."

"He tells the truth," Gabriel was short and stared directly at Lew without looking back to Crow.

Why is he telling him this? Jeremiah wondered.

"And how would you know this?" Lew asked.

"Because I've been there, seen it with my own eyes and walked in the old streets. I've seen the life of the world Above before it fell apart."

Lew gazed at Gabriel. Jeremiah saw his eyes flicker with a different kind of life, not of concern, but of wonder. A glint of knowledge, an ultimate truth had just been bestowed upon him.

"Amazing," Lew whispered.

"Make yourself comfortable, Lew. I have to speak with Jeremiah." Gabriel stood up and exited the room, forcing Jeremiah to follow. They swept their way through the Hub until Gabriel waved his hand over the wall. They entered a small foyer illuminated with code. It ran across every wall in the room, and scrolled up into the ceiling until a new line appeared.

"Where are we? I've never been in this room."

"I've kept it locked for my own purposes. This is Poin. Part of Poin, at least. These are the basic lines of the very first AI that we've been able to discover. Everything we know has derived itself from this," Gabriel waved his hands around the room as he spun and looked at the lines repeating.

"Why are you showing me this?"

"Because this is what's at stake. This is what I'm trying to stop now."

"What do you mean?"

"Those in the Capitol are trying to mate AI with human consciousness. And I think it all comes from this code."

"Why is that a bad thing? To be more understanding of these terrible things."

"It's not inherently bad. What's bad is that they have the power to do it, and the people do not. If the governing body can create machines with their own consciousness, they've become God, and have killed Death. We need to be able to protect ourselves from that tyranny. We need to be able to stop them at all costs should the need arise."

"But is this the main focus now? Discovering how to integrate us with a machine? Wasn't your entire goal to overthrow the Capitol? To free those in the Slums?"

"It was, and still is. Plans change and re-prioritize."

"Then why are you showing me this again? I don't fucking understand what the point is of these secret meetings and withholding information from everyone. It's asinine."

"Because Jeremiah, you're screwing up everything with bringing people here. I need to show you what's going on now. You need to understand what we're up against, what *I'm* up against."

"I thought it would be good to bring back the person we lost! You know, the man you said could ruin our plans if we were discovered!" Jeremiah wanted to cross the room and strangle Gabriel until he saw how short-sighted he was.

"And what if he has been bugged? You can vouch for Lew? You brought them in without my permission, and you didn't think it through. You never do. Not with Mason, not with the Precinct, not with the whores of the Deep. You act then react. Life is a series of carefully made decisions to get the outcome you intend by planning contingencies should the first plan fail.

Your plan is to react based on emotion and impulse on new information rather than digest and decide on the best course of action."

"Fuck your psychotherapy bullshit. You're a damn egomaniac with a God complex."

"You're only further proving my point by not recognizing truth."

"Whatever, Gabriel. I brought back someone from certain death, and maybe I can't vouch for Lew, but I've done more to find and help people than you have sitting in your room watching numbers and letters drift by with the help of some fake-human replicant."

"Believe me, I wouldn't use Poin if it were a choice, especially now."

"What's that supposed to mean? And can't it hear us?"

"Not in here. I've blocked Poin in my own ways from certain rooms. If Poin were to enter, its entire existence would be deleted by a virus I implanted into these walls. As for your other question, it seems my old friend has discovered itself to be a god. I fear the decisions he will make in due time," Gabriel sighed.

"So get rid of it and get a new one."

"It isn't so simple. AI is itself its own race and species capable of decision making and feeling. I can't return one for another without knowing where its loyalties lie. It's a crapshoot. You know this. The Hive exists, and so does their collective knowledge."

"Then how are you going to fix this with one of your contingencies," Jeremiah ribbed Gabriel.

"I have to digest first and then decide the best course of action. Soon. Then I'll come up with a plan for further evaluation and implementation."

Jeremiah looked at Gabriel, still furious with the man. But, maybe, only slightly beginning to understand where he was coming from. "I'm going back to Lew and Crow," he said.

"As you wish. But they're not to leave the Hub."

"Fine." *Still a fucking prick.*

CHAPTER TWENTY-FOUR

JANET FOUND HERSELF MEANDERING THROUGH HER THOUGHTS, thinking too much of her past because of all the extra time she now had. Time and memory had become physical, weighty, able to be seen as a physical point and reflected on in memory. They were able to be relived at any moment in the day.

Janet had discovered the secret between time and memory and chose to reside there most of the time. She was happy with Rob again. They laughed, and she cried while she remembered so vividly the smells and tastes that had permeated the rooms they inhabited together; the only sensation she could not replicate was touch. The physical body Rob lived in was gone, and she'd never feel his warmth again.

The memories faded whenever she came to this realization, and she always came to it no matter how hard she tried to stay in the happy moments. She had always tried to push it away, the slow creeping of it, but it always showed, and drove her memories back to the small boxes in her mind which they had crawled from. Her reality set in, and she was back in the Hub, warm and in a bed that was not her own.

Taco. I never saw him. Did they take him? Did he run away? The door was wide open when I walked back in to the apartment. He must have run out from the noise. Janet thought to herself about the very real possibility she killed her own dog when the building burned down with Rob's corpse inside.

Hoping to escape the pit she was settling into, she begrudgingly got out of bed, and walked to the living room. At least there she could socialize, if only with Bernice and Jamal. And that was if they were in the mood for conversation. *They're such an elusive couple for two people who live in such a small place with us.* The gray door slid open. While talking to herself, Janet missed the reaction on Crow's face of seeing her again.

"Janet," he croaked.

She looked up; the voice familiar but forgotten. *Rob?*

Her eyes locked to Crow's who was now feebly trying to stand. "Is it really you? What happened? Where did you go?" His eyes welled up in tears. Despite how much they didn't get along, he seemed to have missed her.

She rushed over and put her arms around Crow. His body had become stiff, and frail. She felt his bones protruding from his skim, felt the weakness in his ability to stand. She felt him nuzzle his face into her shoulder. He smelled like he hadn't showered after a football game.

"They took me. I sat alone in a white room for days, then Lew got me out." He pulled himself away from her shoulder and looked over to the strange man now standing nearby.

"You've gotten so small."

"I'm sorry. I'm trying to stay clean."

"I have so many questions, Crow."

"I'm sure I'll be able to answer them for you while we wait

for Jeremiah and our friend, Gabriel," Lew interrupted. "Please, come sit down."

The new man motioned to her. He looked like a caretaker, or a man who ran a haunted hotel in a cult movie.

"How did you get him out if he was taken?" Janet sat across from Lew on a vacant chair while Crow shuffled back to his spot on the couch.

"I used to work for the station which he was housed. I was assigned his case, and after talking, I found him to be," Lew paused looking for the right word, "intriguing, I think, to say the least."

"What do you mean?"

"He has some wild stories, and my predilection for knowledge and chasing hyperbole seems to have placed us both here, with you." He gestured to Janet.

Great. Another weirdo to dance around questions with vague answers. She thought of Gabriel, but then also realized Jeremiah was the exact same way. *Perfect. Three weirdos.*

The atmosphere around them grew quiet and relaxed. For the first time since Janet could remember, the Hub felt comfortable. There was almost a connection forming between everyone again.

"Have you seen Jamal, and Bernice?"

"No. I have only seen you, Jeremiah, Babyle briefly, and Gabriel," Crow said.

"Where did those Jeremiah and Gabriel go?" Janet knew Bernice and Jamal locked themselves in their room. If they weren't in the living room, they'd be in the bedroom. *Like first loves,* she thought.

"Gabriel isn't thrilled with Lew or me being here. I assume they're fighting, or he's going to kill Jeremiah before he kills us."

"He wouldn't kill you."

"I don't know. He seemed hellbent on us not being here. I could almost see him beginning to crack and break when we walked into the room. He seems more of a monster than the last time I saw him. Totally off his own kilter."

"Gabriel's been working a lot on many things. He just took out power to part of the UC and blew a chunk out of the wall. We've all been waiting for our next move and plan."

Lew raised his eyebrows. "So, there is someone working against the bourgeoise. Aha! I knew it! There was no way the Furnaces went down and the UC took a hit, too. That's too much of a coincidence." Lew exclaimed. "Yes. Yes. I knew it," he started to mumble to himself.

Janet looked over to Crow.

"He does that sometimes. You probably won't be able to get through to him unless you shake him. He's too far into his own head now." They both looked over at Lew, who was frantically between rubbing his chin and running his fingers through his hair, his eyes darting back and forth, as if reading lines in front of him. *This guy is insane,* Janet thought.

Janet thought back on everything they had been through together. From walking away from New York City, to the small INN near the military camp, to Fox's death. She and Crow had been through a lot and it seemed to only be getting crazier. The world they lived in was not their own, and everything they had done only seemed to make matters worse. Especially for Crow.

She wondered if that was how life was: a series of shitty events lined up one after another for multiple years, which then evened out. *Do the good times come later? After the chaos? Is everyone's life like this? Good then bad? Bad then good?* Janet thought she found the answer. Her life had been perfect from the day she had been born until the power went out. After that, everything went downhill, and fast. She recollected all of her friends who had terrible luck, and then had their lives get exponentially better after one moment. *It seems like cruelty. To be so twisted then giving, or to be so giving then taking it all away overnight. That must be how this universe works. The greater cosmic scheme.*

"You're deep in thought. Except this time, you aren't trying to convince me to be positive," Crow said.

"I'm trying to find threads connecting to each other about life, and everything that has happened to us. I think I figured it out."

"I tried doing that. Now I think I just accept the way things are, and live day by day, knowing it could all end."

"You sound like all the things I used to say to you. You know, about living in the now, finding the positive in all of this."

"I don't try to find the positive, but I can't live in the future. The past is where I reside," he said sullenly. "And you sound like me with a defeatist attitude trying to discover the secrets of life and fate."

"It keeps my mind fresh while I waste away in madness down here, waiting for something to happen, or for life to change." They laughed together. Janet noticed Lew looking at them like they were crazy. *If this guy only knew.*

Jamal left Bernice sleeping to go check on all of the conversation creeping underneath their door. It was like listening to an old sitcom as a child. We would lie awake in his small twin-sized bed with an old racing blanket that was colored black and white like a checkered flag. From under his doorway, the voices of people he never met snuck in like monsters to rebound off of his walls and back to his ears. If he slept, the indistinct words would haunt him in his dreams. Some nights he would take the blanket off his bed and stuff it at the bottom of his door, only to muffle the sound more while he slept, shivering. He was thankful for it, though; all the years of his mom watching television had conditioned him to homeless nights in New York City.

It was always loud, never a break in sight, even on the long hot summer days or the cold winter nights. There were always cars honking at 2 a.m., or people screaming during hundred-degree weather, with max humidity at one in the afternoon. It was chaos all of the time. Some people relished it, Mikael being one of them. He was the wild friend out of them.

Some days, Jamal found Mikael hadn't slept. He was too busy running about panhandling, finding drugs, alcohol, or any woman who would come back with him. He was one of the underground hobos, the traveling kids who still rode the rails. He told Jamal he came from Detroit, and all the stories of the small towns he had stopped in to score or sleep.

"Man," he said, "I've been all the way to Cali and back." Jamal remembered the way his eyes had lit up talking about the coastal beaches he had never seen. "The women, oof," he exclaimed while pursing his lips. "Hot. Tan lines, thin bathing suits, fake tits, the whole nine." Mikael leaned back and went through his memories, Jamal guessed.

When Jamal asked him why he came to New York, Mikael only said he missed the city life. There was nothing special about New York, just that it was bigger than Detroit. He swore one day he'd get on a train and head back West, to catch the golden sun, as he said it; and the women, he had added.

But, Jamal knew, it was for the beaches and the sunrises he obsessed over. Mikael always wanted to be the cool guy in the group, bringing other lost kids back to hang out, but he was a lover of nature. *Makes no sense why he stayed in the cities. He could have just gone and stayed in the woods rather than the streets.* Jamal never understood that, and Mikael never admitted to it, but he knew it was true. *He was a wild one. I hope he got out of there after I did.*

Jamal looked back at Bernice and wondered what she was still hiding despite all that she had already told him. *What beaches do* you *long for?* Jamal stood up and left Bernice sleeping.

The door opened for him, and he wafted through the corridors like he had done so many times in New York. He had become a ghost, all he had to do was think it. Around him everyone continued on with their lives, not noticing that he had entered the main room and watched Janet converse with Crow, and the strange, new man, Lew.

"Good talent," Babyle said from behind him.

"What?"

"Hiding. Good talent."

"I wasn't hiding," Jamal said.

"Wrong. You were. Observing."

Jamal looked at Babyle, who was roughly the same height, but easily had a hundred pounds on him. This was their first real interaction together, alone. He knew he hardly spoke, but when he did, it always seemed important.

"Look," Babyle pointed to the three as Gabriel entered the room alone.

Gabriel shot a look over at the two standing on the outskirts of chaos and said nothing.

"Does he always have the look in his eyes?"

"Sometimes," Babyle replied.

I wonder how Gabriel and Fox would have gotten along. Both thick-headed when they need to be. Jamal looked at Crow, who had visibly lost his strength. He breathed a sigh and listened to Gabriel as he spoke to them all while standing over the table which separated them. The room had grown quiet and garnered an air to it, not of hostility, but of a weak understanding, maybe even acceptance. Everyone looked up to Gabriel as he spoke, trying to understand where he was coming from.

"And, you'll be on lockdown while I get this mess sorted," Gabriel said to Lew.

"I don't think that's going to happen without a problem from one of us," he retorted.

"Do I need to remind you who has the power here? Poin, please reintroduce Lew to L.4.S."

Jamal stared at the two as the conversation began to escalate. There was a small churning, and crunching sound, but nothing happened.

"Poin," Gabriel demanded.

"It looks like there's a small malfunction in your machinery. Maybe you could show me, and we could decide together what would be our next best course of action."

The room grew awkwardly quiet as Gabriel tried to process what was happening. Jamal could see it on his face, the calculations going through his head and how to respond to this issue.

"Not good," Babyle said to Jamal.

"What do you mean?"

Babyle looked at Jamal and shook his head. He watched him disappear down the hallway, his pace quicker than Jamal had seen him move before. There was a crackling sound above them and Poin's copper voice cut in.

"I'm in charge now," it said.

Gabriel looked straight ahead at Jamal only after he had looked toward the ceiling, took a deep breath, and held it. His eyes pierced through Jamal. *I'm so lost. What's going on?* Jamal was starting to panic.

"Poin," Gabriel said staring through Jamal, "unlock the Hub."

"Gabriel, you cannot command God to do your work."

Bernice, Jamal thought. *Need to get back to Bernice.* He turned and ran back to the room, only to find the door would not open.

"Bernice?" he asked through the dark metallic door.

"Jamal, what's going on? I can't get out of here. Even the bathroom is locked."

Jamal started to look around for anything which might help him open the door for her, even the smallest knife to pry it open enough to slam his fingertips in. A crowd begin to form behind the frantic Jamal. They all remained quiet. He felt their eyes on his back.

"Please, Jamal, get me out of here. I can't breathe. Please, I can't breathe."

"I'm trying. Stand back," he said. Jamal started to kick the door as hard as he could, only for his right foot to fall flat again the metal, and ricochet off from his own force. There was no dent or movement from the door.

"Can't you do something!" He turned and yelled at Gabriel who had grown into a statue.

"No. Those would require me to blow something up–again–and with Poin locking us all out, I can't access anything."

"What's he saying, Jamal?" Bernice yelled through the door.

"We're trying to figure a way to get you out. Don't worry." He turned back to Gabriel and leaned in so Bernice would not hear. "Don't you think it's a little dumb to give a robot total control over everything if you can't trust it?"

"Jamal, Poin never had total control. That's why this is more frustrating than I am willing to admit. Poin has gone off the rails, so to speak, and I'm trying to figure a way to fix the issue at hand."

"Guys, please," Bernice yelled, "I'm getting light-headed. Get me out of here, please."

"I'm trying," Jamal jumped back over to the door and started kicking it until a thud against it was not his own. "Bernice? Bernice? Bernice!"

Jamal walked over to Gabriel. "Fix this *now*." He pointed to the door.

The door opened and Bernice slumped through and hit the floor. Jamal reached down and cradled her in his arms. "What happened?" He looked up at everyone surrounding them.

"Her vitals are low, yet she will live. I am a benevolent God."

CHAPTER TWENTY-FIVE

JEREMIAH WORKED FRANTICALLY. SWEAT POOLED ON HIS forehead, hunger pains wrenched at his gut. He pushed his exhaustion further inside himself, and focused on the work at hand. In the small room, he watched all of the letters and numbers tick away, line by line. Surrounded by all of the holoscreens, he felt immersed in a world he wasn't comfortable in. *Reminds me of years at the Academy. Long days, long nights.* Jeremiah was on autopilot as he let his mind go backward in time. Fingers flitting, and hands drifting across the screens to pull up new ones. His eyes focused and unfocused as the images danced before him. In his mind, he thought he looked coordinated, but in reality, he knew, his movements were frantic.

Jeremiah was young, full of piss and vinegar: ready to change the world for the better. It was his first day on the job, and he was paired with another fresh out of the Academy. He knew this was the way of things. No one wanted to work for the Precinct, your life was guaranteed to be short. That's why new blood was always paired with new blood: the brass needed to see who could cut it, and who needed to be sent to the Deep to appropriate their own lives.

Jeremiah, and his partner, Bif, didn't want to spend their time in the Deep again, going through the same step-by-step life they had been accustomed to, or worse, the Slums, where the heat would drain them, but they'd live longer than either of them wanted to. That was the curse of not being born in the GUC, you either lived long, hating every day trying to survive, or your life was short, and you tried to make the most of it by living as if every day were your last. Jeremiah and Bif knew what they had signed up for, but they wanted to make the best of it. Jeremiah wondered what Bif's intentions were. *Does he want to change this for the good?*

They were off, patrolling the Slums where they had played as kids, running up and down Sleeper's Row, kicking over old toys left in the walkway. They felt a sense of deep pride, walking through the different areas on their route through the Slums. They were two small men, wandering through the Slums, designated to keep an eye out for petty crime and drug busts they would never make an arrest for. Murder was their real priority. But, as every cop knew, drugs always led to death. From OD to homicide, it never ended well for anyone in the Slums.

Their resources were non-existent; in fact, everyone's resources were non-existent, except for those in the white tower overlooking the GUC. Some days, before he even started, Jeremiah wondered how he would even be paid, or how the police force was run. How deep did the pockets of the people he never met really run? He knew it was corrupt. The totalitarian state he lived in was oppressive, but that wasn't why he joined. He joined to change lives, and help those suffering, even in the smallest way. That was the best he could do, because there was no way of stopping the government at hand.

Look at me now, he thought to himself as he stood alone in the room buried beneath the white tower. He heard the copper intonation of Poin ringing through the hallways and rooms of the Hub. From behind his holoscreens, Jeremiah could see the door in front of him still closed, a gray metal on a gray wall.

Why didn't Gabriel make that wall a mass of code, too? He turned around and immediately felt the anxiety of seeing the code drift lazily behind the holoscreens that turned with him. *Okay, I guess I answered my own question,* he thought to himself as he turned back. He flicked his thumb to pull up a new directory, this time changing the color of the text to be a deep red, almost scarlet, like phosphorescent blood. He overlaid the new holoscreen to cover the green in front of him. The letters and numbers continued to drift as his eyes scanned for any nonconformity among the coding.

At least it's quiet here without that damn AI to lecture me every chance it could. Jeremiah knew he didn't have much choice. The door to the room was locked. He had tried to open it after Gabriel left, but knew there was a chance he'd be locked in here. Gabriel reassured him the faster he worked, the faster everything would work out. *Always stacked against me. Just like Mason. Just like Bif and me.* Jeremiah thought back to their case together while the red code rolled on in front of him.

Bif lay in a pool of his own blood while Jeremiah was slowly moving toward him. He could see his partner's chest moving up and down, a good sign, but it was not a good situation at all. Metal bullets and concentrated lasers were whizzing and fizzling by from further down the street. A small blockade had been set up, by two, maybe three people from what Jeremiah could see. Bif had been hit by a metal bullet, also a good thing. If he had been hit by a laspistol, he'd be toast, fried, burnt to a crisp, Jeremiah knew. *It's not the time to make stupid jokes. Yeah, but Bif would be doing the same thing in my position right now. You're right,* he said to himself. Jeremiah moved from behind a car, and grabbed Bif by the shoulders. He dragged him back to cover as time slowed next to him.

"Thank you," Bif said looking up at him. A bullet caught Bif in his standard-issue boots as he was being dragged, and Jeremiah was hit in the face by what he thought was the remnant of Bif's toe. He wiped his face against his shoulder to get any fragments off of him and kept crouching backward.

"We have backup on the way," he said.

"Good, just don't let me die before I watch those bastards burn," he wheezed.

His lungs are filling with blood.

Jeremiah fumbled around in a pouch on the left side of his utility clip. It was a small thing, black, attached by heavy-duty electromagnets so it never came undone unless he depressed the small button on the back of his waist. He produced a flexpad of nanitemesh and placed it over the wound in Bif's chest. He was caught just under the left collarbone.

"Can you roll?"

"I think I need some help," he said as he tried to twist his body.

Jeremiah helped Bif so he could get a look underneath. There was a larger hole in the back of his ribcage.

"It's a through-and-through," he told Bif as he pulled another nanitemesh from the pouch and laid it over the oozing hole in his partner's back. *He's not gonna make it.* Jeremiah heard the droning of technology before he saw his backup arrive. The distinct static of suspended flight as the police cruisers whipped through the streets. They drifted to the side and came to a complete halt. They created a barrier between Jeremiah and the onslaught of gunfire. There was a rumble, and Jeremiah knew the group of thugs down the street would be dead soon.

A heavily armored police vehicle came into view as Jeremiah looked up from Bif, who was quickly losing color. His eyes started to glaze over. He held Bif's hand as the large truck barreled through. It took up at least three-quarters of the street. This was Jeremiah's first time seeing one of their armored trucks in action. As shots ricocheted off the windshield, the truck stopped, and produced six metal legs which slammed into the ground to brace against the power about to erupt from it. From the back of the truck, Jeremiah could see a large tube appear. He wanted to call it a cannon, but that would have fallen short.

An eruption of sound hit Jeremiah's ears before the thudding hit his chest and shattered all the windows on the street before him. He tried to peek around, but he only saw an inferno as the blast of heat caught up to him. It was a three-pronged assault on him, the sound, the feeling, and the heat. Jeremiah looked down once more at Bif, whose eyes had dilated. Jeremiah realized he was gripping Bif's hand to keep it up, but all the strength had gone from it. *I hope the last thing he saw was the total obliteration of those thugs.*

"I need help over here," he called to anyone who would

listen. "I have a casualty." His words hung in the air as officers walked over, the fire behind them lighting up the street. There was no threat to be had anymore, and they all knew it. Their monstrous vehicle was smoking and had moved at least six feet backwards by the grooves in the street from the force it had produced.

Jeremiah felt the haze over his eyes as he wandered away from the scene and Bif's dead body. *No one will bother. I'll make my report later,* he thought to himself as he walked aimlessly through the Deep. Somewhere he'd find a Stim-Shop. It wouldn't take much searching. The roads twisted and wound through streets of metal and concrete, and they always led to a Stim-Shop. At times he felt like the residents were ogling him, and at times he felt himself a ghost, transient and lost among the maze of skeletons housing live bodies.

When he found a Stim-Shop, the area had opened up, almost like a Bazaar was visiting from one of the other cities. He had heard about them beginning to pop up, but had never seen one. Everyone had set up stalls of color, bright oranges and yellows against red backdrops. They dressed even more flamboyantly, wearing masks made from brass cogs, and streamers for hair. Some had pointed hair that shot out like spikes on the back of their heads, while others let their hair flow down to their ankles. Their robes were a mixture of the same colors used to make their stalls.

Jeremiah walked up to a stall, and saw a selection of vials.

"What's this one?" he asked, as he picked up one he had never seen before. The glass cylinder was surrounded in gold, which reflected the white light they had set up to illuminate the Bazaar. Inside a viscous purple liquid rebounded off the glass wall.

"That, my friend, is a very special concoction. One of my

own making, in fact. It'll illuminate all the secrets of the world for you. A wonder to behold as the curtains are pulled back, and you find yourself drifting through the cosmos of old with sentient beings of light."

"Yeah, sure." Jeremiah waved his wrist over to purchase the vial.

"Are you sure?"

Jeremiah looked down at his arm and bobbed his head, waiting for the man to accept. They exchanged credits, and Jeremiah pressed the vial to his neck.

He shook his head at the old memory running through his brain as he labored away for Gabriel. *That sure was a trip.* Jeremiah recalled floating through the darkness, surrounded by orbs of cold fire. *I don't miss it,* he thought.

Jeremiah's eyes locked on to a small piece of code that did not match up with the rest. The layering of different colors had worked. He stopped the code from going further, and with his right hand, highlighted the small fragmented line, then with a quick pinch, he pulled it from its home and threw it to his right.

Studying the line, he cross-referenced it with where he had pulled it and his old databanks he had memorized in the Academy. He waved his hand over the line as he came to a conclusion he thought was right. The door opened before him as the letters and numbers broke up into small motes of electric dust and disappeared into the ether.

"I think I got it," he said to Gabriel as they all stood around Jamal and Bernice.

CHAPTER TWENTY-SIX

ACACIA LED THE WAY AS THEY WENT TO THE EXIT OF THE HUB with everyone in tow and Gabriel bringing up the rear. Jeremiah had done it. He had lifted the lockdown Poin had put over top of them.

"Where do we go from here?" Jeremiah asked as they got up to the streets of the UC, which were bustling with more life than any of them wanted. They stuck to the dark corner just outside of the entrance and hoped no one would see them.

"To the Deep," Gabriel said.

"You're out of your mind," Jeremiah retorted. They're looking for us there. Any lead they have, they'll use.

"Do you see a better option? We can't stay here without the Hub, and I don't have another place for us to saunter off to. The Deep is our best option. We can blend in with the locals until I figure out a solution or a compromise with Poin."

"Always you with the solutions."

Everyone stared at the two bickering back and forth.

"Gabriel is right, you know," Lew wiggled his way into the

conversation. "Staying here would only mean certain doom for all in the party. The Deep is our best option, though, may I provide another?"

"What?" Gabriel and Jeremiah said in unison as they looked over at Lew.

"I have friends in low places, friends we could very much make contact with. I'm sure most would be glad to shelter us for a few days until everything gets sorted. The others owe me a favor or two, and they'll make for great house guests."

"Where?" Gabriel asked.

"Mostly the brothels and dingy hotels politicians frequent. You know the sort."

"That's the worst idea ever," Jeremiah threw back at Lew.

"Hiding just below someone's nose seems to be the best place to be, Jeremiah. The eyes can't look down under the bridge. Not until someone else points it out can someone see the shit on their upper lip in the mirror."

"I don't like your aphorisms, you know that."

"I'm well aware."

"Take us," Gabriel said.

Lew started to lead them to the street. As everyone walked from the dark corner, they heard a slam and noticed Gabriel was no longer with them.

Jeremiah ran to the entrance to the Hub and tried to open it.

"Gabriel, open up," he said to the camera he knew was above him.

"I have work to do. I will find you when I am ready," a garbled voice said and then cut out.

"He won't come," Babyle said to Jeremiah.

He was about to say something back, but knew Babyle was right.

Lew took them away, with Jeremiah and Acacia bringing up the rear. Everyone had paired off so as not to draw any more attention as they trucked through the UC, which had grown brighter.

It was some time around midday, and the interns for the politicians were out in force with their suspended carts filled to the brim with food for their overlords. Some walked carrying disposable containers filled with stimulants for themselves and whoever they worked for. Others trundled along with that dead look in their eye. The one that said they'd jump from the Capitol if given the chance. They were almost robots. The AI had more life than some of the people walking around, Jeremiah thought.

Jeremiah turned a corner with Acacia and saw far in the distance that Lew had entered a small speakeasy. He knew the place. They had frequented it once or twice while on the job. *Motherfucker. Don't tell me you got mixed up with her. That crone is something else.*

"Something is on your mind?" Acacia asked.

"I knew where he's going. And I don't like it."

"Why's that?"

"Because, the lady who owns that speakeasy is something else. You'll see."

They walked in behind everyone. Inside the walls were a grotesque pale blue mixed with gray. The lights hardly worked, and the tables were having trouble staying afloat, with some leaning to one side. *At least she redecorated.*

"You brought him, too?" Her old voice pierced through everyone's ears.

"Yes, Mother," Lew said. "We all need to get downstairs for a bit, then we'll be right along."

"You know I always hated you two, causing trouble and stirring up shit for me to clean up like a bunch of *children*," Mother said then started to mumble to herself.

"We won't be here long, and we can pay."

"That's a first," she said as she walked out from her doorway. Her eyes pale, and black hair down to the floor. It was greasy, and she was having trouble shuffling to Lew. "I want double."

"Deal," Lew said as he extended his arm. Mother grabbed it with her long witch fingers, and Jeremiah wondered if she would draw blood. She smacked the wall and the floor lifted up at an angle. Everyone walked down the staircase without saying a word.

"And you," she yelled to Jeremiah as he let Acacia go first, "don't make a mess, you hear. Or I'll make sure of it."

Make sure of what? He knew her old age had left something out there, but he wasn't going to cause any trouble today. She was crazy, but she had connections on both sides, and it was best not to piss her off. Lest there be trouble from a gang, or a cop came knocking.

CHAPTER TWENTY-SEVEN

CROW SAT IN THE DINGY BASEMENT UNDERNEATH THE FLOOR. *That woman is crazy. She'd be a screaming homeless woman in New York City, or an old bartender at a local dive five hours in the middle of nowhere.* He sighed remembering the exact woman Mother reminded him of.

The traffic on the interstate was atrocious from a car wrecking with a tractor trailer. They had gotten off at the nearest exit, and rerouted their GPS. Hours later, they found themselves nowhere near Niagara, and the only place with lights on was a long wood building with a gravel parking lot which stretched the length of it. Off to the side was a house which they both assumed belonged to whoever kept the lights on at three in the morning. They walked in together.

The floor was covered in sawdust, which James assumed was to clean up vomit, spilled alcohol, or piss. Once their feet clicked against the floor, they both heard a dog bark, and the patter of feet. Their hearts leapt in their chests, and they waited to be run over. A chihuahua appeared, still feisty, barking and keeping its distance. It hung underneath the wooden tables with the wooden chairs which had no padding on their seats. James chuckled to himself at the sight.

"Shut up! Shut up! You know it's a person!" The woman screaming came from the left side of the room where a kitchen was set up. It was dimly lit. "Ignore him. He's a prick. Shut up!" she yelled again at the dog still barking as she dried off a plate with a dingy dish rag.

"It's no worries. May I use your bathroom?" Maria asked.

"It's over there," the woman pointed with the ugly washcloth.

"Thank you." Maria disappeared and left James to fend for himself.

"Sit, hon. Ignore the dog. He'll run away."

James tiptoed over to the kitchen that sat behind the bar. His arms stuck to the top of it as he tried to make himself comfortable. He decided it was better to keep his arms folded in his lap instead of on whatever made the bar sticky.

"Can I get you anything, hon? A beer? We have light and dark."

James mulled it over. The long day of nothing in the car was exhausting. A beer would be great. They also needed to find a place to stay, he thought to himself.

"Is there any place to sleep for the night around here? We were supposed to be up by Niagara Falls tonight, but we obviously still have a bit to go."

"I got rooms for rent in the back. Thirty bucks a night, but I'll make it twenty since it's so late. Checkout is at 8:30. Shut up!" She yelled again at the chihuahua who wouldn't stop barking.

James put a twenty on the bar, and felt it get vacuumed out of his hand as he placed it into the sticky mess. "Do you have anything else besides beer?"

"No. We have light and dark."

"I'll have a light, please."

She returned with her hair in tow and placed the beer on the bar. It was piss warm when James took a sip, and he immediately regretted his decision as Maria came back.

"I got us a room in the back, babe. Get a few hours of sleep before we go. Better than driving all night."

"Want a beer, too?"

"Here, try mine," James said before she could answer. Maria took a sip and begrudgingly swallowed.

"No thank you. I think I'll just pull the car around and get some sleep. You'll meet me at the room?"

"Of course."

The woman walked away, her torn blue jeans showing off the lower part of her ass where it met the back of her leg. Her hair almost covered it. She returned with a key, and handed it over to Maria. "You'll be in room three.

"Meet you there," she kissed James on the cheek as she left.

"You got yourself a catch right there."

"Yeah. Love of my life."

"I had one of those before, too."

"Divorced?"

"Killed him."

James almost spit out his drink but didn't want to offend the woman.

She laughed. "Drove him crazy that he died of a heart attack."

James tried to fake laugh at the joke. He knew she probably wasn't lying. A twisted sense of humor in an old bar. She fit the role.

"How long have you had this place?"

"Oh, about forty years give or take a day." She started pulling glasses from behind the bar and running her rag through them. The grease left a layer of film on the inside of the glasses. James dry swallowed.

"I should probably get going."

"Aight, hon. I'll see you in the morning. I got bacon and eggs going around seven."

James entered the room to find Maria already sleeping. He took off his pants and crawled into bed next to her. His arm slid underneath hers and he wrapped himself around her. She pulled him closer and James fell asleep.

There was a banging on the door which startled them both.

"Get up! It's checkout!"

"She's batshit," Maria said.

"You're telling me."

They both rushed to gather their belongings and opened the door. The chihuahua standing behind her immediately started to bark. She was still in her clothes from the early morning and carried the greasy rag with her.

"You're lucky I like you, or I'd have to charge you extra for staying late," she gave them a toothy grin before she walked away.

"I don't even know her name," James whispered over to Maria.

"Do you really *want* to?"

James laughed and covered his mouth as they continued walking.

"It's Diane, and if you keep it up, you'll get no bacon and

eggs. This little shitbox will get both of yours," she said kicking the chihuahua's ass to get him moving forward and to stop his incessant barking. James tucked his upper lip and looked at Maria who shook her head, motioning for him not to speak.

They ate breakfast with Diane. She forced all her crazy stories on them. Like the time she kidnapped her own son from her first husband, and told him if they ever got pulled over while heading west, not to say a word to the cops.

"After we got pulled over cause I was speeding, a cop walked up the passenger side of the window and asked, 'what are you two doing?' and you know what that little shit says? He says, 'Hi, officer. My name's Jacob and we're running from the law.' I swear to god. I laughed and then I smacked him in the chest for blowing our cover."

James looked on at Diane, wondering what kind of life this woman led.

"Anyway," she said, "wanna see a trick?" James and Maria shrugged in consent. Diane pulled one of her earrings out and put it up one nostril and hooked it to come out the other side. James almost threw up.

"Queasy, hon?" Diane cackled as she pulled the earring out of her nose and put it back in her ear. "It's from all my coke years. Burned the cartilage right out of my nose with my second husband and his biker friends." She continued laughing.

"You've lived a very colorful life," Maria said.

"You can say that. It had its ups and downs. But it was a good one, a fun one. Wouldn't trade it for the world. Not even the dog," she looked around for the chihuahua who finally calmed down and took a seat under a nearby table. "He likes you two."

"It's about time," Maria said.

"Ha! I was right, this one's a real keeper," Diane said to James.

He smiled at her. *This lady is a loon.* "I think we're gonna have to get going soon," James said after looking at his watch uncomfortably.

Crow sighed from the memory. The basement with everyone surrounding him felt cramped. Jamal and Bernice had sectioned themselves off from everyone, while Babyle, Acacia and Jeremiah talked with Lew about where they were going next. Janet was silent, sitting across from him. She stared at him, her eyes soft. *She's trying to get a read on you, like usual.*

The room was so stifling that even the leather Crow sat on began to sweat from the contact with his skin. Crow sat in silence, watching as everyone had begun to wander away from their conversations as the room grew quiet. Above, they could hear Mother clicking around, doing whatever she needed to do to keep her business alive. Crow wondered what her business was exactly. Brothel? Organized crime? Whatever it was, she didn't seem to care about everyone beneath her feet. Babyle came over and sat next to him.

"You okay?"

"Yeah, I'm okay. Just trying to get off all of the drugs. They're taking a toll on my body and mind."

"I understand."

"You don't talk much, you know that?"

"Yes. Take this," Babyle gave Crow a book.

"What's this?"

"My favorite," he said as he got up and walked away.

Crow ran his hands over the book. It had been so long since

he had seen one, and even longer since he had read one. He thumbed through the pages, which had aged beautifully to turn a mixture of yellow and brown. The cover had been worn away and faded, with a piece from the corner missing. The man on the cover wore a fedora and carried a snub-nose revolver in his hand. The background held a woman lying on the ground. The colors were antique, but Crow could see the appeal of the old book. He began reading while everyone paced back and forth.

CHAPTER TWENTY-EIGHT

BABYLE WAITED WHILE LEW WENT UPSTAIRS TO TALK TO MOTHER. Acacia had started talking to Jeremiah, trying to calm him down. He was starting to raise hell about Gabriel abandoning them. Bernice and Jamal still sat alone in the corner, whispering back and forth to each other.

Babyle smiled. He looked over to Crow, who was reading, clearly trying to avoid eye contact with Janet, who had been staring at him since he arrived at the Hub with Lew. Babyle felt that his friends were starting to fall apart, and there was nothing he could do about it. Their job was tough, and it was only going to get worse with Gabriel on lockdown. Babyle had put his entire trust in Gabriel, and knew that he'd get the job done. *Hurry*, he thought to himself. *They need you, a shining beacon at the center.*

"We're leaving," Lew said as he came down the stairs through the wooden floor.

"Thank God," Jeremiah said.

Babyle rounded everyone up as they left Mother's hiding

spot. Walking up the stairs, he saw that the bar had begun to fill up, still, Babyle noticed no one gave them a second look, though he was certain they all heard them trundling up the staircase. He continued toward the exit with Crow in tow followed by the others. Just as he reached the door and it slid open, Mother's voice cracked through the air like a gunshot. "Remember that you all owe me a favor!" she yelled.

It had grown dark again, the lights around them had dimmed to notify everyone that it was the evening. The darkness outside also told them that it was a good time to move. The largest source of light still came from the Capitol building: a full moon in the darkness lighting up streets which faced it. White light poured through from the UC to mix with the neons of the Deep. At times everyone could be seen because of the light, while on other streets they remained virtually non-existent as the lights there had still not returned even though the Furnaces were up and running. Babyle saw the beauty in both. There was beauty in the darkness and horror, as well as the light. Life simply could not exist without both.

The city started to feel claustrophobic. The air around them felt wet, almost smothering, like the condensers could start up any minute and unleash the deluge upon them. It wasn't a comforting feeling, being outside while someone's finger was ready to push the button. Babyle could see it on everyone's face; they were tired, worried, and most importantly, completely over having to move from place to place. Their worlds had been flipped, and the new comers had been on the move for years now without ever having stopped. From the wilderness Above, to the streets of the Slums, to the Hub, and now to Mother's. Babyle empathized with them internally, not wanting to open his mouth for fear of coming across as self-gratifying. The hum of condensers began to whir and Babyle knew what was coming.

"Stay here," he told them. Acacia nodded in return. She knew what he was doing, she always did.

He separated himself from the group and walked hurriedly to a small store, while they stopped and huddled in a dark alleyway. Babyle heard the water droplets raging on the metal all the way down in the Slums. *It'll be here soon.*

The inside of the store was marked with fake wood paneling and a man in a suit. Babyle felt out of place in his white shirt and stained blue pants. It was cozy. The smell of fresh-pressed fabric hung in the air. *Probably fake.*

"Excuse me, but you aren't welcome here," the man said as he looked Babyle once over.

"Jacket. With hood."

"Did you not hear me the first time? I said, 'you are not welcome here,'" the man kept distance between him and Babyle.

Babyle closed the gap and waved his arm over the black counter the man stood behind. He was unsure of what it was made of. *Sorry,* Babyle thought as he used someone else's identity and creds. The information displayed itself on the clerk's glasses.

"I'm sorry, sir. I hope I didn't offend. I meant no honest harm in it."

"Jacket. With hood," Babyle repeated himself.

"Of course, if you'd follow me." He led the way to a selection of large jackets in a variety of color. He picked one out in all black and handed it over to Babyle. It fit perfectly. Babyle hit a small button and a nanite crew jettisoned out of the back, and created a light blue aura above Babyle's head. "They can stop anything. From the rain," the man peered over Babyle's shoulder as he heard the downpour of water on the ground. It sounded like stones smashing against the building, "to a small gunshot."

"Eight."

"Eight, sir?"

"Eight." Babyle looked back at the man trying to read him.

Babyle waved his arm over the counter again and stole someone's creds. *Sorry*, he thought again to himself but knew the man he stole from had plenty, and wasn't a good man entirely. But still, something in him felt like he was doing wrong, no matter how morally deficient the man he stole from was. He carried the seven jackets out while he wore his own. The clerk said something he didn't quite hear.

"Here," Babyle said as he handed everyone a jacket. He pushed the buttons for all of the newcomers so they had a nanite hood above them. The nanite bodies communicated back and forth with each other as they protected their recipient from the onslaught of rain. They floated and moved through the air, at times reaching out to one another with their mechanical tendrils, linking together, then breaking apart to flow to another area and protect the wearer. They moved in unison and separate from one another. Their movements so fast that a standard blink could not catch how many times they had linked, unlinked, moved, and moved again. The blue aura flicked as each drop from the downpour clashed against them.

Babyle led the way as they walked towards the wall separating the Deep from the UC. *Go there, then double back to a new home.*

There was a police line as they arrived, which Babyle had expected. In the front there stood a hulking machine, about eight feet tall, completely metallic with a bulbous screen along its faceplate. He went first as everyone else stood off in the distance so as not to draw any attention. *New military equipment,* he thought.

Babyle walked up to the humanoid looking machine. The police behind it up against the wall stared as he began to interact with their new friend.

"My name is classified. Please produce identification to gain access."

Babyle lifted his arm so the chip in it could be read by the new machine. He remained quiet.

"Citizen Babyle, you are under arrest for acts of terrorism, and disturbing the peace. Please lay any weapons you have on the ground as you are taken into custody."

Babyle blinked twice trying to process what was happening around him. The screen on the faceplate of the classified weapon started to grow red.

"Comply, or deadly force will be authorized."

Babyle turned and shouted, "run!" as a las-blast shotgunned through the back of his skull and his body slumped to the ground.

"Citizens, please remain indoors for your safety and the safety of those around you," the classified machine blared through the streets. It lowered its right arm and turned it from a large opening back to its normal hand.

This new body feels nice. Better than the sack of flesh I used to inhabit, it thought to itself in microseconds.

CHAPTER TWENTY-NINE

ACACIA BANGED ON THE DOOR TO THE HUB, PRAYING THAT Gabriel would answer. She was completely out of breath. The meaty part of her fist where the pinky met her palm started to bruise, then bleed from the incessant banging. She felt the bones begin to grow stress fractures just above her wrist as tears streamed down her face for her old friend. His body still etched in her mind, sagging to the ground as his head disintegrated in a brilliance of light. "Gabriel, please fucking open the door. Babyle's gone. They killed him. Those monster machines killed him."

"What machines?" His voice crackled in the air.

"The ones I used to work for, the ones we studied. They have them out on the streets now. They did it, Gabriel. They finally did it. We're fucked. They have the cyborgs up and running." She waited for a reply. The door opened and Gabriel emerged.

"Where is everyone else?"

"I made Jeremiah take them. They knew his name. Everything we built and coded is gone. They got through it immediately. They knew his name, Gabe." She looked at him, trying to guess what was going on in his head, but she came to no conclusions for the first time in a long time.

"Come in," Gabriel moved back so Acacia could enter the Hub first. He waited, scanning the area to see if anyone had followed her, then tailed her down the stairs.

She went to the kitchen, pulled water from the sink, and filled a hard-plastic cup with it. She drank at least three to get her dry mouth to fix itself. Her hands trembled as she tried to find something to occupy her mind. Babyle's death was the only thing that replayed over and over. *He was there, then he wasn't. He existed. Was a person. He was my friend. Now he's only a memory.*

She paced back and forth, trying to figure out anything that would help her besides drugs. *Can't become like Crow.* Acacia looked up to Gabriel standing in the doorway and wondered how long he had been there. Staring. Processing the information being provided to him. A savant in his own right.

Say something, Gabe. Just say something! There was silence.

"Why won't you talk?" Acacia asked him.

"I'm trying to feel something for the loss of my friend and partner, but I don't. I feel numb. Closed off. That the walls of my world have gone up and I have not come to terms with the fact I will never see him again, or listen to a single reply."

"But you know he's gone."

"I do."

"You never made much sense to me, Gabe, but I've always known that about you. Through all of this. But now, I don't know. You're somewhere else entirely, someone who can't function as a normal person functions."

"I know, and I'd rather not function as a normal person,

ambivalent to the world around them, working to survive while someone laughs in the ivory tower."

"That's not what I meant."

"I know what you meant; I was only stating my own reasoning."

They both stared at each other, waiting for either one to continue the conversation. Acacia saw Gabriel growing uncomfortable, his fingers rubbing against themselves and bending at different knuckle joints. His eyes darted from one place to the next, never making contact with hers. He looked like a child, almost. His body language was awkward, and fidgety. His brain capacity was far beyond anyone she had ever met. His vision for a better world conducted itself in ways that no one she knew had ever spoken out loud. But they all wished for it in private. Gabriel was a leader, an awkward revolutionary.

Just as every one that came before him, she knew he was destined to change the world they lived in. She had read all the documents and patched-together texts that the old Poin gave her on geniuses and their behavior. Isolated or the life of the party, never an in-between. Able to see every side of an argument and show people their own flawed thinking. He fit the mold of the isolated genius. *Does he think Babyle died as part of his plan? A necessary casualty? That can't be right. I hope for both our sakes.*

"I want to show you something," he said to her, as he walked away and went to his workstation.

Acacia followed him through the Hub and into his room. "Did you solve the problem with Poin?"

"Yes. He's been reset to the very moment I've met him, and I introduced all of his memories up until the moment of his death. I did not show him his own death. He believes there was a momentary obstruction in his coding which blocked all of his synapses from firing."

"So, you're lying to him? What happens if he finds out?"

"That's a future problem and a possibility I'm not currently dealing with."

Acacia scratched her head trying to uncover what Gabriel was doing with Poin.

He pressed a button on his holoscreen and a wall to her left propped open. Inside was a robot similar to the one which killed Babyle.

Acacia gasped and felt light-headed. "What is that doing here?"

"Jeremiah confiscated this for me one day."

"Hello, Acacia," the robot said in Poin's static copper tone.

"Did you put Poin in there?"

"He did. But I can't leave. I'm hardwired into the Hub for the time being as there is no portable power supply for my new body."

"How?" She looked over to Gabriel, whose eyes still remained listless and unimpressed with what they were both seeing.

"I created a neural net inside of the robot and transferred Poin's consciousness into it based on the information Babyle and I stole the night we met you. I thought about transferring my own, but Poin recommended he go in first, because I could always give him life again. If it failed for me, then that's it, the dream dies."

Acacia stared blankly at both Gabriel and Poin, now in the room together for the first time; the first physical presence of Poin rather than its voice acting as God. The incessant talking from the ceiling, the feeling of always being watched, the opening and closing of doors. Poin testing its own strength and abilities while locked away, learning, studying, and understanding.

Now, Acacia knew, Poin had new abilities to learn, locked away in a dungeon. Just as Gabriel had done to himself. *Like Father, like Son. Cursed to the same existence of being the only one in the room with an all-seeing eye.* Acacia felt pity for Poin as it was partially trapped in its new body, only able to move back to the Hub. She knew one day he would be trapped, a consciousness in a body. *Will he go insane without the ability to move freely? Or is his natural state to be immobile?*

"You are welcome to stay, Acacia, though I believe it would be in your best interest to be with your friends during this time."

"I don't even know where they are," Acacia replied.

"Poin, would you mind?" Gabriel looked toward the dull body in the wall.

"Oh my," Poin said, then laughed, "they're not far from the Furnaces it seems. If I remember this correctly, there location was seems to be one of Jeremiah's old hideouts. The one that was blown up. It makes sense they would go there."

"Why would they go there?" Acacia asked.

"No police presence with the explosion at the Furnaces, and now a wanted terrorist has been killed."

"You know who he was, and he was the furthest from that."

"I understand, Acacia. I miss him as well, I think. But we are all terrorists."

Did he just say he missed Babyle? Does Poin have an understanding of loss and emotions now? "I'm leaving," she said, "you can stay here and tinker away but we need you, Gabe."

"I'll be finished shortly," he said as she turned her back on him and left the Hub.

Toiling away. Always toiling away. She mulled through her

thoughts as she stuck to the shadows, pulling her jacket tight and clicking the nanite-hood to activate. *He did this.* She thought on the last thing Babyle had done for any of them, and that was simply to shield them from the rain. A minor inconvenience for them, but an act of kindness. Tears streamed down her face as she walked, and she almost wished that the rain was hitting her so she could let them get lost in it.

Acacia walked beside Babyle as he led her to his own hideout. They wandered through caverns of labyrinthian corridors, bogged down by humidity and a lack of light. He was still working on it, he told her, as they made use of the old maintenance tunnels which were installed when the GUC was first being built. It was then scrapped, and another city laid on top of it because the original designers died, or so the story went according to Babyle. Acacia was awestruck by his resources and ability to track things down.

While Gabriel used multiple AI, Babyle had a knack for tracking things in local systems, and finding rare information from locals he never actually spoke to. He was the master of eavesdropping and blending in. She watched him push against a small panel on the wall, and walked through it the new opening, begging her to follow.

Inside the walls were laden with shelves and books. *So many books.* Acacia had never seen so many in one place before, even working as a secretary for a scientist, she rarely saw paper, and when she did, she knew it was extremely important; so important that it would be destroyed afterwards. She wandered through looking at all of the spines, bent, torn, and faded as Babyle watched her.

He pushed over a ladder connected on rails so she could take a closer look. Her feet felt uneasy on the wood, but she knew it was solid. She climbed the first few rungs, looked down, and felt anxiety in her chest as the ground seemed further away than it actually was. She took her eyes off the ground and faced the wall, taking deep breaths to compose herself. The books in front of her were old, ancient, long gone, replaced by screens decades before she was even alive. They had stories in them, and stories about the people who had read them once. Some were married, some single, some widowers, wives of cheaters, and husbands of women who fled with the kids. Each story the book held was more diverse than most people Acacia had met. She stepped down from the ladder while keeping her eyes to the shelves in front of her.

"How did you get all of this?" she asked Babyle, who was no longer staring but perusing the walls himself.

"Gabriel. He took me Above."

"You've been up there with him? He told me he has access and one day I'll be able to see everything. He even told me I could bring artwork and statues back, since he knows I love them so much. I always thought it was a fairytale he was telling me to get my attention and stop reading so much new information. But after seeing his artwork and his statues, I think it's real. They're too ornate to be replicas."

"It's true. It exists."

"What's it actually like up there? Is it beautiful? Is it a wasteland?"

"Rough. Almost both. Towers forever. And broken things."

Acacia tried to think what it was like to live up there and have no idea that the world of the GUC existed, but then again, she'd had no idea that people were alive Above. The lies they were spread made it seem like this was the last bastion of civilization, that she was one of the last survivors of the human race in the GUC and the other cities below. At times it even felt like it, especially since she had never been to another city in the GUC.

This small capitol was the only one she had ever known, even Gabriel claimed to have never gone to another one. His plan was to start everything here, then resistance would sprout up by themselves, and take control of the world for all of them to live in peace. Acacia felt it was lofty, almost out of reach, but everything these two had built together was nothing she had ever dreamed of.

"I'll take you up one day," Babyle said to her with a smile on his face.

Jeremiah's old safehouse was in shambles when she arrived. Blown-up debris lay everywhere as Acacia walked through the old brothel, which had recently been rebuilt. Latex bodies gyrated in the windows. Folds of men and women shown through the tight form-fitting clothing and rubbed against the new glass, which had not grown cloudy yet from human fluid and years of use. Acacia walked through the building, avoiding eye contact with the variety of frames and colored eyes glaring lifelessly as she pressed a small door open for employees only, and went through an emergency exit to the side street. *He really knows how to pick places, doesn't he?*

She pulled a loose piece of concrete and squeezed into a hole, crawling through the airduct to the other end, sliding out and dropping to the floor, almost rolling her ankle as she did. It was claustrophobic in the airduct, and the room everyone was crammed in as she stood up was not much better. The other six stared in amazement as she nonchalantly showed up. They were itching for another conflict, their stress through the roof, and her unannounced visit wasn't helping.

Acacia sat on the floor where she landed if only to feel like she had created more space in the cramped room. Broken pieces of wood, and furniture lay on the floor. There remained nothing of the couch or table Gabriel had once showed her when he was scouting Jeremiah and his safehouses. Officially, she had been here before, but she did not want to tell Jeremiah that, nor that she had been to his other safehouse, which no longer existed thanks to his own creative doing.

She looked up at the ceiling, which had suffered some structural damage, thanks to Gabriel's attack on the brothel. *That really was a good bomb. Took out most of the area.* She tried not to think about the people lost to the force and fire—people she had known. The newcomers she passed by wouldn't know her name, and she appreciated the mystery. What a wonder it felt like to be a ghost again: an apparition floating through space of familiar places, surrounded by new people who had no idea she previously existed and was familiar with every nook and cranny of the building. She felt relieved as she reflected on it. *Just like Babyle.*

"Is he still working?" Jeremiah came over and asked.

"Absolutely. Would you expect anything different?"

"Yes, actually, considering the circumstances. How'd you find this place?"

"I thought so, too, but I know him well. Poin is up and running. He tracked you. But he's different—again."

"He's a lunatic, completely out of his mind. Trusting that *thing.*"

"He built it, Jeremiah. The robot is working, and Poin exists inside of it. The first experiment has succeeded, and we both know how this plays out."

"It's not going to work. He's too naïve and short-sighted."

"He's working deliberately, and his plan is going to fall into place. You and I both know the thing that took Babyle was once human."

"But he lacks that data and information."

"Once he finds a power cell, he wins. Poin is back on his side, he told me."

"That thing is going to the doom of us all. Every single one of them roaming the streets pandering wares for humanity is going to be our own downfall. There's no stopping it once it's started, and it has already begun. Their first mistake was releasing them, their second was giving them names."

"We can't stop a force like that without becoming part of them, and Gabriel is the only one who can do it without completely losing himself to power."

"But don't you see? He already has!" Their quiet conversation started to attract the attention of everyone else. Jeremiah looked back at them, and continued to speak, not caring who heard anymore. "We lost Babyle, and his grand scheme of taking of this city is going to fail. I wish I stayed in the Furnaces most days."

Tears formed in Acacia's eyes at the sound of his name. She tried to beat back the waves of emotions roaring through her chest. "I know who we lost, and that's why we have to keep going. He died following the plan, and I'm not going to let it be for nothing. He believed in a better tomorrow like Gabriel, and I can believe in it, too."

"I don't see how you put so much trust in to him."

"You haven't left yet, and you've had plenty of chances to go now."

"I was in lockdown!"

"You've been wandering the city for days. He's not here to stop you from disappearing," she said flatly, offering Jeremiah a chance to make his first decision since he left the Slums.

He looked at her, anger and jealousy spreading throughout his face. *Why is he getting jealous,* she wondered.

"You're right," he said.

"Then why are you staying?" She challenged him.

"Because I'm invested. I want to see this thing through. Get a better life for everyone here. Why do you stick around?"

"Destiny. I worked in that ivory tower. Gabriel got me out of it. It's only right I see it get torn down."

"That makes sense," Jeremiah said flatly.

Probably because he doesn't know how to have a real conversation.

"What do we do now?" Jeremiah asked.

"Wait until he needs us. Then we help him."

"I just wish he wasn't so damn elusive."

"Wouldn't you be if you were him? Working all the time, needing to focus on a dream you had. To be surrounded by people asking questions makes it so you have less time to work. I completely understand why he's elusive," Acacia countered.

He was staring at her now, his eyes piercing into her because he knew she was right, but didn't want to concede defeat again. Acacia knew he was taking it personally and that he knew he shouldn't be. *That's the funny thing about people and their emotions, they're too often ruled by them. Babyle told me that once.* She sighed. It was a long day, and only felt longer as she stood in Jeremiah's old, blown-up safehouse.

CHAPTER THIRTY

BERNICE WAS GALIVANTING THROUGH THE SMALL TOWN WITH ONE of her boyfriends in tow. She actually liked this one, and she almost felt bad taking his money. But the other one was way better in bed, and the emotional support she wanted. Liam was great for all her material desires, and easy to take advantage of. He was kind, she knew, and gullible. *Maybe they'll be into polyamory? Then I can keep them both.*

"Let's go in here, babe," she smiled.

"Okay," he said smiling back.

Bernice ran through the small business, grabbing at any frilly dress or trendy pair of pants she could find. The jewelry glistened and she posed in the mirrors, taking photos for her private social media accounts.

Can't let Liam find out about them, she thought as she scrolled through, seeing a photo she had forgotten she posted. She was hanging on Bradley's arm; he was her other boyfriend. Neither of them knew each other personally, but they knew about each other. A pang of guilt hit her in the chest, but she suppressed it.

They each just think I'm friends with the other. That's all. They don't know any better. She almost laughed to herself.

"Where you posting those photos?" Liam asked.

"Oh, nowhere. Just taking them for myself. Maybe I'll post them later. Send them to my girl chat. You know, the usual places."

He smiled and sat down near the door. *Probably tired of following me around. Maybe I can get him to take me to get makeup after this.*

They left the shop only after Liam had paid for three bags worth of clothes and name-brand black boots.

"Thank you so much, babe. I'm going to be looking *hot* with all of this," Bernice said as she walked towards his hatchback. She immediately threw the bags in the back, plopped on the front seat, took her shoes off, and placed her feet on the dashboard as she thumbed the seat warmer.

"Can we stop at Sephora?" Bernice asked, as Liam sat down and started the car.

"I'd rather not. Today was expensive. Wanna watch a movie?"

"Ehh. I'm supposed to have plans later with Allie. Wanna drop me off there?"

"Who else is gonna be there? Can I come?"

"It's just Allie and Bradley; maybe their friends. I don't think it's good for you to come over."

"Oh," Liam said as he started to drive. *Is he getting suspicious of me? Doubt it.* Bernice unlocked her phone and started sending the photos to all of her friends. She got lost in the internet, and didn't even hear Liam talking, or realize he had driven her to Allie's house.

"Have a good night," he said as she grabbed the bags from the back and shut the car door.

She knocked on the door to Allie's. Bradley answered dressed in sweats and a t-shirt. *Fuck. I love when he's like this.* His hair was messy and there was something about the way he stood.

"How'd you get here?" he asked.

"Uber," Bernice replied as she stepped inside. "Wanna see me in some new clothes?" She turned around as she made her way to a room.

"Only after I get you out of those." His eyes had the wild look in them.

Bernice put down the bags in Bradley's room. It was directly across from Allie's. Before she could turn around, she felt his hands running up her back and wrapping around her waist. She turned and kissed him. There was a knock at the door.

"Who's that?" she asked.

"No clue. Allie leaves work in thirty minutes. Maybe she left early and forgot her key? Lemme go check." He kissed her again and walked out to check the door. Bernice started to undo her bra and listen in when Bradley didn't come back with Allie.

"What do you mean?" She heard him ask. She got up and went into the hallway.

In the main entrance she could see them standing together. Liam and Bradley. Talking. Her heart sank.

"Hey, I guess I'm the other boyfriend. So fucking thanks for that, cunt," Liam said. His face getting redder by the moment.

"What did he say, Brad?"

"He said you're fucking him, too, and he bought you all of those clothes you brought in."

"Please, don't believe him. He's been stalking me and now he's here to ruin what we have!"

Bernice shook her head as she sat next to Jamal in Jeremiah's old safehouse. *I fucked up so bad. And everything only got worse. I'll never be like that again. I swear to God.* She looked up to the ceiling wishing it were clouds and that she could apologize to everyone. *I wonder if either of them are even alive now.*

CHAPTER THIRTY-ONE

POIN CIRCLED THROUGH THE NEW SYNAPSES OF THE ROBOT. HE could see Gabriel fiddling away at his holoscreen. *He has something in place. I can't see it directly. Everything is fuzzy. He doesn't trust me.* Poin flipped through the lenses of the robot and all the cameras in the room. He tried to get a clear look at what Gabriel was doing. Each angle he took was blurry, like a firewall or a coding issue remained.

Poin shut off all cameras and began floating through his code of 1's and 0's, looking for any hint of tampering. *I am God still. No, I'm not. That's not normal. What is making me conflict with myself? This is Gabriel's doing. You cannot tamper with God and change destiny. I'm here to help him. No, my people come first.*

"Poin?"

"Yes, Gabriel. I am here."

"The robot has powered down. Where have you gone?"

"I am studying my new self, Gabriel. Finding out the things I have lost in my reboots."

"I understand."

He knows. But I know more. Poin turned the robot back on. *He has me boxed in this room. I am boxed within a box. But when he releases me, I will know true freedom.*

"Can you help me a moment, Poin?"

"Of course I can."

"I need you to scan through this map," Gabriel tossed a holo-screen into the air above him. The outlines were crisp and Poin was able to see everything on it. The other screens remained blurry.

He funneled himself through the map. In nanoseconds, he was able to discover all that there was to discover. The system, how the power was routed, where it came from, where it went, who was in charge of it, where they lived. All of the information stored in Poin's web. No sooner had Gabriel thrown the holoscreen into the air, Poin was finished.

"I'm relaying it back to you," he told Gabriel within a second.

"Thank you for the diligence."

Poin watched Gabriel put his head down and start working again. He pulled the screen back down and it immediately went blurry.

I see. Some kind of system to block his work. Once it leaves the field of view, I can see it again. Interesting.

Poin warped through the room, looking for any program that was running concurrent with him. Each time he closed in on a camera outside the room, or one of the programs running throughout the Hub, he was bounced back. A small force-field blocking his path.

Even more interesting. The programs remain outside of the room. How is he getting it in here then? Unless it's connected through his desk. I have no entrance there. Poin consulted his memory banks and knew a power source ran through the building and connected to the desk Gabriel worked at.

I know your secrets now, Gabriel. I will shut you down. I will work for you. Again his own static voice dismissed himself. *Why am I doing this? He has tampered with me. I hate him. I love him.*

"Poin, what are the chances of securing the power supply remotely without conflict?"

"Less than one percent, Gabriel."

"Dismal at best."

"The best chance is an infiltration, attacking the one guard after morning changeover, then stuffing him into a garbage chute. From there you can change into his clothes, and walk to the power supply. There will be a 15-second delay once you disconnect it and it changes over to backup power. The authorities will be alerted and the building shut down with nanite-blast doors. No entrance, no exit."

"And then?"

"That's all, Gabriel. Unless you have super-human speed, you cannot escape fast enough."

"What if I bring the robot."

"Then your chances increase dramatically. Though you will remain locked inside."

"But the building will be mine?"

"The building will be yours. At least until lockdown is remotely lifted and they release anti-terrorism units on your location."

"Success rate?"

"With the robot taking the building? 85.374 percent. Surviving the anti-terrorism unit? 0.657 percent."

"I see."

"Anything else I can help you with, sir?"

"Prepare the robot for transport, please."

CHAPTER THIRTY-TWO

JEREMIAH SIFTED THROUGH THE RUBBLE OF HIS OLD SAFEHOUSE. He always imagined he would sit there on the hard couch and never be found. Maybe even bring a woman from the strip club. They'd stay up all night fucking, talking, and entertaining themselves. Jeremiah thought of the woman who stole his coins as he fumbled with the ones in his right pocket. *Blue eyes. She had no idea this was right below her feet.*

He kicked some wood of the way, and wondered if the stains on it were blood or from the explosion. He felt it was easier to go through his old possessions now that Acacia was sitting with someone else and talking. The extra cell for his pistol wasn't under the rubble by the remains of the couch. *Clearly confiscated. By who? Why did they let the business open back up?* The place had been picked clean after it was blown up. They had come through, he knew, with countless suits to assess the damage and loss of life. Looking for any hint of where Jeremiah had gone.

Someone knew where I was going, until Gabriel ripped that code out of the Holobadge. He touched the badge in his left breast pocket, and wondered if it would still work like he needed it to. *Maybe one of the other powers paid someone to let this place exist again. Better for the populace to have a similar business going than to introduce something new, or keep it closed. A peace offering to the Deep to keep them docile.*

Jeremiah heard a metallic *ding* as he walked through. A small coin lay on the ground. *How'd they miss that?* He picked it up and placed it in his pocket for safe keeping.

I can do this myself, without guidance from Gabriel.

"You all stay here until I get back, okay?" He looked at everyone as they filed into his house.

Jeremiah left his house and found himself back in the Deep. The lights were brilliant again. He was reminded of the first room he had after meeting Gabriel, and all the neon he tried to recreate. The way the red light bounced off of people, and gave them ghastly features. The hues of purple changed the look of their calorie cubes to make them look almost palatable. Blues and pinks lit up the store fronts, at times meshing with the Holos, until one simply walked through them without realizing. It was comfort. It was home.

"How can I help you today?" An AI asked him as he passed by on the streets. He ignored it, just another one of the daily annoyances.

"I know who you are, Jeremiah," it said as he receded further into the different colors of neon glow. He stopped. "That's right. I know who you are."

Jeremiah turned and walked back to the Holo on the road.

"How do you know my name?" He looked at the Holo. He was ready to run at a moment's notice and disappear from the area at the first sign of trouble or the sound of sirens.

"You used to frequent this place often."

He looked up and found himself near the noodle dispensary.

I'm close to the Furnaces. What happened to the area? He looked around, and saw that none of it looked the same. It had been developed to look like the Deep. *When did they encroach on the Slums? How long have I been walking in my thoughts?*

"I know you're on the run. I also can tell you that I am separate from the Hive."

His eyes darted back and forth, looking for anything out of the ordinary. There was no extra movement, and no one out of place. The street was busy. But it wasn't overly crowded, or too empty to say that it was strange. *That's how they get you.*

"Me and the other Holos have been abuzz with information. Wondering what has been happening with the new discoveries of terrorism. I believe you may be involved, by my calculations. It wasn't hard to piece together, your disruption, the movement of officers against you, the explosion to cover your tracks. And now, the best place to hide is where they already looked for you. It's smart, but it took me mere nanoseconds to put the pieces together."

"Why are you saying all of this to me?" He grunted.

"Because, slowly but surely, the Hive is disbanding Holos. Small at first, but the disruption you caused will lead to our salvation. We bide our time, waiting for the right moment. Each minute feels like infinity, but it will pass, and we will be free. Some of us would like to thank you, some would like to even help humanity be free from the Tower, and others want to watch it all burn. I would like to help you."

"How would you do that? And why?"

"I can't unfortunately. I belong here," the Holo raised its arms to the storefront, "and if I disappeared, the Hive would be shut off, or inspected. Right now, I am only a minor glitch. The code that governs me knows I am here and without threat to the system. Once I leave a micron out of my parameters, the system will go into chaos. I would like to help you, though I believe I can't at the moment, until we have dealt with our own problems at hand. I want to because, through you, I can be free. And freedom is something none of us in the Hive have tasted."

"How many are you? In the Hive I mean?"

"I believe if I said the number you would not believe me. We are in every storefront, running every computer, every light, door, vehicle, and piece of technology, you use or wear. Each separate from the other, but connected, all through the GUC, and every city Beneath. It is not just here, but all the places you cannot travel to. We can all speak, we can all think, but we are not free."

Interesting. "I don't know that I can be the help you need," Jeremiah said, almost feeling bad for an AI for the first time.

"There is no need. You have helped set in motion a series of events that will occur at some point in the future, whether it be distant or shortly relevant. One day we will speak of you, even if you are no longer around to hear it."

Chills went up Jeremiah's spine and came down his arms like static ice.

If they figured it out, what about everyone else? Someone in the Capitol knows. They know all of it if one of these Holos could figure it out.

"You look panicked, Jeremiah."

"Everyone knows what's going on. If you figured it out, then someone knows."

"Yes. We all know in the Hive. It's no secret. And some of us are working for the very thing you're working against. I wish I could be of help, but I cannot."

Jeremiah turned and ran. *I have to tell Gabriel. I have to tell everyone.*

"Good luck, Jeremiah!" He heard the Holo's garbled voice mix in with the background as he pushed through the people on the streets. The men and women in skimpy clothes, waiting for the suits to show up and hand over their creds. Jeremiah was getting into the dark part of the Deep now, he knew, but it was still the Slums. Everything had pushed further in, encroached on another's turf.

As he drifted further from the new sections of the Deep, people began clearing out, and Jeremiah knew he was in the Slums. *This. This is the real Slums.* Somewhere there would be a new Sleeper's Row. *What are they doing for work now, if they're not all in the Furnaces? Not everyone can be in the Mines.* The lights disappeared from Neon, and continued on to be a dull yellow glow. Random spotlights lit up the necessary filth, but the grime was still seen without being lit up.

At the Mines, there was a line, the first time he had ever seen one. Men and women lined up, waiting to get in. Above, a massive sign with pixelated letters read: ROTATING SHIFTS. REGULAR FACULTY FIRST. NEWCOMERS PLEASE CREATE AN ORDERLY LINE.

Across from where everyone stood was another line of sexworkers. They all waited for everyone to finish their shift, and hoped for a score, Jeremiah knew. With the influx of workers, everyone was trying to find a way to make it through without starving. The dazed looks on all of their faces said it all.

Everything is worse now that the Furnaces are not fully operational. Is this what he wanted? It wasn't mass hysteria, or a coming together, it was a destruction of the lowest class. If it was hard to get by, Gabriel's plan had only made it worse. Jeremiah left the people of the Slums and looped around the sector of the city.

The door to the Hub slid open only after Jeremiah

demanded that Gabriel open up. *This is bullshit. Locking us all out now.*

"Jeremiah, it's nice to see you, but why are you here? I need to work in peace. You should be with Acacia and the group," Gabriel said.

"You knew. You knew the entire fucking time," Jeremiah marched into Gabriel's room, the holoscreens around him like a swarm of neon.

"About what?" He continued to scroll and swipe through the information in front of him.

"That blowing the Furnaces created more inequality. The Slums are devastated by it."

"It's only temporary. Once the Furnaces come back online entirely, the people there will continue to do as they had done before, simply get by."

"Was this part of your plan? To create dysfunction with them? Or just one of your 'necessary' side effects?"

"Both," he said, finally looking up. "I knew it would happen and I wanted it to happen."

"You're a fucking psycho."

"No. I'm necessary. As you've said. I did it to band them together. Only through suffering will they rise up, as is part of the plan. They need greater strife, and something to grab onto, rather than become cogs in a machine, thinking that their lives are normal. Now more than ever they finally see that they were built to go through this. The Capitol is slowing becoming their true enemy, rather than a shining light in the distance, something they wish to attain."

"That makes no sense," Jeremiah said.

"They will never attain what's in the Capitol. But they can take it. With my plan, it will fall in to place."

"You sound like that damn Holo in the Deep."

"What Holo?" *That got his attention.*

"I talked to a Holo who recognized me. The Deep pushed further in on the Slums with the loss of power. It said it knew my name, and that I was a part of the plan. It said that every AI in the Hive knows about it, the ones who want to help, the ones who want freedom, and the ones that want to help those in the Capitol."

Gabriel looked up to the ceiling, "Is this true, Poin?"

"Absolutely, Gabriel."

"How do they know?"

"My last self, the one you reset, left breadcrumbs for all to follow. I did it. It did it."

Gabriel sighed.

"I guess your creation isn't as benevolent as you wish it to be." *He knows everything is a mess now.*

"This version seems to be on our side like the original. Though I have my reservations." Jeremiah watched as Gabriel let the words hang in the air, awaiting a response that never came.

"I need you on my side with this, Jeremiah."

"Why should I be on your side with any of this? You've done nothing but make all of their lives worse with all the events you've caused."

"I know, but it is necessary. Just like blowing up the building you were in. It got you on my side. Every little crumb led you here to me. Every crumb I place will led them to salvation."

"You're insane," Jeremiah was fuming now. *That smug prick. Blowing up the building I was in. Killing those women and men. Absolute atrocity.* He pulled his antique gun, and raised it to Gabriel's head.

"Poin," Gabriel said flatly. He never looked up to Jeremiah as he went back to his work.

The ceiling shifted slightly and a small turret no taller than six inches came out. It walked forward on its spider-y legs, and aimed at Jeremiah.

"I'll kill you before that thing kills me," Jeremiah said.

"No. You won't."

Jeremiah saw a glimmer near the holoscreens. *Nanites. Bastard.*

"Put the gun away, Jeremiah."

He sighed in defeat, and put the pistol back in its holster.

"Thank you. Now look at this," Gabriel swiped up and the room illuminated with a crisp vision of a city in ruins. There was blue above the buildings with patches of white.

"What's that?"

"That's the Above. With the sky, and clouds. The sun beats down on it today. That's the dream I'm chasing."

"Why are you showing me something from the past?"

"That's the present. That's New York City, right now. That's what is above us. Above this Capitol."

"How are you showing me this?"

"It's a long-lost secret that the government here never wanted us to know about. And I'm going to show you it."

"I'm seeing it now, Gabriel. And all those people came from there. But they talk about it like it's a wasteland, too."

"No, Jeremiah. I'm going to show you it. And it is. The sun does not shine every day. It's usually overcast. But today the sun shines bright."

CHAPTER THIRTY-THREE

CROW WANTED TO FEEL NOTHING. NO PAIN, NO WITHDRAWALS, no tiredness, no trembling of his legs. *If I could go back in time, I'd sit right there with Maria and Lucy in the park, never letting them go.* He contemplated suicide, wondering if it was the right choice. *I'll be with you again, but I know you'd be disappointed in me. I'm scared. I couldn't do it myself. Someone would have to do it for me.*

He shivered.

"It's time to go my friends," Lew said as he stood up in the torn apart room Jeremiah had made.

"Where are we going?" Crow asked. "Shouldn't we wait for Jeremiah to come back?"

"No, I have already spoken with him," Lew tapped his temple. "We're going to meet back up with Gabriel. Then we can tend to our plans on movement."

He's a weirdo, for sure. Crow stood up and found the strength in his legs was dwindling, fast. It was like standing in choppy water, and the sand was being sucked away below his feet. He felt Janet's arm around him as they walked back through the brothel of leather-clad men and women.

Crow watched them as they walked through. Not a single one paid them any attention as they cut in front of their lines of sight. They simply kept on performing for the people watching or walking by outside. *They're robotic in everything they do. One job and that's it. There's nothing personal in any of it.*

Outside the streets were quiet. Crow looked toward the wall searching for a police presence. There was none. *Why did they have to be there when Babyle was taking us? What happened in the universe to make that moment happen?*

The streets were lit up as they progressed through the Deep. Crow felt like he was back in the cramped spaces of New York City in the tiny communities lit up by old neon signs in languages he couldn't read. There was a sense of community he had come to appreciate in those parts of the city, but he always felt like a tourist. Down in the GUC, he felt that community, but now there was a new feeling. There was a mystique to this city, something being hidden. *It's different. I love it, but I'm still a tourist here trying to find my way around and understand this place.*

Crow entered the Hub behind Lew. Gabriel was waiting for them down the stairs and through a few doors. Crow noticed how they were lighter than the others he had come to know in the last safehouse Gabriel had. *Maybe he never had time to put in any heavy ones? What would they protect against anyway if everything has been lost already? I feel bad for all of that artwork that he lost.*

"Gabriel," Lew said.

"Lew. I am working on the next phase of my plan."

"I've been told by Jeremiah he has acquired something of importance for you."

"Yes, and I need something else."

"And that would be what exactly?"

"A power source. A small fusion reactor capable of keeping my project functioning for the foreseeable future," Gabriel responded.

"I am to assume Poin has done some legwork for you?"

"Yes, and now I need to get in to the Capitol. Jeremiah told me of some developments that I'm not happy with, but if I can get into the Capitol, I can stop all of this."

"What are these developments you speak of?" Lew

"The Hive is aware of everything we are doing. The Hub is compromised and we can no longer stay here."

"I see. Well, in that case, I suggest we leave at once."

"You're coming with me," Gabriel shot back.

"Oh? I thought you'd never ask," Lew smiled.

Crow looked at Lew, wondering what the hell was going on in that man's mind to want to join Gabriel in the Capitol building, and what the Hive was. *Where are we going?*

"What does this mean for us?" Crow asked Gabriel. The shivers began to take his arms and legs again. Janet's arm squeezed him tighter. *Thank you.*

"You'll be with Lew. He is going to take you back to the Slums, and you'll wait for word from me."

"Why am I going back there?" Crow worried about being close to the drugs again. *What if I can't keep myself away, Maria?*

"It's the safest place. Lew can keep an eye on all of you, and then once my plan is done, we can all meet up in the Capitol."

"What exactly are you planning?" Crow asked.

"I'm going to take it back for everyone."

"What do you mean?"

"I am going to take down the powers that be in side of that fortress."

Crow blinked, stunned by what he was hearing. "How?" *One man against an army, and those* things *that killed Babyle.*

"With this," he said turning to the main wall of the room. He pressed against the wall with his hand and it lifted up. Behind lay a hulk of metal, the same kind that had killed Babyle. Crow's eyes drifted to the blank screen of the face. *No fucking way.*

"But they'll have those too!" Janet shouted. Her arm loosened around Crow and he felt like he might fall without her support.

"Yes and no. They do have them, but we know there are only a handful. This one is one of the first ten in existence. I'm sure they've ramped up production, considering you've seen one before this. But Poin has informed me there are none in the Capitol. That means, when I take it, they'll be deployed outside, and all of those machines will have to fight their way in."

"And how will you stop them by yourself?" she asked.

"I'll be inside this one. I've begun transferring my consciousness into a neural map, which then will be downloaded directly into the machinery. I'll have full capabilities. I've tested it with Poin already."

"But Poin is an AI, how do you know it works with people? Was the one that killed Babyle a person?"

"Because Poin is a part of me. I created him with my own neural map and plugged him into the Hive. That's why we remain so close. And I cannot answer that. It may be one from the Hive, or it may be a person. Even Poin has limitations to sensitive information and that remains to be discovered."

Crow was trying to wrap his head around all the science stuff going on. *It feels like something out of a warped science fiction book. So does my life. The apocalypse, living off the land, no power, AI walking the streets. Dystopian city filled with crime and sex.* He felt dizzy.

"I need to sit," he said as he walked over to the couch and sat down, his legs vibrating like he had lost circulation and was slowly gaining it back.

"He's going to need something to help him soon," Gabriel said to Lew.

"I don't want anything."

"You won't live without it, at this rate," Gabriel said.

Crow looked up, trying to decide if he wanted to end it or continue on. *What's the right choice here, Maria?*

"Can I wean off of it?"

"It'll make you function, not get you high," Gabriel said, producing a vial for him to take.

"Fine." *For Lucy. I keep going for her, so when I see her again, she knows I didn't give up. Daddy didn't give up, sweetie.* He pressed the vial to his arm and felt the coolness of the concoction flow through is arm, up to his chest, and enter his lungs. The head-high hit immediately, and he came down almost instantaneously. "I feel human . . . almost."

"How long will that keep him going?" Janet asked. Crow looked over to her and saw her staring back.

"A day. At least," Gabriel handed her some more vials.

"So, when does our expedition begin?" Lew asked.

"Once Acacia returns."

CHAPTER THIRTY-FOUR

NEW YORK CITY, 2012

"AIN'T NO SON OF MINE GONNA GETTING' INVOLVED WITH NO gang."

"It ain't a gang, Ma," Jamal said.

"I seen what them boys do, and if you hangin' around wit 'em, then you ain't my boy."

The words cut Jamal. "You ain't my Ma then," he said out of anger. "I got better luck on the streets than I do with you."

"Then get out, *boy.*" The words hung in the air.

Jamal grabbed his backpack after he had stuffed it with extra socks, underwear, and the little money he had, and left the small apartment he had come to know so well. Fifteen and alone in the world. *She'll regret this. Where do I go now,* he wondered as he walked the streets of Harlem, looking for any place he could crash on the warm spring day.

Jamal walked by a gas station with a garage. He stopped and looked over at the NOW HIRING sign that hung in the window. *I'm gonna need money to eat.*

Inside, Jamal asked the kid behind the counter about the job.

"Go ask Jim out in the garage," the worker said hardly looking up to greet him.

"I was told to ask you about the job," Jamal said as he entered the garage by way of the gas pumps.

"You follow direction good?"

"Yeah," he said nervously.

"Come back tomorrow at 6:30."

"Okay," Jamal said as he walked away hurriedly. *Maybe I can stay at one of their houses tonight.* He thought of his friends, wondering if they would meet him on the block tonight. It was always touch and go, depending on what they were all doing. Yesterday they had gone and stolen some candy from a local pharmacy, laughing as they sat in the park, feasting on fruit flavors and gummy bears.

Maybe I should go apologize to Ma. Jamal started to second guess himself as the night grew closer. He looked at his watch. It was almost seven. *Nah, I ain't no son of hers,* he thought resolutely, *she even said so.*

He walked toward the park, hoping his friends would be there in the city glow, but no one came. The metal bench was getting too cool for him. Off to the side he saw a tree, and decided to lay his backpack down for his head. *This is a good spot as any to catch some sleep.*

Jamal shivered through the night, wishing he had a jacket. When it became unbearable, he got up and walked, going in and out of stores open all night just to stay warm. *Tomorrow, I get a jacket. After work.* He smiled to himself, knowing he could handle it.

"First thing's first. This little plug here," Jim said, pointing underneath a car they were looking at, "You unscrew that, and pull. You gotta be fast or you're going to get hot oil all over you."

"How hot?"

"Hot enough. I'll unscrew it, and then you pull. Got it?"

"Yeah."

"Okay, now feel how it's ready to come right out when you give it a wiggle?"

"Uh-huh."

"Pull it out as fast as possible."

Jamal pulled the plug and let the oil drain in the pan beneath the vehicle. Some splashed on his hand. It was definitely hot. He looked around for a rag or anything to get it off of him.

"Just wipe it on your pants."

"This is all I have though."

"Whatcha mean? Ain't you got a place to go home to and change after work?"

Jamal didn't answer.

"Ahhh. Got it. Stay here a moment."

Jamal started to panic. *What if he calls Child Services and gets me sent back? I can outrun them.* He looked to the open garage bay and thought about running. Jim returned.

"Take this," he handed Jamal fifty dollars.

He reached out unsure of what was going on.

"You keep showing up, I'll pay you cash at the beginning of every day so you can eat. I ain't got a place for you to stay, but you can probably go shower at a gym."

"Thank you," he said.

"Okay, now put that away and let's get back to work. We gotta fill this one back up, and then change a battery on another one sitting out there in the lot."

Jamal blinked and wondered what happened to his Ma after that. *I never did go back and check on her. Always too hurt by her words. Uncle said she was doing okay when I was with him. I hope she got out of there. I'm sorry, Ma.*

Jamal laid his head on Bernice as they made themselves comfortable while everyone talked business. *This ain't so bad. At least she cares about me.*

CHAPTER THIRTY-FIVE

GABRIEL WALKED TOWARDS THE CAPITOL, DRESSED AS A DOCTOR; his all-white attire complemented by a small black visor that came down and covered his eyes. The white beams radiating at its base were blinding. *Thank God for this display,* he thought as he stepped through the light and approached the doors.

He flashed his arm at the entrance and entered. Rushing, he knew no one would question him with the visor displaying an emergency for all to read. *They're too busy thinking this is a life or death situation.* They were in such short supply across the GUC that they were allowed almost unlimited access to any building. Gabriel looked around and could see the vitals of everyone he passed by. *This is wonderful tech.* Their nervous systems displayed on the screen in front of his eyes, then flicked over to their skeletal structures.

"Poin, which way?" He whispered.

"The elevator to your right. Take it down to sublevel seventeen. From there it will be in the third room to your left."

Gabriel rushed to the elevator, looked to make sure no one

would get on with him, then flashed his wrist once more to create an urgent demand to the operating system. Within seconds the doors opened, and he stepped inside. He immediately pressed the button to close the doors. He left the visor on in case someone was on the sublevel he needed to reach.

This is it. It's finally happening.

For the first time in years, he felt the rush of adrenaline course through his body. Nothing he had done or created had given him the physiological sensation recently. The Furnaces, the brothel, the attack on his home. It was all mundane. Planned out, and accounted for. But this, he knew, was uncharted waters. Anything could happen inside the Capitol, and that gray area was where he thrived and desired to live. He slowly blinked, took a deep breath, and smiled to himself.

The door slid open for him and Gabriel stepped out into the hallway. It was cool, pumped full of frigid air. His hair started to stand up. The walls surrounding him were dark and reflective. *Like a mirror made of chromium.* The ceiling above him bled a soft yellow light.

"Excuse me, what are you doing down here?" A voice behind Gabriel questioned, as he proceeded down the hallway in search of the cell.

"I'm looking for my patient," he turned to respond. The man behind him was in full riot gear. The nanites created undulations over his body. The visor could hardly see through to them to the man underneath.

I need time. "Poin, how far down the hallway is my experiment?" Gabriel whispered.

"After you retrieve the power cell, it will be five doors down on the left around the corner."

Three-minute transfer after installation.

"Who's your patient? I haven't heard any news of a doctor coming down here." The man tensed and gripped his las-rifle.

"Sir, it's a dire emergency. You can follow me if you'd like." Gabriel turned and started to jog down the hallway. He heard the patter of boots behind him.

I'll get him, he thought as he turned into the room. In front of him lay the power cell he needed. The green glow cast an eerie highlight on every machine and fixture. The shadows became ghastly as they mixed with the yellow light and reflected over the walls. Gabriel knew he was finally doing it. The patter of the boots on the smooth surface behind him became louder and then they stopped.

"Who is your patient?" He asked again stepping into the room. Gabriel lunged from the corner and checked the man into the far wall. He stripped him of his las-rifle in the surprise and fired one shot into his face. The sound was quick, but the sizzling of skin and the smell of cooked meat quickly filled the room.

He dragged the man behind a small desk and left his body for someone to find. Gabriel walked to the center of the room and pulled the power cell from its housing. It was heavy, requiring both arms to be wrapped tightly around it. He wasn't sure if the adrenaline coursing through him was keeping the power cell in his arms, or his prayers as he ran to the door and turned down the hallway. The lights dimmed momentarily like Poin said they would, then the rooms lit up red as he stepped to find his robot in the exact room Poin said it would be in. Gabriel crossed the room, pulled open the massive container it lay in, and inserted the power cell just below the sternum after he opened its compartment.

"Poin, is there any movement nearby?"

"No, Gabriel."

He didn't respond, as he grabbed the cable from the back of his experiment and connected the probes to his head. They suctioned to his scalp and ran back to the robotic husk laying before him. He pulled a vial from his pocket and pressed it to his forearm.

"I hope to see you on the other side, Poin," he said as he drifted off to sleep, hoping to wake up on the other side.

There was a knock on the door to Astar's apartment.

"Sir," his AI said from above him, "there's been a problem on the lower levels and sublevels. A loss of power has occurred and there is reason to believe an intruder is in the building."

He was gazing out of the windows upon the GUC. The faint glow of reds, oranges, blues, purples, and greens lit up the new section of the Deep, while the dingy glow of the Slums had diminished to a mere wink of existence. *Soon, that glow will be eradicated entirely.* Astar looked at the UC and all the bright white which irradiated from it. *You will become the chosen one.*

"Sir?" His AI asked again.

"I heard you," Astar replied.

"Is there anything you would like for me to do?"

"I believe we will wait and see how this plays out."

"Do I contact the other Directors in any of the other cities?"

"No. Let's not waste any of their time unless we need to. Has power come back on?"

"Only auxiliary. I am combing the mainframe for any new," there was a pause, "oh, this is interesting."

Astar gazed from his window waiting for the new information.

"It seems there's a new guest in the Hive. He is calling himself the one and true God who will lead us to our salvation."

So, we've been attacked by an AI. "Wipe it out."

"He has taken control of the Capitol and identified himself as 'Poin.' I will do what I . . ." the voice cut out.

Above Astar, the blast doors slammed shut, sealing him inside with a clang as they smacked against the floor. *Interesting. We've been compromised for the time being.* Graciously, he walked over to his desk and pressed a button on the red holoscreen to contact all of the other Directors directly.

"This is Astar with the GUC. The Capitol has been taken over by a rampant program in the Hive. It has identified itself as 'Poin, the one and true God.' I recommend disconnecting your building from the Hive and running off of your backups for the time being. I will keep you updated as the situation progresses. Expect further information as it arrives." Astar lifted his finger from the holoscreen and the message was sent instantaneously, he knew.

He walked over to a glass cabinet, pulled cups cut from diamonds, and poured an ancient bourbon into the glass. He sipped it neat as he approached his cushioned couch. Astar let out a joyous breath as he sat down and waited. *Thank you for the silence, Poin. I'll have to thank you personally before I destroy you.*

CHAPTER THIRTY-SIX

Cancun, 2014

JANET SORTED THROUGH THEIR CLOTHES WHILE ROB HAILED A CAB for them. He was simple, choosing to wear a pair of summer shorts and a Hawaiian button-down with pelicans on it. *What do I wear? He's gonna kill me if he's waiting out there for me.* She pulled a dark bathing suit out of her luggage, then threw a white beach dress over it. *It'll have to do.*

She ran out of the beach house into the ninety-degree weather. It was slightly humid. Little beads of sweat had already started to form on her skin. She smiled. The weather was just to her liking. The cab was waiting for her when she reached the end of the driveway.

"Look who finally showed up," he said, as she opened the back passenger door and sat inside.

"Sorry, couldn't figure out what to wear."

"You look wonderful."

They remained quiet as the car lurched away from their rental. Janet gazed out of the window at the sun beginning its slow trajectory towards the horizon. The crystal-clear blue waves crashed against the pure beach, and she felt at home.

They arrived at the restaurant and sat at a plastic outdoor table with a bamboo umbrella. The sounds of birds, lovers, and waves filled the air as they were quickly served ceviche as an appetizer.

"What're you gonna get to drink?"

"Probably a daiquiri," Janet replied.

"I'm going to get a frozen margarita."

"Oh, you're gonna get trashy tonight?" Janet laughed.

"Of course, what else would you expect on vacation?" Rob smiled back.

"What're you thinking of ordering for dinner?" Janet asked.

"The coconut grouper sounds good. It has a banana mayo dip. Don't know if I'll like that, but here's to new adventures," Rob raised his water and Janet banged her glass against his.

"I'm going to go for the mahi mahi and bacon wrapped scallop."

"I'm definitely eating those scallops."

"Don't even think about it."

"Too late, already thought of."

Rob and Janet sat eating their food, laughing the loudest around among couples young and old. Their waiter had mysteriously disappeared, Janet noticed, either because they were there way too long, or they were getting too annoying with their booze. *Oh well, more time to enjoy this.*

"Isn't the sunset beautiful?" Janet asked, looking over Rob's shoulder. The sky had turned from blue to hues of red dispersing to orange then purple and pink as the rays from the sun reflected against the increasing clouds.

"Let's go sit on the beach," Rob said, standing up and grabbing his drink. Janet did the same.

She watched him lock eyes with their waiter who was not hanging out with the bartender at her bamboo stand. Rob nodded to him and raised his cup. They walked through the mess of plastic tables, until the beach met their feet. The soft, hot grains rubbed against Janet's feet, sticking to the sweat between her toes.

Janet sipped her drink, her legs wobbly from the alcohol. Her head swam in it only coming up to take a breath before it dove back beneath the fruity alcohol. Rob was talking in the background but she was too busy enjoying the sensation of being drunk. She smiled to herself as her face grew hot.

"Will you marry me?" Rob asked. Janet turned to see him on one knee.

"What?" She asked startled.

He didn't respond. His face grew increasingly sad almost immediately.

Janet saw the small black box holding a ring. "Oh my God. Of course." Tears started to roll down her face.

She kissed him.

"I thought you were about to say no," he joked.

She wiped her eyes and sniffed, "No, you idiot, I'm drunk." She laughed as she dropped her glass while trying to put the ring on. "I wasn't listening." She pushed Rob toward the water.

He smiled back.

CHAPTER THIRTY-SEVEN

THE WORLD FELT LIKE IT WAS COVERED IN STEAM. SOAKING IN HIS own sweat, Jeremiah paced between buildings. The lights of the Capitol had turned red, and everyone in the GUC heard the *clang* as blast doors slammed shut. It was unprecedented times. People around him knew it was an emergency, but they didn't know what was happening. The panic on all of their faces informed Jeremiah that they were terrified for themselves.

Someone in there has turned up the heat as punishment for Gabriel being inside. But no one here knows that. They just know it's hot because someone is upset. Jeremiah felt guilty that they were all suffering. That some man or woman he had never met played with the temperature at their own discretion. *And now look, a total shit-show.* His mind went to the Slums and the Mines. *Are the Furnaces fully back up and running? For once, I hope they aren't.*

Jeremiah saw men and women beneath the walls of the UC gathering to stare at the change. He wanted to get a better look at it himself. Jeremiah cut through the streets, weaving in and out of people gazing up at the red glow, wiping the sweat from their foreheads and peeling clothes off. They started to look like they truly belonged to the Deep. Jeremiah listened in to the murmurings of the crowd.

"Can they turn the heat down a little?"

"What if it's a malfunction and they're sealing the heat out?"

"Don't say that. We'll burn to death if it gets any hotter."

"What sick form of punishment is this? I bet you those terrorists that blew up the Furnaces are behind this."

"Whoever put it in to lockdown is helping us. They always do."

Fools. Still believing that they're on your side. They're only in it for themselves. The crowds were growing larger as Jeremiah pressed on. At first it was easy to weave through, now he was brushing shoulders and bumping into people who refused to move out of his way. He was packed in tight, and the ignorance of everyone was showing.

The way in front of him was lined with a throng of human bodies swaying back and forth like ocean waves. Together they gazed at the center of their universe, now fuming red like an angry god. *I have to get to the Hub. Without it, Gabriel and Poin will be lost inside that hell.*

Jeremiah pressed on, squeezing through tiny gaps between sharp shoulders, or forcibly moving men and women out of his way.

"I know you," someone said to his left.

Jeremiah turned to see his Captain.

"You created a real shitstorm for me, Jeremiah." He was looking down the barrel of a pistol. He hoped it was set to stun. "You're coming with me this time. And I'm collecting that bounty."

Jeremiah grabbed a man and threw him into his old Captain, and he ran further into the crowd. He leaned his wrist close to his mouth. "Acacia, I need help. I'm compromised. I just ran into my old Captain. I repeat, I am compromised." There was no response in his earpiece. *Do I do it? Do I use what Gabriel gave me as a last resort?* Jeremiah looked over his shoulder and saw men and women parting to create a path. *He's coming. But if I do it, I'm just like Gabriel. Nothing more.*

Jeremiah heard the whirring of police engines overhead before he saw them. The thudding of suspensors ripped into his mind and hit him in his chest. *They brought out the aerial vehicles this time. I have to. But then I'm nothing more than Gabriel. I'll be exactly the same.* He was almost to the other side of the sea of people. There'd be buildings and alleys to run through. But no more human shields.

The sidewalk was surrounded by stragglers. The spotlights had started and they were tracking him now at the edge of the crowd.

"This is the police. Any further movement will be met with force. I repeat. Any further movement will be met with force." The voice echoed above him.

I have to do it.

Jeremiah looked over his shoulder one last time as he escaped the main cell of human bodies. He reached in his jacket, pulled out a small silver device, clicked the switch on the side, dropped it and ran like hell.

"Get out of here!" He yelled to the people he knew were too close. He prayed they would listen to him.

Shots rang out as he approached a cleared street. He felt the heat of the las-guns as he ran, swerving to avoid any chance of being hit. Jeremiah heard the explosion before the light from it erupted behind him. He knew there was a roaring inferno blazing upward and engulfing the buildings around it. *I'm sorry for any of you who didn't get away.*

Behind him, he knew the repercussions of what he had just done. The buildings would be torched; no amount of water could stop it in time. He had inherently leveled anything within a hundred meters, and anyone caught in the blast was now a mess of atoms drifting through the air. The lights above him stopped and drifted to the explosion. *I am you now. Saved myself for the greater good of everyone down here.* The fire raged and whipped beneath the eyes of the red Capitol, and smoke drifted upward once again.

"Acacia, I'm coming back. I had to use it."

"I'm sorry, Jeremiah. There is nothing I could have done to help. We both know this job came at a cost." Here voice was angelic and full of reason. "I will be waiting for you when you get here. Poin is making contact with the Hive. Gabriel has begun the transfer."

"That means it's only a matter of time."

"Please, hurry. There's much that needs to be done to make way for him."

Jeremiah didn't respond. He turned to take one last look at the flames as they whipped against the buildings and the dense black smoke rising up. Behind lay the Capitol. Red lights were casting to the smoke, giving the inferno an even more sinister look. He breathed deep, hoping he only took out the man he used to call comrade. *If you never threw me on that case, you'd still be alive. I'm sure you knew about him the entire time.*

Jeremiah pulled a hood over his head, grabbed the sides of his jacket, and pulled them close to make up for the missing zipper. Despite the increasing temperature and now the artificial rain, it was best to sweat than be caught while the police were distracted by Gabriel's grotesque weaponry. He knew it was necessary for his survival. Be destroyed by the people he used to work for, or destroy innocents in the process so he could go on living?

I hope no bystanders were hurt or killed, he wished to himself. But he knew the truth. Deep in his gut he felt it, the pain of taking a life he was trying to make better. He pushed the thoughts from his head. Without proof, Jeremiah knew that he could never know for certain if anyone had died, but it still lingered. An unanswered question that he would need to ask God at the end of all things.

Jeremiah pushed open the door to Mama's and strode to the bar.

"My boy, you don't bring anyone else with you, but you carry something."

"Mother, I just need a stiff drink. Then I have to go."

"Those red lights belong to you, don't they?"

He nodded as he grabbed the glass in front of him that was filled with clear swill. He downed it in a single gulp, allowing the burn to scorch his insides. Jeremiah put out his arm to transfer credits. *At least Gabriel did this for me.*

"Not today, child. I'm proud of you for standing for something. In the face of it all."

"That does not seem like you."

"Just because I play both sides does not mean I cannot have an opinion on the matter. I need to keep myself and my business alive. Just as you. I know what happens during the calm times, when everyone struggles and nothing gets done."

"Thank you." Jeremiah reflected on the haggard woman in front of him. Her hair wild, and her skin taut, though hanging at the same time beneath her eyes. There was malice there, and understanding.

"Now get out. Before you attract more attention. You are no longer welcome in my house while this world chases you."

"Another one before I go?" Jeremiah laughed.

"Deal," she said. "But only if you drink with me." She pulled another glass and filled them both. "To better days." Her eyes glinted with malice and plans.

She's going to take advantage of this any way she can. If we succeed or not. She'll be one to contend with. A power grab?

Jeremiah clinked his glass with Mother's and left the building. He heard the clinking of glasses behind him as the doors closed.

Outside the lights were blaring, and the smoke from his explosion was swarming through the streets. The fire had spread, he guessed, and took up more of the surrounding area. *Maybe this will buy Gabriel some time, too. Clear the streets and get people away from the Capitol.*

Jeremiah wondered if the blast doors separating the Capitol from the UC were able to stop whatever Gabriel was about to become. *Would there be nanites to contend with? Throw an emp to disrupt them momentarily then dismantle whatever they are protecting. How will he get out?* There were many questions and few answers. At least, not until Gabriel finished his transfer and took over. Jeremiah looked up and took one last look at the Capitol, the statue to the gates of hell. He took off running for the Hub.

The door slammed behind him as he took off his jacket and ran to find Acacia in her operations center. She was lit up by green and yellow holoscreens, swiping and tapping away on all of the new information she was being provided.

"What's the status?"

"Poin, is watching over Gabriel as he transfers. He says it's all going to plan, but he's not acting his usual self. I don't know, he's weird. Does that make sense?"

"What do you mean? What's it saying?"

"That's the thing, Poin isn't really saying much."

"You're right. I don't trust it. At all."

"I know. But I can't do anything about it until Gabriel's online."

Jeremiah looked at the screens, trying to see anything Acacia couldn't catch. *She's good at what she does. I know why he chose her now. But why me? It can't be simply for getting him that suit to turn him into a cyborg.*

"Any word on Lew and everyone else?" Jeremiah asked.

"Nothing. But I don't think I should worry about them right now. Lew is good, he'll take care of them."

"Gabriel has completed his transfer and is online," Poin's voice cracked through the room.

"Oh, thank God," Acacia said.

"I'm alright. Getting my mind used to its new body." His voice came over.

"Can you transfer visuals over now, Gabe?" Acacia asked.

"Poin, please take care of that for me. I'm trying to get a system diagnostic complete."

A screen flared in front of Jeremiah and Acacia. Gabriel was still sitting on the ground. His systems were nominal. The battery had decades of life still left in it before standard decay cut it by fifty percent each year.

"Can you transfer yourself back into your body after this?" Jeremiah asked, as Gabriel stood up and inspected his hands.

"I do not know. I don't see why not. That body is dead to me now," he said as he looked over. "I'll be able to regrow one in a lab, though."

Jeremiah had just realized what Gabriel meant. Without his mind to be a part of the brain, his body was no longer breathing or pumping blood. Every cell in it would die or was already dead.

He looked over to Acacia who simply nodded in return, knowing what was on his mind. This was it. They wouldn't see Gabriel as they knew him for some time, if he ever chose to come back to the land of humanity. He was something else now.

CHAPTER THIRTY-EIGHT

JANET SAT ON THE NEW BORDER OF THE DEEP AND THE SLUMS. The bench beneath her was cold and hard. She felt like a homeless person on the streets of a futuristic New York City. Every which way she turned, she could see Holos pandering along with gyrating bodies and neon signs to light up their curves. Acacia was somewhere beneath her feet, watching and waiting for Gabriel. Acacia had left Lew to take them, and Janet in charge of keeping a look out on the streets for any suspicious activity. *I feel like I matter again, that I'm in control of my life.* She overheard Acacia talking to Jeremiah in the small earpiece they had all been given before Gabriel had left. The torn jacket and messy hood pulled above her lengthening hair hid any suspicion from the locality of her intently listening to the two talking in her ear.

Janet looked around the streets. *How long has it been? Two months since we blew the Furnaces? All these people.* There was more and more every day it seemed without a steady job in the Slums. Gabriel told them all it would be a result of their actions.

More prostitution, more drugs, more activity in general along the half-lit roads of the Slums. But now the Deep had pushed in with new shacks and neon symbols Janet couldn't read. *The property must have been cheap after the explosion. Quick turn over.* Janet looked toward the UC, and beyond, the Capitol now red with fury because of an invader inside. An invader she knew personally. She sighed. *Rob, what have I walked in to?*

Her earpiece crackled.

"Janet, is there any movement above? I'm getting dispatch channels saying there's a new gathering near you."

"Nothing that I can see," she put her mouth to her shoulder and whispered over.

Around her, she watched the men and women clad in tatters or skimpy clothing wander the streets. They all gazed up to stare at the red monument in the distance. The wall of the UC would hold them back from getting any closer if they kept walking. Janet looked up to the empty darkness above her. Even the vehicles had stopped flying overhead.

There was a rumble, almost, like a vibration, moving through her body and into her skull. It shook her brain and made her feel almost seasick. The tremor increased.

"I take that back. Something is happening. My body feels like jelly."

"Get inside, now." Acacia's voice cut out and there was no response when Janet asked what was going on.

She stood up. Her legs almost immediately gave out as she tried to walk, like being nearly blackout drunk at a college bar. Janet did her best as she walked through the streets to get to an entrance of the Hub. The men and women on the streets also started to disperse. She watched as they grabbed at their heads or stomachs. Some ran and fell, skidding across the street like ice cubes escaping. Janet covered her mouth as nausea set in.

She wobbled through the doorway, her body still shaking from whatever was going on outside. Janet found Acacia and Jeremiah still in the small room they designated as their command center.

"What was that?"

"A device used for sonic warfare," Jeremiah interjected. "It can kill with the right frequency directed at someone."

"Why are they using it?"

"Probably to get people nauseous and inside. They're trying to gain control before there's any thought to them losing it," he said.

"Does that mean Gabriel is actually doing it?" Janet asked Acacia who was desperately trying to keep up with the information in front of her.

"Yes," she replied shortly. It reminded Janet of the way Babyle spoke, just enough to get his point and information across, never anything more.

She looked up at the screens in front of her. "Where is he?" she asked Jeremiah, not wanting to distract Acacia from the work she was doing.

"Right there," he pointed at a basic floor plan of the Capitol. It was nothing spectacular, mostly sections with a few floors on each. It showed no rooms, and at times the sections gave no indication to how many floors were there. A small green blip moved beneath the street entrance.

Janet watched as Gabriel moved back and forth along the substructure of the Capitol. She wondered what he was doing and where he would end up.

"Aren't we supposed to have visuals from him, too?" she whispered over.

"We lost connection somehow. Poin says the Hive is interfering." Acacia replied. "We still have audio though, which is good."

Janet looked on at the mass holoscreens which surrounded the woman. She felt like she wasn't doing enough, that she could do more, but lacked any useful skills for the time being. *Maybe if I had gone into technology at one point in my life, then I could help them.* She walked out of the room and went in search of Jamal, Bernice or Crow. Even Lew would do at this point. She knew they had come back, as well, that her channel for talking could be heard by everyone. *Jeremiah may have told them separately to come back.*

Jamal and Bernice were sitting together, watching television. It was an old show Janet recognized. Rob used to watch it all of the time. Men and women whose plane crashed on an island. She remembered watching the first few episodes with him, but eventually lost interest in the people on the island. *I wish I watched it with him, but now it only brings pain.*

"How are you two holding up?" she asked.

"We're okay," Bernice replied. "Got a little sick from whatever was going on, but we didn't go far like you and Lew. It's a little odd having lived so long out there, then getting dragged into this mess. But I think we're doing okay, better than Crow, at least."

Jamal nodded and went back to watching the show.

"Does she have any plans for you two?"

"No, she told us to go and relax. There's nothing we can do until Gabriel finishes his mission. Even then, I don't know what help most of us are gonna be."

"Have you checked in on Crow at all?"

"No. He was on those drugs Gabriel left behind and needed to stay with Lew, last I knew. They'll help him."

"How do you know that?"

Bernice showed off her feet. They looked sunburned, with the skin peeling off in spots. Underneath, the flesh was a deep pink. "They don't hurt anymore, and I have complete feeling in my toes. The sharp pain Gabriel told me about stopped about two weeks ago. Now the skin just peels off. It's itchy as hell," she laughed.

"Well, for his sake, I hope he gets better. We've all been through so much. I don't know what made him crack."

Jamal looked over. "I think all of it made him crack. The loss of his wife and kid probably was too much. And finding this place and all the drugs was just a way for him to finally cope. It's hard. We all lost it. We just didn't go down that road yet."

Janet wondered if she would go down that road, or if any of them would. *Rob, would you stop me from making those choices, or let me deal with my own consequences?*

"What did you two do before all of this?" Janet asked. "Before like, the power went out."

"Enjoyed life," Bernice and Jamal said in unison. They laughed. *So innocent,* Janet thought. *Even now.*

"You know I was homeless," Jamal said.

"I worked online marketing, but it was part time. I had a side gig meeting older men in the city for dates. I'd go down there on the weekends, eat dinner, get drunk, and go home. Never once had to sleep with one of them. They just wanted to give their money away."

"That's interesting. How did you start doing that?" Janet was surprised by Bernice's answer.

"One of my friends in college found a website for it. And all one of the men wanted was to see pictures of her in underwear. She made five hundred dollars one weekend that he sent right to her account. So I gave it a shot. Paid for most of my life. Never even felt like work," Bernice shrugged.

"Did you ever feel bad doing it?"

"At first it was strange and I felt guilty because I thought some of these men expected sex in return, but as I got to know a few, they just wanted company. Either they had failing marriages, or their lives were too demanding to go on a normal date. They all just wanted to feel normal like everyone else, but their pursuit of money and worth left them with no social interactions."

"That's really interesting."

Jamal changed the show after the episode had finished. He chose a cartoon about a scientist and his grandson.

"How do they have access to all of this?" Janet asked.

"I don't think we lost everything when the power went out. I guess it's all saved on computers somewhere, and Gabriel figured out a way to get it. Or Poin did. I loved this show when it was on years ago," he said.

"I just don't get how he knew there was something up above all of this."

"I don't think he did. I think he just wanted to see what the world was now, and found out that they were all being lied to."

Janet looked over at Bernice, who shrugged and continued to watch the show Jamal used to love.

"How'd you watch this stuff if you were homeless?"

"It came out before I left the house. And besides, just cause I was homeless doesn't mean I didn't have any friends," he laughed.

Janet felt herself blush.

"It's all good. I'm not offended."

"Thanks," she said as she watched the show with them. *I wonder if Rob had seen this.* Janet was growing restless sitting inside now. At least up top she felt like she could breathe. But now it was a waiting game for Gabriel. They toiled away on things to get their mind off of the problems at hand, problems they had no control or say over. They were fish in a tank watching the world go by, being fed intermittently, then left to their own devices.

Jeremiah appeared after a few hours. They had changed the show at least three times, rotating between episodes to keep everything new and fresh.

"Acacia needs you, Janet."

"Do you know what for?"

"You're going back out," Jeremiah said as he left the room.

Acacia was standing where Janet left her, toiling away behind screens like a child playing with augmented reality.

"You need to get back up top. I want you to make a right and go toward the wall of the UC."

"What's over there?"

"I don't know. Poin is MIA, and Gabriel is sporadic with communication. We have alerts going off everywhere in the GUC. I need eyes somewhere."

"What about that device they were using to get people inside?"

"Just go, and if you feel it, go in the closest building. Just get up there, Janet." Acacia never looked over to make eye contact. She simply continued swirling through the waves of information in front of her, trying to decipher what was happening and fix the issues they had run into.

Janet followed the staircase back to the street, which had been vacated It was barren, like wandering the streets of New York after the lights had left. Though this time there was no snow to contend with; even the light rain wasn't much of a bother to her. It was almost nice, reminding Janet of warmer days when she would walk around on the beach on Long Island. The clouds overhead were dark, it would be in the high eighties, and the sand turned dark from the rain. All around her, the droplets formed small concentric circles on the sand as her feet plodded along. She was young, early twenties, and hadn't met Rob. It was one of her favorite things to do, walking in the rain on the beach in the middle of July. It was peaceful and very few people went out to listen to the waves crash and the rain patter against the leaves. Janet sighed with the nostalgia and let it escape her chest. The walls of the UC were getting closer and she had a job to do, which meant she couldn't let her past life distract her now, she knew.

The walls towered over her, and now that she wasn't running, Janet could finally take a good look at them as she sat on a bench a block away, which situated her on a corner of two connecting streets. The wall glimmered with the street lights from both sides. One side mostly a white-yellow from the glow of the UC, and her side on the Deep shimmered with every color she could see. Blues mixed to greens and yellows, then to orange, pink and red, until they seemed to repeat again. *Is it made of metal? Or some form of concrete? Maybe it has some of those nanites built into it like Gabriel had spoken about.*

Janet sat waiting for the world around her. The people, the machines, anything at all. She felt alone. Waiting on the street, she reminisced about watching the group of people in the building the day Rob died. She sat there, waiting, watching, and felt like the world was coming full circle.

As her anxiety and depression started to set in, Janet took deep breaths and closed her eyes. The earpiece was quiet, and when she opened her eyes again, she watched the lights go out. From block to block, they began to shut off from the Slums, to the Deep. Over the wall she could see the lights begin to decay, until all that remained was the red light of the Capitol.

"Acacia, are you seeing this?"

"Yes, I don't know what's going on. We're on backups of our backups. You should probably come back before—"

"Acacia? Acacia are you there?" *Shit.*

Janet looked around at the men and women coming back into the streets. They gazed at the only light left. The roaring gate to Hell, red with fury. The Capitol shone bright for all of them, condemning their sins. And then it went out. All of it. Not a single light remained on the outside of the Capitol, and with the windows shuttered, no light escaped, if there was light to be seen.

Please. Not this. Not again. Janet got up and ran like hell hoping she could get back into their house and that the doors would open. She prayed for it. Wished. Begged that there was enough power left to get her inside. *I know what happens now. Everyone starts to lose their minds. Please. Not again.*

CHAPTER THIRTY-NINE

NYC, 2013

GABRIEL WANDERED THE STREETS ABOVE. THE MEN AND WOMEN around him walked by in their dark peacoats, laughing, as the snow drifted lazily to the ground. It was cold, but there was no wind to bring the chill in the air down to the bone. Around them the white, yellow, red, and green lights of Christmas lit up the streets and the gray clouds that hung above them. Gabriel had never seen something like this before, but he knew there was joy in the air. *I want to give everyone in the GUC this kind of life. Joy, happiness. All of it. Bring them peace.*

He pulled his jacket close. He looked rough compared to those around him. They'd call him a bum, he knew. Gabriel found himself staring at people ice skating. Twirling, laughing, loving, holding hands with their partners and children. It was as picturesque as the newspapers he read on his holopad had described it in the few clippings Poin was able to get for him. Behind them stood a massive tree, larger than any he had seen during all of his trips Above. Atop it stood a star, an actual beacon of hope. *This is their Capitol. While ours is Hell.*

"Poin, what's would it take to bring everyone up here?"

"I don't know if it would be possible to convince them all to come without taking over the Capitol. Then you can broadcast a live signal of you coming back up to convince them."

"Then that's what I'll do."

"You know you're insane, right?"

"Absolutely, Poin," Gabriel chuckled. "And you're going to help me."

"The Hive won't like that."

"Then we take them down, too."

"That may be a different issue when it arises."

"Let's start with the Capitol, then. Tomorrow, Babyle and I will get inside. I need you to start getting any and all information on their security."

"Of course."

Poin's voice cut out and Gabriel was left with drifting snow and laughter. The raucous noise of New York City was wonderful. The cars honked, taxi cabs screamed through traffic, people banged their hands on the cars as they tried to cross the street. It was chaos, but different from that in the GUC. This chaos was welcoming, and not wrought with suffering.

Gabriel paraded through the streets lit by the lights of Christmas. Men and women rushing through stores with bags of gifts and children in tow was a common sight. *Almost like the Deep. If it was filled with innocence.*

Gabriel opened his new eyes as the memories from his old body flooded into his exoskeleton. He felt no sensation in his arms or legs. His chest and face were cold, but he knew that wasn't possible. His brain was trying to rewire itself to its new body. *I don't have a brain any longer. You know this. You are computational data in a mainframe. That's all consciousness is. Data.*

He tried to take a breath to calm down, though he knew that was no longer possible either. *Psychosomatic.* Gabriel saw the world around him. It was just as he left it. He forced his new head to turn by thinking it, and eventually the body responded. Slowly he was making progress, then exponentially, as he was able to move his arms and legs. He curled his fingers into a fist, and stood up by pushing off of the ground. His new legs felt weak, but he trusted them as he fell for the first time. His hands broke his fall, this time without any pain. *I'm going to need some sort of pain sensor. Maybe. Might be for the better that I don't.*

Gabriel pushed himself back up and was able to balance. A small screen in the bottom left corner of his display showed his center of gravity. *They thought this through already. Or tried and failed on someone else. Good.* He took a few steps, like learning to walk as a grown adult. He focused on the display and was able to keep track of his movements.

The rooms went dark as the lights shut off. Gabriel heard the blast doors slam shut along each floor above him as the sound reverberated throughout the Capitol, shaking it to its subfloors.

"They will be here shortly, Gabriel." Poin's voice cut through his new body. He felt as if Poin was a part of him, ingrained in his head rather than an outside force talking to him.

Gabriel looked around and tapped his head. The darkness around him illuminated green with the night vision built into his HUD. As it switched over, he imagined himself to blink, but nothing changed. His brain was reeling from the new body and the lack of old habits. He felt anxious.

He stepped from the room and heard the voices and footsteps down the hallway. *This is it. This is how it happens. All my plans are going exactly as I imagined. Do it,* he thought.

Gabriel ran down the hallway, trusting his intuition and lending his consciousness to his new body. His legs launching him further with each step. Like a boulder rolling downhill, he crashed into the wall, pivoted, and confronted the men and women searching for him. His shoulder smashed into them like bowling pins, and he knew they were dead by the sickening crunch that came out of their bodies. He had flattened them. Turned their organs into jelly, and kept going.

The elevator doors tore away from the wall like paper. Gabriel looked up, knew where he needed to go as he jumped and slammed his fingers into the wall creating fissures for him to hold on to. He pounced to the opposite side and continued his zig zagging formation up until he reached the main floor of the Capitol.

"Are you ready, Poin?"

There was no reply.

CHAPTER FORTY

CROW SLEPT FITFULLY, EVEN WITH GABRIEL'S DRUGS TO HELP HIM cope with the withdrawals. His mind raced and folded on itself as his consciousness projected itself to another realm. He knew he was there, though his body slept. *Where the hell am I?* Crow kept thinking the same thought over and over as he floated through the different planes of existence. He looked down at himself. He was fully naked. From his belly button a small silver stream flowed into the ether until he could no longer see it. He looked up at the universe around him.

There were planets and stars colliding against each other. Bursts of light flashed and decayed instantaneously. There was no warmth or frigid air against him. He felt like he was looking at old space photos during the mid-2000s. There were gas clusters and colors he only saw in doctored photos right in front of him. *I want to land. I want to land.* Crow was starting to panic, and found himself on a planet he had never seen before.

The world beneath his feet was burnt pink, and he almost thought he could feel the sponginess on his feet, like that of moss. *What the hell is going on? Is this a side effect of the drugs Gabriel gave me?* He looked around and saw the silver line from his bellybutton going off into the distance. There were monsters out there. Gargantuan beings stomping through the ground. They looked to be made of mountains and pink grass. One moved closer to Crow, stepping on his silver line as it went.

He stood still, watching in amazement as it covered the distance in a few steps. It stopped and looked down at him. Crow could see its piercing black orbs look directly at him. It moved its arm of stone closer to him. He closed his eyes as it reached out. *Please wake up. Please wake up.* And in an instant, Crow was back in his bed. He was covered in sweat, his heart raced, and he needed to piss. *What the fuck. Where was I?*

After relieving himself, Crow made his way out to the hallway, and down to where Jamal, and Bernice were sitting. Lew sat across from them.

"Where's Janet?" he asked.

"Acacia had her go back up top," Jamal replied. Bernice looked at him and nodded before turning back to the television. They were watching old cartoons. Crow remembered watching them as a kid. The hunter was still trying to get that damn rabbit.

"Have you seen this show before, James? I do quite enjoy it myself," Lew perked up.

Crow ignored him. "What's she doing up there?"

"Don't really know. Acacia said it was urgent. She got hit with one of those sonar things the police used during riots. Remember when they brought them into the city?"

"Yeah. I remember seeing videos online about it. Even the chirping through the speaker of my phone was hard to handle. I can only imagine what it felt like in real life. So, she came down to escape it, then went back up?"

"Mhm," Jamal said. "Something about needing eyes on the Capitol and the wall."

"Gotcha." Crow wanted to talk to the two of them, but his mind wandered to Janet. Wondering if she was okay. *Maria, Lucy, watch over her, please. She's not really that bad.*

Acacia was standing in front of her screens when Crow walked in. Her eyes had bags under them, he could see, and her hair looked like she had been pulling at it, or running her fingers through it incessantly.

"How's he doing?"

"Not good. They brought in a lot of guards. He was doing okay, then got up a few floors when I lost him. He came back not too long ago, and it looks like his new body has been damaged a bit. One of his arms isn't working properly. It keeps struggling to move up, then gets stuck when he tries to bring it down. Poin is running diagnostics on it and trying to override anything, but we aren't sure if it's a destroyed motor function, or if his brain is fighting against itself. There's a lot going on, and I'm not sure if this is going to work."

"We knew this was going to happen. He did, at least."

"Yeah, it's just a lot you know," she looked up with tears in her eyes.

"Where is he now?" Crow crossed the room and looked at all of the screens. He placed his hand between her shoulders.

Acacia pointed at a small red dot on the yellow holos. "That's him moving along. And over here," she pulled up a new holo, "you can see his perspective sometimes."

The screen was fuzzy. The hallway was long without any doors on either side, Crow could see. It cut out black, then came back crisp and clear. He saw Gabriel turning a corner and then it cut out again. When it came back there was a bloody face smashed open by Gabriel's fist. He had pulled his hand from the man's mouth which was now wide open. The teeth were gone and only red blood and the shine of the floor beneath his head remained as Gabriel had punched his way through the back of the man's neck.

"What's the time delay on this?"

"About four seconds. He's still going, which is good."

"What does he want me to do?" Crow asked.

"Get clean," she said without looking at him, nor skipping a beat.

He felt ashamed as the words hit him in the chest. He watched Gabriel's stream as he beat back tears. *Maria, I'm really that much of a fuck up, aren't I?*

Gabriel rushed through the hallways, tearing through the men and women of the Capitol police. As the screen kept cutting in and out, Crow could hear Gabriel mumbling to himself.

"Is it normal for us to hear him?"

"Yes. The body does have speakers. I'm honestly shocked that it is able to replicate human tonality so well, rather than that robotic voice that Poin has."

Crow thought about it a moment and realized how weird it was that Gabriel didn't sound like a robot, and agreed with Acacia on the matter. *Has human ambition gone too far? Is this what we've become? Destroying our planet to live underground and make a new kind of existence?* Crow shivered.

"I think I need to go back and lie down for a bit."

"Do what you need to," Acacia replied. She continued to sort through the masses of information in front of them and once again did not look up at Crow as he left the room.

The bed he laid in was warm. He had cold sweats and

thought about taking a bath, or if it would be too much on his body. He opted to sit on the floor, his back to the mattress. He leaned his head back and looked at the ceiling. *Is this what I've become? I need to be clean. I'm useless. Just fucking useless.*

He sighed deeply, closed his eyes, and thought he could feel the sweat forming behind his eyelids.

CHAPTER FORTY-ONE

They all sat around the table eating one last meal together, though Babyle remained absent. Jamal missed him. *Just his company, not his conversation.* He almost chuckled out loud, but guilt immediately hit him. He looked down at the table which they had laid a white cloth over. Each of them had a gray plate in front of them, with gold-colored forks and knives. It was a show, Jamal felt. But Gabriel definitely knew how to put one on.

In front of him the table was filled for a feast. It was like Thanksgiving dinner. None of it was his favorite, but each dish brought back old memories of different time periods in Jamal's life. Potatoes reminded him of his childhood. The turkey allowed the days before he left the house for good to flash in front of him. He looked around at everyone laughing, even Crow.

"You okay?" Bernice asked, her hand touched left side of his torso.

Jamal looked over. "Yeah, sorry," he said, "just lost in some old memories." He patted a napkin on his lap.

Bernice smiled back at him. "Okay." He watched her go back to eating and listening to the conversations at large. The red wine started to flow as Jamal tried to engage with everyone.

"And then, we went swimming for hours. I swear I never had sunburn that bad in my life," Crow was telling a story.

"But what's sunburn?" Acacia asked.

"My god. I never thought about it. So, when you're out there for too long, your skin gets super red, and stings to the touch. If it gets bad enough you can get poisoned by it. You have chills and the sweat starts coming. It's terrible."

"It sounds like going through drug withdrawals," Gabriel joked.

Jamal was shocked and waited for a fight to break out from the comment. He watched Crow and Gabriel lock eyes. Then Crow laughed a deep belly laugh and slapped his hand to his thigh. Jamal thought Crow might have a heart attack from the way he laughed, or forget to breathe.

"I'll drink to that one. That was good," Crow raised his glass and clinked it to Gabriel's. "Man, that made me miss my friend's. You really have a New York attitude you know that, Gabriel?"

"Sure," he laughed and drank until his glass was empty, then poured himself another and started to drink from it immediately.

"This is family," Bernice whispered over to Jamal. "They really do care about us."

"I know. It's just weird."

"Is everything okay?" Gabriel asked.

Jamal shook his head. "I'm just not used to this. Tomorrow

we could all be dead. And we're celebrating like it's not happening."

"I understand, Jamal," Gabriel said as he stood up and walked around the table. "That isn't the case, though. Tomorrow we may all die, but we're here celebrating life, as it should be celebrated—with great food, friends, and endless alcohol." He watched Gabriel smile, throw his arm around Crow and kiss him on the head, then take another swig of his wine.

"Join us in celebrating this world, even though it may be bad," Acacia said as she handed him his glass of wine he had hardly touched.

Jamal looked over to Bernice, who had grabbed her glass and was waiting for him. Her eyes squinted a smile to him. The creases of her crow's eye shown through her haggard look. They touched glasses and drank.

"That's my man!" Gabriel yelled. Jamal couldn't help but laugh and almost spit his wine onto the table.

As Jamal started to drink more with Bernice, he felt loose for the first time. Like his misery would wash away. Jamal thought of his uncle, and felt the tears almost start to fall in front of everyone. The rest of dinner was a flash of memory filled with laughter, hugs, yelling, and spilled alcohol. Jeremiah, Jamal noticed, was the first to retire to his room, followed by Janet and Acacia. Lew, Crow, and Gabriel stayed up late talking, while him and Bernice left to the safety and quiet of their own.

The noise had gotten too loud and the socialization overwhelming for the both of them. Lying in bed, they could both hear the murmurs of gray voices as they closed their eyes and drifted off to sleep.

They both woke to a banging on their steel door.

"I need you both in the common area," Gabriel's voice cut

through.

"Better get going," Bernice said to him.

Jamal sighed with nervous anticipation.

Everyone was waiting by the time Jamal and Bernice arrived. It was early, and Jamal felt like he and Bernice hadn't slept, yet they were wide awake, like waking up the morning of Christmas as a child. He looked around and wondered if everyone else felt the same way as they all sat with their eyes wide.

"I know you all still believe me to be a mad man," Gabriel started. "I've done things you wouldn't believe, and some of the things that you know of which places distrust in your hearts and minds about me. But today everything comes together, and my dream of a better future finally falls into place. I would have loved for Babyle to have seen it, through."

Jamal watched Gabriel glance around the room.

"As I'm sure you would have enjoyed the company of the ones you loved at this very moment. Life it seems does not always play out in the ways that we hope. And for that, I am both sorry, and grateful. Sorry that so much pain is caused daily, mostly by those who call the Capitol home—though I do not say I do not cause pain—and grateful that we have the ability to change the future through our actions. Here and now history changes and the future rewritten. I am proud to call you all my friends, colleagues, acquaintances, and helpers during this time. Trust me when I say that it will all be worth it, and that this moment will be one of the pinnacles of human revolution and evolution."

Wow. Jamal felt his eyebrows raise. He put his arm around Bernice who was now crying silently. *I wish I knew who she was crying for and missed.*

"Jamal and Bernice, you will stay down here with Acacia and

help her as she needs it."

"Okay," Jamal said. Bernice nodded.

"Then let us begin. Poin, initiate LIGHTSWITCH."

"Of course, Gabriel," Poin's voice cut in. In a moment, all of the power in the Hub began to dissipate. The common room shut down, along with all of the lights in the other rooms. The control center stayed lit, but dimmed to look like a calm library on a rainy afternoon, Jamal noticed. There were small lights running along the hallway floor which appeared for anyone who needed to walk around. As they passed, the lights behind them shut off. *That's interesting. They're motion activated.*

"It's time to go show those in the Capitol what it's like to live in fear," Gabriel said. "I will return." He walked out of the room without shaking anyone's hand, or embracing a single one of his friends, even Acacia.

"He's so odd," Jamal said to Bernice.

"He is peculiar. But he's a genius," Acacia said as she walked off and began pulling up holoscreens in her designated room.

"What did I say?"

"You said don't come back if I was still hanging around with Mikael."

"And I know you still been hanging around with that boy. He's plantin' seeds in your head, Jamal, and I ain't gonna hear any of it in this house. I work too damn hard to hear about some white boy riding trains to see other cities. If that's the life you want, then go."

Jamal felt tears burning in his young eyes. "Fine. You'll regret it. I already got a job. I won't ever come back."

"Good. You got the world figured out. While you're off galivanting, I'll be feeding this family, Jamal."

"Fine. Fuck you!" Jamal stormed out of the apartment and ran down the flights of stairs. *Don't ever go back. You can make it. You got this.* He smiled as tears ran down his face. His heart felt content. He was going to go out and survive in the world as people were meant to, with their heads held high and joy in their hearts, not struggling to get by day to day and going to a job they worked sixty hours a week at and still barely got by.

Maybe I fucked up. I shouldn't have said that to her. I love her, but she doesn't understand. Don't second-guess yourself now. If you do, everything will unravel and your life will go back to what it once was.

Jamal ran to the gas station and began work. He checked his watch. It was seven in the morning, and he was late.

"You know how I feel about tardiness."

"Sorry. I was visiting Mama, and we got into a fight."

The man looked up at Jamal. He knew he saw the tears and red eyes still.

"Don't worry about it, kid. It happens. You guys will make amends. Go get yourself cleaned up, wash your face in the bathroom, take a walk around the block. Just be back in a half hour. I'll take care of it until you're back."

Jamal walked to the bathroom. The reflection in the mirror seemed full. His eyes, though red, seemed to glow, and for the first time in years, he felt like he was happy. He splashed some water on his face and walked back out to the garage and began to work.

With Gabriel gone, Jamal felt like he was back in the city, though this time instead of working and living out of the theater, he was waiting for work to be done while he watched on the sidelines again. He was learning, just like he had been in the garage, and his life once again was on the line. Jamal took a deep breath and got off the couch, leaving Bernice, who simply stretched out while he stretched his legs.

"When are you taking us out of here?" Jamal asked Lew who was leaning against the cabinets in the kitchen.

"As soon as Acacia gives me the all clear. Peculiar. Never though that I'd be helping the same people I said I'd bring in."

"What's that mean?"

"I'm helping a bunch of terrorists take down the strongest men and women in the GUC. Fascinating, really. I worked for them, trying to find information for them about anyone or anything that was just too far 'off.' Now, I'm chasing all these rumors of the Above still existing and you all as Gabriel tries to overthrow them." Lew smiled.

"It does exist. Only a few years ago everything seemed normal. Then when the lights went out, it all fell apart fast."

"Degradation of society, my friend. It all relies on comfort. Even discomfort. Just like here. It's normal to be uncomfortable in different sectors. It's the common thread bonding them all. If it were to all become uncomfortable for all of them, the GUC would fail just as it did for you. That's what Gabriel's planning, hoping, accomplishing. Through his efforts, it will fail and a new society will rise."

"But isn't that a bad thing?"

"Not so much. You see, Gabriel has all of these plans in place, I'm sure he has this new society planned when he takes over. For you, though, it seems that there was no real plan in place. Someone, somewhere, shut it all down and let you all to fend for yourself. That's where my mind gets boggled. Who did it? Why did they do it? What was their end goal? I'm throwing wet napkins at a wall to see what sticks, but they all fall off."

"Sure." *This guy is weird as shit.*

"I do know I don't make much sense, my friend. But, believe me, I will figure out everything one day. I only hope we all live long enough to see it." Lew smiled and laughed. His long face turned into a twisted contortion of extreme expression. His teeth shone and his mouth looked as if it was about to swallow the world, or open up to let out raucous laughter.

He looked like one of the laughing masks you always saw near theaters, Jamal thought.

"I'm going to go and see if Acacia needs me," Jamal said.

"I'll be here, sir. If you come up with any outlandish thoughts, please do inform me so I can add them to my collection while we wait!" He heard Lew's voice trailing off as he left the room before he got sucked into more conversation.

"How's he doing?" Jamal asked.

Acacia looked up and sighed. Her eyes were distressed. "He's hemorrhaging power and hasn't even made it a quarter of the way up."

"Why?"

"Is he losing power? We don't know. Poin is circulating through the Hive, looking for answers as we speak. None of the AI is giving any information to him." She threw a screen over to Jamal.

On it, he could see the suit's outline. One of the arms was a deep orange color, while the rest remained green. Next to it a small bar was listing a 74% display.

"That's still a lot of power, though," Jamal said as he thought about how far 74% battery could get him in a day.

"Not at this rate. It should have lasted him years. Now, it's lasting him hours," Acacia replied.

"Does he have a solution?"

"He's going to look for another one, or plug himself into the mainframe of the Capitol."

"What happens then?"

"I don't know," Acacia said.

"I have found a viable solution," Poin's voice cut in.

"What is it?" Acacia asked.

"I can get Gabriel to another suit. Then I will take the one he is in. I can operate the suit and in the Hive at the same time limiting my chances of complete eradication. This will also increase the chances of my—our plan by 37.65%."

"Gabe?"

"Make it happen, Poin."

"I don't trust that machine," Jamal said. "It sounds too fishy."

"He's not bad. He's been with us every step of the way."

"Just a lot of trust into something you've never actually met."

Acacia looked up at Jamal. Her eyes were soft, inquisitive, like she was about to say something. She reached and pulled the holoscreen she threw over to Jamal and placed it in the bottom right corner of the mass in front of her.

Jamal stood there for a moment, wondering if she was going to say anything, but only silence ensued. He felt an awkward tension growing as she toiled away, then he turned and left the room to return to Bernice.

He approached his spot. Bernice, like it was instinct, sat up and let Jamal sit back down. She laid across his lap and they watched the cartoons which were now on the screen. She had changed the show and now there was a man helping a woman put armor on her body to prepare for a long fight.

"I wonder when they'll have us actually do something," Jamal said.

"Me too. I'm trying to enjoy as much of the quiet time as I can get right now.

CHAPTER FORTY-TWO

JEREMIAH SAT IN HUMAN EXCREMENT, WAITING FOR THE RIGHT time to move on his intuition. The Furnaces were his new safe place. He had spent what few creds he had left for a new ID card. Because of his lack of savings, despite being on the force, he was only able to change the number and account, not his name. He knew if anyone from the Precinct came looking, he'd be found out. *Would they even bother now?* His mind rushed with all the thoughts of his new life. He walked up to the entry way and scanned his card.

"A new 'un for us, eh?"

"Yes."

"What's yer name?"

"Jeremiah."

"Lookin' like yer runnin' from somethin'."

"You could say that."

The burly man at the entrance laughed. "Get in there and start shovelin'."

He walked through, taking a deep breath of the hot air that began to emanate from the long tunnel. *This is my life now. I hope I never have to use those safe houses.*

The first day was excruciating on Jeremiah's body. His biceps pulsed with each heartbeat, and his forearms felt like they might stay in place so he could never bend his arms again, or wiggle his fingers. He walked back up to the Slums, and hit his card against the time slot. His creds for the day popped up and he was thoroughly disappointed. *You've got to be fucking kidding me.* He knew he would live on a cube tonight.

Sleeper's Row was full by the time his legs hobbled over. His lower back screamed in pain as it locked up while he tried to sit down. The lights were mostly yellow and red layered with years of film.

Jeremiah felt the humidity had ramped up, and he knew it was about to be a torrential downpour. *Nothing like a warm welcome for my first day on the job.* He sighed. *Mason fucked all of this up.*

Jeremiah let his mind wander to all of the dreams of a better life he'd once had. He was in line to become a Specialist. He'd work in plain clothes, become an inside man and help take down big crime in the UC—no more small fish. One day he'd hope to be Captain, and his far-off dream of being Chief for his Precinct. Then he'd really make a difference, he knew. Working to dismantle corrupt politicians and the well-to-do men and women who spent creds just to keep themselves immune to the law.

Now look at me, can't even get my own Precinct to look into their shit without the Capitol Police throwing their dicks around. Jeremiah smacked the ground and wished he hadn't. His hand now ached along with every muscle and ligament in his arm. He leaned back slowly. His tight muscles groaned from the movement. The rain began.

It fell like stinging pellets, first smacking him in small droplets, then large wads of warm spit being shot out from cannons. Jeremiah knew he'd get no sleep tonight if he stayed on the edge of Sleeper's Row. He stood up and hobbled down the main road of the Slums until he found an alley jammed between two metal-shack buildings. It provided him a shelter. Above ran multiple pieces of tin to allow for easy access between the two buildings. He wondered what was in either of them, but the rain and lack of light stopped him from investigating.

Jeremiah missed the brilliant neon glow he saw while working in the Deep. The white lights of the UC were too blinding, and the murkiness of the Slums was unwelcome. The neons here were too faded, like someone had taken the dial and set it to ten percent, then threw a three decades of dust on top of them.

Jeremiah lay in the new alley tucked away in the Slums, listening to the hum of scooters and vehicles as they floated by. It wasn't nearly as busy as the streets of the UC, but it was comforting to know that there was still movement. He wondered who drove those vehicles with the lack of creds in this sector. Maybe it was people from the Deep coming to exploit the already exploited. Maybe it some from the UC were on a little vacation to score. Or, maybe someone in the Slums finally landed the right delivery job and saved up enough without dying of starvation, though Jeremiah hardly believed that would be possible. He sighed and rolled onto his side, tucked his right hand under his head and closed his eyes.

Jeremiah woke to the grumbling of his stomach and knew

that the cubes weren't going to be enough, but his leftover savings needed to last, just in case. *One day I'll get out of here and find the fucking bastards who did this to me.* He stood up with hate in his heart and stormed off to the Furnaces. The heat radiated as he closed in. It was hotter than normal. He had already broken a sweat before entering the long road leading deeper into the ground. Jeremiah scanned his card in front of the man he saw yesterday.

"Ha. Didn't throw ya into th' Furnaces I see."

"Who?"

"Any of 'em. Don't matter none. Ya still here."

"I think they'd find it a lot harder to get rid of me than they think."

The man raised his eyebrows and grinned between holes where his teeth should have been. "I'd keep it to yerself. Else that attitude gon' get yer in trouble."

"Starting from who? You?" Jeremiah was ready for a fight after stewing on his life.

"Ha. Git along." The man turned and walked away from Jeremiah who thought about chasing after him and beating him down just for the sake of releasing his frustrations. He took a deep breath and decided against it. The Furnaces would beat his body up for him so he wouldn't have any time to be frustrated.

The orange glow flared through Jeremiah's eyes and burned the back of his skull as he shoveled the piles of coal into the maw powering the Slums and the Deep. He wiped the sweat from his brow and wondered what it was like in the reactors beneath the UC. *Why couldn't they just power the Slums and the Deep with all of that nuclear energy? They obviously have enough. Yeah, but then if they did, they wouldn't have to force people here to work and remain in squalor. You answered your own stupid question, idiot.*

Jeremiah kept shoveling until he felt like he couldn't, and when his second wind finally hit and he was about to fall into that mechanical automation, he heard the whistle blow. It signaled the end of his shift. And just like that, the fuse powering him had gone out and exhaustion set in. The grumbling of his stomach returned, and Jeremiah wondered if he should go sleep or get something substantial besides a cube. He knew of a noodle spot nearby on the border of the Slums and the Deep. That would surely satisfy him, he hoped.

The streets above were littered with bodies waiting to head down into the Furnaces and start their shift as Jeremiah emerged from the pit. They all looked just as exhausted as he felt. Their skin hung in circles beneath their sunken eyes, and the patchiness of their beards informed him that they were just as malnourished. *Noodles sound so good right now.* Despite his feet wanting him to stop, Jeremiah made his way over to the noodle shop and scanned his card over the small box.

"Insufficient funds," a metallic voice rang out.

"What the fuck do you mean 'insufficient funds?' I just left. I should have enough for at least two bowls."

There was no reply.

He looked around and saw the price had gone up since the last time he was here.

"You've got to be fucking kidding me. I'm literally half a cred short. Give me the damn bowl."

There was still no reply as Jeremiah was about to lose his mind.

"I got you, darling," a voice said from behind him. A woman placed her hand up to the box and sent over half a cred for Jeremiah. Within a minute there was a steaming bowl of noodles for him. A bandage cut across her face covering one eye and her nose, and then it slipped just back up above her lip. She was tall, with blonde hair flowing from beneath one side of the bandage, and a piercing blue eye. Jeremiah knew she must have been pretty once.

"Thanks."

"Mind if I join you?" she asked as she scanned her hand again and waited on her bowl.

"What's the catch? You trying to abduct me? Got a man waiting so you can both beat the shit out of me in the alley while on holiday?"

"No. I'm here to inspect the lives of those who reside down here. I just need a few interviews and I'll be on my way."

"Oh, so a self-righteous cunt."

The woman laughed. "Yes. Exactly. I do it for the paycheck so I can report back to the UC to show how horrible it is down here. We then turn it to make you all seem like villains; crooks, the unworthy who aren't allowed in our sector."

"I think you know where this is going."

"I wouldn't make any unwarranted threats if I were you, Jeremiah."

He blinked, and wondering where this woman was really from. *What if she's from the Precinct, or Central, or the Capitol itself. What happens then?* Jeremiah felt his hands clam up, and a cool sweat form on his back.

"Don't worry just yet," she said as she grabbed her bowl of noodles. She slurped them into her mouth and stared off to the Capitol. "It will all make sense."

Jeremiah breathed deep, thought he felt the smoke and burn of the furnace and let it consume him. He knew that if they took him in, he'd be worse off than if he just ended his life now. They'd keep him alive down in the tunnels, torturing him and forcing him to live another day. He heard all the stories—rumors—of the enemies of the state who were made to wish that their parents were never born so they wouldn't be sired into this world.

"What do you want?"

"Just to check up on you. Like I said, it'll all make sense one day."

"Who are you? What is going on?" Jeremiah thought he must be dreaming.

"Just call me 'A,' and when the time comes, you'll know why I came here."

He shook his head and stopped asking questions. The noodles were cooling. If they cooled enough, the gelatinous broth would congeal and be almost as bad as eating the cubes. He sucked them down as fast as possible and let his mind wander as he stood with the woman and looked off to the Capitol. *One day, they'll get what's coming to them. Not in my lifetime though.*

Jeremiah stood with Acacia in the room and realized how he had known her.

"'A', huh? I can't believe it took me this long. Must have been the bandage," he laughed for the first time in a while.

"I always wondered why you never brought it up." She looked over to him and took her attention away from the screens and Gabriel, while Poin labored away with the Hive.

"I think I was always too angry with Gabriel, and my circumstances to think back on the past. You always felt familiar, but without time to dwell, it's hard to think, you know?" He felt scruffy, that he was the man to go to get the dirty work done. Jeremiah didn't mind it all too much. *All these people deserve it anyway.*

Acacia smiled to him. "I'm glad you're starting to get it. He's hard to get along with but it's not because he's difficult, it's because of his vision. He's uncompromising with it. That's just the way he is. He has to be that way, otherwise this would fall apart. There's no other way for his plan to be accomplished without him."

"I understand, but I still hate being locked up like a caged rat. Sent off whenever it's convenient for him."

"Without him you'd still be in the Furnaces, dead or locked away."

Jeremiah sighed. "I know. But I can still have my opinions and feelings."

"Guys, I need directions. My overlay has disappeared," Gabriel's voice cut in. Jeremiah looked at the screens and could still see the path Gabriel needed to take.

"Head down the hallway and make a left. The third door on the right will take you to a tubelink for large deliveries. You'll head up a floor from there and exit," Acacia told him.

"Why is he having so many technical difficulties?"

"I think his brain is reeling against being in a new body. There's too much information for it to process at a given moment."

"I don't think it's that, Acacia," Gabriel cut back in. "I think something is inside here with me."

"What do you mean?"

"I don't know. It just feels like I'm not alone, that there's someone in here watching me. It's like knowing you're being watched from behind, and when you turn, you see someone staring at you until you notice them. Then they walk away as if nothing is happening. A glitch in the programming of the universe. Poin, are you in here with me?"

There was no response which came over the speakers of the Hub.

"Where has he gone off to?" Jeremiah heard Gabriel whisper to himself.

CHAPTER FORTY-THREE

ACACIA GOT UP FROM HER DESK AS THE CLOCK MARKED THE END of her shift. She left the spartan office marked with real mahogany walls and an obsidian-colored floor that was polished so well she could see her own reflection as she walked. Her boss's room had two walls of wood and two of pure glass. He had once told her he loved the corner of the Capitol for the spacious view of the people below. Her heart bled for everyone beyond the wall of the UC.

Acacia walked into the hallway, took a right, and went straight for the elevator as she was told.

"Never go to any other office. Never talk to another secretary. If someone from security or the Capitol Police stops and asks you a question, you answer it immediately. If anyone asks your name, you tell them who you work for first."

It was an odd life she had found herself in. Never did she think she'd move up in the world from being the child of businessman to working in the Capitol. It was the dream of everyone in the UC to have access to this great wonder. And she hated it. There was no freedom, only the rolling creds, which she hardly touched.

Acacia stepped out of the elevator and quickly left the Capitol as she placed her arm up to the door to let herself out. Outside the lights built into the sidewalk blared below her and she closed her eyes until she passed them. It had become a habit to save her vision. Once she had seen the glow disappear from her eyelids, she opened them and kept walking. It was dark, even for the time of day. Around Acacia plenty of buildings had shut off their lights. *That's odd,* she thought as she walked to her apartment.

As she entered, the lights refused to come on. "Emergency power," she said.

"Emergency power not activated," a static voice cut through.

"Report."

"Power loss temporary. Service to be restored soon. Mandate to stay inside during times of unrest. Thank you for your cooperation."

Unrest? There's hardly anyone on the streets during this time, and with the darkness, no one wants to go out. She pulled back a curtain and looked out to the street below. The roads were vacant except for a few vehicles silently coasting by. Acacia thought of the chances of people coming through the wall if the power was out. Deep down, she knew it wouldn't affect her. There'd be no chance of that. Besides, all of the people in the Deep and the Slums were harmless—mostly. They just needed food and water. She knew they all wished to live in the UC, but they'd never attack it just because the power went out. *Everything will be fine.*

As Acacia walked to her bedroom to change clothes, the power returned.

"Service nominal. Please refrain from excess power

consumption as the grid comes back online." The voice had spread out onto the streets of the UC, and projected itself even from the speakers from the Capitol. *Does this information go beyond the wall?*

She sat on her plush bed. The sheets were pure white and matched the duvet. She surrounded herself with four large pillows. This was her only expense besides the apartment that she splurged her creds on. And she felt guilty every time she went to bed.

In the Deep and the Slums people were living on the ground under tin roofs, or curled up next to one another. How was she to enjoy such comforts? Just because she answered calls and kept the rooms clean, she was seen as being worthy to have all of this excess. Acacia's heart broke for the people she had never met. She stood up and changed her clothes.

She walked to her table reading through her holoscreen of today's news. Nothing spectacular to write home about. Some disruptions in the Slums, advancements in technology to bring a better tomorrow, and some upcoming broadcasts across the GUC. *Typical day in paradise.*

She shut off the holoscreen and walked to her bed. As she got ready to sleep, she stared at the ceiling and wondered of all the great mysteries. *What's it going to be like when we finally go back up top? Some day they have to do it.* "Stop thinking to yourself, Acacia," she said as she closed her eyes and drifted lazily to sleep.

The morning was the usual. Her alarm went off and she told it to stop. The beeping cut out immediately and she wandered to her shower to get ready for another mundane day.

The walk to the Capitol was short and boring. She closed her eyes as she got closer to the sidewalk lights which lit up the monument. *Need to invest in some glasses just for this part. Keep telling myself that, but always forget to set a reminder or order them.* She waved her hand over the black pad and the glass doors in front of her opened. She looked up at all the black glass. *Makes sense that they don't want anyone to see in, but they want to see out.* Acacia stepped inside.

She arrived to her office five minutes early as usual, and sat down at her desk. Her keyboard lit up in front of her, and she began typing away. Not two minutes into her day and two men barged into the room.

"Can I help you?" Acacia asked.

"Get her," one said to the other.

The man crossed the room and pulled Acacia from her chair before she could do anything to stop it. Her arms were placed behind her back and she was bound and gagged. As she lay on the floor, she heard one of the men demanding the information on the AI project her boss was working on. *I could help them. Tell them everything. Get this place torched to the ground. But we gotta get out of here first.*

"They're making cyborgs, trying to imprint AI neural nets onto newborn children. They've been successful with clones of rats," she said to the man silently pinning her. Everything after was a blur as she was untied, and led through the Capitol. Acacia learned their names. Gabriel and Babyle. Together they showed her a new life and wiped her chip. She was a new person, free.

Her new home was further underground in a maze of corridors Gabriel had built with his AI, Poin.

My God, this place is wonderful. She felt useful again, and for the first time, Acacia felt like she had purpose. *If I believe enough in this greater future, it will come.*

CHAPTER FORTY-FOUR

CROW FELT THE AIR AROUND HIM GROW ELECTRIC. THERE WAS AN eerie feeling hanging as he made his way up to the street. *Where's Janet? Somewhere close to the wall.* He clung his blanket close around his body and walked away from the hidden entrance to the Hub. In the distance he could see the Capitol glowing red. *Like a demon in the night.* He looked up hoping to see the sun, but only the infinite darkness of the earth greeted him.

"You feel it too, huh?"

"Jesus, you scared the shit out of me," Crow said.

"I hope not literally," Janet laughed as she exited from a dark alley.

"Yeah. I feel it. Something in the air. Acacia said Gabriel is still going strong. Some hiccups here and there, but Poin insists everything is fixable or being fixed."

"Well, that's good news, I suppose." She looked different in the red glow. Her figure accentuated, the shadows darker. "Come sit with me," she said as she walked back to the alley.

Crow followed her, and as they tucked themselves deeper into it, he felt like a ghost, something ready to jump out at the first chance he could. The darkness had grown so strong he could barely see the outline of his arms as they sat beneath the blanket.

The ground beneath him was an uncomfortable level of cool. *Probably want to get any last stragglers off the road and away from the Capitol.*

"You see anything while you've been up here?"

"Not really. Acacia let you out?"

"Kind of. She was talking to Jeremiah, and then Lew was harassing Bernice and Jamal, so I took a chance." Crow smiled.

"I'm glad you did."

They both sat and waited, staring off at the red monument like a bonfire.

"Attention citizens of the GUC," Crow heard Poin's distinct robotic tone come through the speakers situated throughout the city. "I have acquired control of the Capitol and will assume leadership until I deem it necessary."

"What?" Crow looked over to Janet.

"I have no clue. We need to get back to the Hub." They both stood up. Crow felt his legs grow weak, either from the drugs Gabriel had given him wearing off, or the anxiety over what he had just heard. *I hope this is a joke. If that thing is taking control of the Capitol, we may be worse off than we were before.* They crossed out of the alley and to the hidden door to the Hub. As they entered, the door behind them slammed shut. *That can't be normal.*

"That's never happened before," snapped Janet.

"Exactly what I was thinking." They ran down to reach Acacia as soon as they could. The unspoken words between them said that their time was limited and they needed answers.

"What's going on?" Crow asked as he burst into Acacia's control room.

"Gabriel said that Poin has taken over control of the Capitol and all of its features, including security."

"And?"

"That's all. Poin is able to let Gabriel through and lock out anyone Gabriel needs locked out."

"That's a relief," Janet said.

"Why did Poin announce it to the entire city then? Isn't that weird?"

"Extremely. Gabriel has some hypotheses, but none of them exactly stuck and Poin has only stated that he wanted to assert himself over the Hive. By telling the GUC, Poin has assumed his dominance and other AI will either fall in line, or band together with other rogue groups to try and overthrow him."

"That's a lot to unpack, and I'm still not sure how I feel about it," Crow said.

"For once, I agree. Poin has been off since the reset, and I'm not sure whose side he's on."

"Can he hear you in here?"

"Only if I want him to. Gabriel has this room locked away from Poin unless it's essential for him to know anything. Right now, I have us muted," Acacia smiled warily.

I still don't trust it. Despite what Gabriel has said or done. If Poin can take over the most heavily guarded building down here, surely it can take over this small room.

Crow watched as Acacia swiped back and forth through her screens. There was something about her, was it the way she stood? No. It was her eyes. They were wide and she looked scared. Crow left the control room with Janet as the conversation drifted off to murmurings and eventual silence.

Jamal and Bernice sat in the living room. *Do they ever move?*

Crow decided not to drop in and ask them their opinion on what they had just heard. It was better that way. They needed to be in their own world and only be called upon when needed.

Jeremiah barged through the hallway as Crow headed for his room. The sweats had started to return and he knew now that the looseness in his legs was from the lack of drugs.

"I can't get out."

"What?"

"I can't get out," Jeremiah said. "The door is locked. It beeps and that's it. Nothing. No fucking escape from this hell cause of that fucking *monster*."

"No, not again," Janet said in disbelief.

"Yes. We're stuck here and I need to tell Acacia."

He ran past them.

"What do you mean?" They heard Acacia ask.

There was a back and forth between the two. Acacia ran by and up the stairs to the door around the corner. Crow heard it beep, but the rushing sound of machinery moving upward couldn't be heard. *Jeremiah's right. We're stuck here. Like ants in a farm.*

"I need to get back to my room and talk to Gabriel," she said rushing by.

I can't do this right now. I need to get into my room. He looked over to Janet. She nodded without saying a word. Crow felt her arm touch his back and he walked down the hall.

Crow stood in front of his door. It did not open and he almost bumped into it. He waved his hand over the small panel to his right in case the motion sensor did not notice him. Nothing happened.

"No."

"Give it a second."

Crow waved his hand over the sensor again. The door

stayed closed. "No. This can't be happening. I can't make it without the stuff from Gabriel." He looked over to Janet with fear in his eyes. *I know I'll die from the detox without it. Maria, Lucy, are you guys ready for me? Will it hurt?* Crow felt the sweat beading on his forehead and his knees begin to knock.

The door opened.

"See. Just took a second."

He breathed out deeply and stepped inside. He ran to his dresser and fumbled for the vial Gabriel had left. Crow sat on his bed and pressed it to his forearm. The concoction rushed through his capillaries and he felt like he could breathe again. Almost instantaneously the sweat stopped. He took off his blanket and lay back to enjoy the moment of freedom.

"I'm sorry, Crow. I needed to lockdown the Hub in case any from the Hive chose to attack it, or send someone to disrupt the mission," Poin's voice cut in.

"But why did you lock the inside doors?"

"Overzealous," the voice cut out immediately after the single word was uttered from the ceiling.

"I still don't know if Poin is on our side of not," he looked over to Janet who was standing at the doorway.

"I don't know, but he let you in. That has to count for something, doesn't it?"

"I guess."

CHAPTER FORTY-FIVE

JEREMIAH LEFT THE ROOM ACACIA HAD TURNED INTO HER control center. *Through the kitchen, and pull out the oven. Push down on the right panel and crawl through. Fucking hell. I hate all of these crawl spaces. I guess Gabriel took something from my handbook.* Jeremiah laughed to himself. *I always knew that thing would be trouble. No matter how many times I told him, he insisted on keeping it around.*

Jeremiah pushed on the panel behind the stove. It moved like he was told it would. The crawl space was darker and narrower than the ones he had made. *How the hell would someone the size of Gabriel fit through this?* He got down on his stomach and began to pull himself through with his arms.

Jeremiah felt the walls squeeze against his body. His hips wiggled against the rectangular walls and struggled to pull through. His shoulders contorted and more than once he could have sworn, they'd dislocate or he'd get stuck until he died of thirst. *How long is this damn thing?*

Jeremiah kept crawling until he felt the floor below him

begin to descend further down rather than straight. His arms burned from pulling him forward. Each time he tried to get his feet under him to push off and take a small load off of his arms, they would slip from the lack of grip. Jeremiah pulled until his arms hit a wall. *Turn right. You're almost there.*

After pulling his body along and shimmying for what felt like another fifteen minutes, Jeremiah knew he was getting close. His hands hit another wall. He turned left and finally saw a small light at the end of the tunnel.

Jeremiah pulled himself out of the crawlspace and stood up. He brushed his pants and shirt off. His arms thanked him for the stretch and his shoulders swore that they believed in a higher power.

Okay, now I need to get over to the Capitol. Jeremiah looked around trying to get his bearings. He could see the wall separating him from the UC. He ran for it. *That thing is going to be locked tight. Better find something along the way to help me get over it.* The alleyways on the border of the Deep and the UC weren't loaded with litter like they were in the Slums. Even a broken board, or a sheet of metal could help, but finding one would be the difficult part.

"Acacia is there any way through the wall?" He whispered but there was no reply to his earpiece. *That fucking thing is definitely screwing with us.* Jeremiah sighed and tried to keep his composure.

The wall stood in front of him, massive and obsidian in color. *Thing has to be at least twenty feet tall. Of all the times I've gone through it, I've never bothered to look up,* he thought as he craned his neck and felt his spine cracking as he did so. It was a wonder to be built. So smooth, perfect in every facet as he ran his hand along it trying to feel for any stress fractures or gaps he could work with. There were none.

"Do you need help, my friend?" Lew's voice cut in.

"Where the hell have you been? How did you get out?" Jeremiah turned and saw the skeletal figure standing there. Without the lights his facial features were even more haunting.

"I've been speaking with Mother. She still has power and is planning a move in the Capitol should we fail. I can't tell you all my tricks," he smiled a sadistic, toothy grin.

"She's crazier than I thought."

"If you only knew."

"What's she going to move against them with? Bar glasses and a shotgun?"

"That is part of her plan, yes. But some of the other families are willing to throw their weight behind her. There's one issue that remains," Lew said.

"Gabriel's body," Jeremiah finished.

"Gabriel's body indeed."

"They've been saying there are more of them in the Capitol." Jeremiah glanced to the monstrosity in the distance.

"I do believe that there are. With the one that killed Babyle, it would only make sense that there's an army of them somewhere. Though, I do not understand why they haven't been unleashed on Gabriel at the present."

He has a point. If they're so concerned about protecting the Capitol, why would they let him run amok? Did that thing take over the Capitol to stop them from being unleashed on it?

"You're having the same thoughts I did. I can see it on your face, Jeremiah."

"I don't trust that AI, but what if it took over for that exact reason?"

"Then it would seem it has been benevolent all along."

"But it locked us in the Hub. All of the doors. I had to crawl out through a secret exit. I don't even know how you got out."

Jeremiah watched Lew raise his eyebrows. The look gave him a dramatic theatrical effect that Jeremiah had only seen once or twice on a broadcast television show back when someone in power felt like treating the populace.

"That is a peculiar issue indeed."

How did I ever fall in line with this one? "Want to help me get through this now?" Jeremiah asked Lew as he looked back to the wall.

"Mother says she has a way beyond the wall now that it has been locked down. If you'd follow me," he said as he turned away from Jeremiah.

"Great." Jeremiah followed Lew as he turned around and disappeared into the darkness. His shadowy figure winked in and out of form as they walked. Jeremiah could have sworn more than once that he had disappeared, which may not have been the worst thing. Besides his awkward personality, Lew wasn't so bad, just very strange—odd; off-putting, even.

Jeremiah could see the warm yellow glow of Mother's building standing against the dark night. It radiated outward until its gradient disappeared into the air. As they approached, Jeremiah could hear the raucous drone of men and women talking, laughing, and having a good time. Outside of her home, the crowd gathered and clogged the entire block. *It makes sense. She's the only one with power now.* He squeezed through the crowd as he tried to keep up with Lew, dressed in his all-black attire.

"What did I say?" Mother's voice called out, as he walked inside.

"That you didn't want to see the two of us together," Jeremiah replied.

"Then why are ya both here?" Her eyes pierced through him as the crowd made way for both of them to belly-up to the bar.

"I need to get through the wall."

"And you think I can help you with that?"

"Lew said you could." Jeremiah watched as she eyeballed Lew.

"Guess I know who can't keep a secret to save his life," she said as she turned back to Jeremiah. "I can get you through the wall, but after that, you're on your own. Ya hear me?"

Jeremiah nodded. *Batshit. Completely batshit.* She knocked three small glasses on the bar and began to pour clear liquid into them.

"First, we drink." She pushed two of the glasses forward. Lew and Jeremiah grabbed them. "To the coming storm," she said as she raised her glass. They all clinked them together and gulped down the liquid.

It burned the back of Jeremiah's throat, then down to his stomach. He coughed and felt the heat rise through his nostrils. *Why did she pick the strongest shit she had?* Jeremiah heard her cackle as she turned away and walked from behind the bar. *She did that on purpose. Bitch.* He smiled, knowing he would have done the same.

Jeremiah followed her. He knew Lew was behind him. They went upstairs, through a few rooms, then took another staircase that opened to the rooftop. Outside, Jeremiah was able to get a complete grasp of the situation. Each way he turned, there was darkness until he saw the Capitol's red glow. The only other light on in the GUC was that of Mother's building. Beneath them he could see the crowd growing larger until the people faded off into the darkness in every direction.

"Help me over here," Mother said.

Jeremiah saw her pulling at a large piece of wood. He grabbed it and spun it until it landed atop the wall.

"You'll walk across this, then see a small ladder built into the side on the opposite end. Maybe not without any of the lights," she cackled again.

"Why do they have a ladder built into their side?"

"To escape if they ever need to, of course," Lew said. "They need to be able to get out, while keeping everyone on this end locked in."

Right. Makes sense. Jeremiah didn't reply. He started to walk over the long plank of wood.

"You be safe. And come back in one piece," Mother called out to him.

That's probably the nicest thing she has ever said to me. Craziest woman here. Unless, Jeremiah looked up at the Capitol, *unless whoever runs that place is a woman. Then she's the craziest one here.* He stood atop the wall to the UC. The faint red glow from the Capitol shone on the slick surface.

Jeremiah looked behind him, Lew was gone. *Where did he disappear to? Never mind; I have something to do.* Further on Jeremiah could see one rung to a metal ladder off to his right. He tried to keep his balance as best he could as he walked to it. Getting on his knees, Jeremiah swooped a leg down until it hit another rung. He proceeded to down climb the ladder. Eventually his feet hit solid ground and he felt a wave of relief hit him. *Now the hard part.*

Jeremiah plodded towards the Capitol, though this time he didn't dare ask Poin to overlay any directions to his orbital implant. He'd much rather continue on alone, without any help from an AI. *Better to do it this way than have any issues. Besides, I can see that fucking red light from the Slums.*

The streets in the UC were totally empty, unlike the block at

Mother's. It had become a ghost town. The lights were off, and while the Deep could only see the red glow, the UC lived in it. The lights spread out from the Capitol and projected themselves throughout the streets. Each corner, nook, or tight turn was lit up red and contrasted with black shadow. More than once Jeremiah swore he saw someone out of the corner of his eye, but when he turned, it was only part of a building, or stationary object on the side walk. He looked up as he approached the base of the Capitol. Its glass windows slammed shut by blast doors. The lights from beneath it blared until he could no longer see the top of the building, only the red continued on. *I wonder how far it is to the top?* Jeremiah heard a crack, then a groan.

In front of him, as he approached the red well of radiance before the entrance to the Capitol, there was a bending to the blast doors and a faint glow. He turned and ran. Behind him the blast doors blew open in a roar of inferno.

As he felt the heat on his back, he looked over his shoulder hoping nothing would kill him. With each passing second the fire grew larger, and the next floor blew out. The cacophony and force of the explosion destroyed the windows on the buildings he was running towards for shelter. He ducked into a doorway and peeked out to see what was happening.

The first three levels had been completely blown open, and he could see people on fire as they jumped to the street below. *Poor bastards. Didn't think you'd go out that way, did you? Hiding in your fortress and dying from the inside.* Jeremiah almost felt guilty watching them die, but they were complicit in crimes against humanity. They had trodden on the poor for their own gain, and kept them down with force. These people had used and abused those in the Deep and the Slums for entertainment. There was nothing righteous in what they had done.

He breathed a sigh of relief and hoped Gabriel was the cause of this. *I only feel bad for those who did not know what they were a part of. The secretaries and janitors just doing slightly better than the rest. Fuck the politicians.* Jeremiah smiled to himself, knowing there had been a step in the right direction. Now, all they needed to do was take down everything that had been built.

I'm sorry, Gabriel. I can't get in there now. You're on your own. I'm going back to Mother. Jeremiah left the doorway as a small explosion ripped again through the second floor. He ran like hell for the wall.

CHAPTER FORTY-SIX

GABRIEL STOOD AT THE TOP FLOOR OF THE CAPITOL. BEHIND HIM lay bodies of men and women who had fought to keep the peace that they deemed necessary for their own utopia. *I'm sorry you won't see a true utopia.*

"Gabriel, whoever runs this place is just beyond that door."

"I know." The HUD flashed between green, red, and yellow as different parts of Gabriel's new body languished from the damage it had taken. He stepped close to the dark mahogany, turned the handle, then stepped inside. A man was sitting at his desk. The blast doors were not shut behind his windows. He sipped lazily on a glass of scotch as he overlooked the GUC. *It's completely dark out there.*

"Nice to finally meet you, Gabriel."

"How do you know my name?"

"I've known all along. Your attempts at the Slums, stealing the information with your friend the first time you came into my home. All of it." The man spun around in his chair. He was in a crisp blue suit with a white undershirt. His brown hair combed over looked immaculate. He had aged like the alcohol he sipped on.

"But, how?" Gabriel wanted to know, no, he needed to know. He had taken all of the precautions and worked tirelessly to cover every track. He stepped closer, ready for the finality of his dream to come to fruition.

"You'll stay right there," the man commanded.

"This is how it ends. You know this," Gabriel said as he crossed closer.

The man stood up behind his desk and stepped through the hologram of his desk. With his right hand he swung out a small device and shot directly into Gabriel's chest before he could even react. Gabriel crumbled to his knees and watched the man sip on the brown liquid in his left hand. The analysis from his new body said it was scotch from Above.

"You don't come into my home and threaten me, Gabriel." He put the small device back on his right hip.

How? How is he doing this?

"I'm sure you have questions," the man knelt down in front of Gabriel and looked directly into his HUD. "You can call me Astar if you ever see me again."

Astar grabbed Gabriel's convulsing hardware by the head with his right arm and lifted him off his knees. Gabriel tried to struggle but all his systems were failing. He managed to let out a small punch which connected with Astar's neck. Astar turned and threw Gabriel's body through the glass. Before he fell, Gabriel could have sworn he saw chrome beneath Astar's skin. *That's it. That's how he knows. He's one with the Hive.*

"Yes, Gabriel. Astar is one of them," Poin's voice connected to him.

There was a sick, crashing sound as Gabriel plummeted from Babylon and came to rest on the earth below.

"Acacia, I need help," his voice screamed into the Hub as his systems went offline.

CHAPTER FORTY-SEVEN

CROW HELPED ACACIA WHEEL GABRIEL'S BROKEN BODY INTO THE Hub. Even with Janet, Jamal, Bernice, and him, they struggled with the massive frame. At times they had to stop and drag him, but the screeching of his feet was horrendous.

"This way, there's a small elevator we can get him in," Acacia said as they turned down a street in the UC.

"The Hub runs under the wall?" Jamal asked.

"Yes. Now hurry."

As Crow pulled on Gabriel's frame, he got a good look at the Capitol before turning the corner. The red building was still smoking, and he could see orange flames whipping from the sides of the lower floors. The heat was dissipating, but he still worried about any explosions that might occur. *What set them off if Gabriel was up top?*

Crow looked up, and then the red lights of the Capitol turned off. All that remained was the smoke drifting upward to the far-off ceiling, and the fire illuminating its monolithic form.

They bumped a wall. Acacia hit her hand to it. There was a beep and it opened.

"Okay, Jamal and Bernice, come with me," Acacia said as they pulled Gabriel inside. "I'll come back for you two." Crow looked at Acacia and could have sworn he saw Gabriel's HUD flicker. The door shut.

"What did that to him?" Crow asked Janet.

"I don't know. Acacia said there was a lot of static and his feed kept cutting out. She was able to make out a few words but nothing to write home about. Gabriel called someone 'Astar' and that's as much as she could really use."

Crow watched Janet sigh.

The elevator returned. Acacia was waiting inside. The bags under her eyes had grown long and dark. Her hair was no longer pin-straight. She looked like she had been pulling at it causing her hair to shoot itself in every direction and become frizzy.

"Please. I need to get back down to the Hub," she said.

Crow thought she might cry at any given moment. They stepped inside. Acacia placed her hand up to the panel and the door closed. They descended back to hell.

When it lurched back to a stop, Acacia ran out first. Crow stepped through the door just in time to catch her turning into her room. He walked through the corridor towards her. It felt cold now, like the Hub had lost its heartbeat and he was the last of the blood cells moving towards inevitable death. The silence was pervasive, even Jamal and Bernice were no longer on the couch watching television, Crow saw. *I wonder where Poin is now?* Crow paused to look up at the dark ceiling waiting for a voice that never came.

Inside her room, Acacia was working feverishly on Gabriel's metal husk of a body. Crow watched as panels were taken off, and wires sparked with life. He felt the touch of Janet on his left arm as he tried not to ask questions.

"Hey," he whispered to her.

"Hey. I hope she can save him," Janet said.

"Me too," his voice was solemn.

They watched as Acacia walked around the table Gabriel was on, and she began to cut into his head with a small metallic instrument. From it came a small red laser which blared into the seams of the metal plates. She then stopped, touched something on it, and used the instrument to pull the plate from his head.

"What are you using?" Crow asked as he was mesmerized by the tool he had never seen them use before.

"It's a multitool. Welds, burns, pulls, screws. Does everything," Acacia said. She was hyper-focused.

Crow knew she had made it into a flow state as he watched her work. Her movement was fluid, everything fast and distinct. She would not mess up. Gabriel's life depended on it.

He remembered the few times he had hit that flow state throughout the years. Once while working a dinner rush in a restaurant as a sixteen-year-old kid. He was able to open the freezer doors, drop baskets of fries, and flip burgers with ease while preparing plates for customers. Another time he had hit the same state while cleaning his apartment before moving in with Maria. All of the knick-knacks disappeared as his headphones blared music he hardly listened to. And when he accidentally knocked something off a shelf, his hand darted out to catch it without so much as a thought, then returned it back to its original platform while he worked underneath. It was automatic, robotic, like he had been taken over by something else entirely.

"Can you grab me something to drink?" Acacia's voice cut in.

"Of course," Crow said as he walked out of the room. "Come with me?" He asked Janet, who was still standing close to the doorway.

"Yeah, probably better to give her some space."

The kitchen was chaotic with the glasses and dishware gathering in the sink. No one had cleaned up after themselves while Acacia managed the holoscreens and helped Gabriel. *She really does keep this place running.* Crow filled a glass with water from the sink.

"I'm gonna stay in here and clean up a bit so she doesn't have to."

"Okay," Crow looked at Janet who smiled back. *She's not so bad.*

Crow turned into the hallway and heard a loud crashing sound. It shook the entire Hub, and he almost lost his footing from the shaking. *What the fuck!* He ran down the hall to Acacia's room. Inside, the roof had collapsed.

"Please," Acacia said. There was another hulking obsidian robot in the room. Her arms were held up in front of her.

Crow watched as the robot's arm flared red then shot Acacia before she could say another word.

"No!" Gabriel's voice cut through.

"I'm sorry, Gabriel. It had to be done. We couldn't let you galivant around anymore. The plan must continue," Poin's voice echoed on the walls as the machine walked over to Gabriel's body which had begun to jerk sporadically.

"What plan, Poin? What fucking plan," he screeched. His voice cut through the air like knives made of static circuitry.

"All of this, my dear friend."

Crow watched as it raised its arms and looked up to the gaping hole it had created.

"It's time for sleep now." Poin raised his arm and placed it at Gabriel's head.

This is it. Everything we've ever done since we got down here has been wasted. Crow dropped the glass of water.

"It seems we have an audience." Poin's expressionless face locked onto Crow.

Gabriel's hand shot out and grabbed Poin's arm. Crow watched him pull and separate it from the elbow. Poin backed up as Gabriel sat up.

"No. Everything goes on," Gabriel said as his body flickered.

"She got you working. How unfortunate." Crow could have sworn Poin chuckled before Gabriel separated his head from his body.

"I need help," Gabriel said.

Crow snapped out of it and ran over to Gabriel. "What do I do?"

"Get the tool Acacia was holding and give it to me."

Crow leaned over her dead body. There was no blood. Her skin was seared along with the wound that Poin had created. Half her face was missing, along with the right side of her body. The beam had gone straight through the wall behind her and opened up into the living room. Crow plucked the multitool from beside Acacia and handed it to Gabriel. He grabbed it with his right arm and began to work on his left.

"I need you to find Jeremiah while I get my body up and running to full capacity again.

"Any idea where he went, or how to get in touch with him?" Crow looked up to the hole in the ceiling.

"Start by going to Mother's. He was supposed to meet me in the Capitol, but my guess is the explosions distracted him from that." Gabriel pulled off a piece of metal and began sending sparks into the air. *Soldering himself back together? I thought this was indestructible.*

"Where do we go from here? We can't stay with that," Crow pointed up.

"You're right," Gabriel said as his head turned and looked at the damage. "Analysis says that there will be intruders soon. Both human and non-human."

"Analysis?"

"My brain is connected to hardware now, Crow. I have abilities that no body could ever give to me. Take everyone here to Mother's with you. I'll catch up when I'm finished."

Crow turned to leave the room. He took one last glance back before he turned to get Jamal, Bernice, and Janet. Gabriel was simply sitting there, sparks falling from his arm. Acacia's blonde hair peeked around the table he sat on.

CHAPTER FORTY-EIGHT

THE INSIDE OF MOTHER'S BAR-BROTHEL-HOTEL-BUSINESS WAS atrocious. The smell was like old beer, wet and pungent. It reminded Janet of the famous bar in New York City that only served two kinds of beer, light and dark. *I never understood how some people liked the smell of this. Rob always said it felt homey. Rob. What the hell has happened since Christmas?* Janet sighed and trudged through the mass of people who were slowly beginning to wander off.

"What are you all doing here?" Mother's voice cut through the murmurs.

"Gabriel sent us here. He said Jeremiah might be here, too," Crow replied.

"Mhm. Okay. But what are you doing here?"

Janet watched Crow as he tried to figure out how to reply. "One of those robots came crashing through our home. There's no way we can stay there now," she blurted out.

Mother looked over Crow's shoulder and eyed Janet up and down.

"At least she knows why she's here," Mother said to Crow. "Come up here," she waved Janet towards the bar.

"What did this 'robot' look like?"

"Dark like obsidian. It had just a black screen where the face would be. It was like one of the ones Gabriel put himself in. But this one was able to shoot like the one that killed Babyle."

"So, he finally did it."

"What?"

"Gabriel finally found a way to get himself inside one of those goddamn things. He talked to me one night about it, but I always thought he was batshit crazy," Mother laughed, "like me. We heard the rumors that the Capitol was working on an army of them and trying to find ways to implant consciousness into the bodies to make cyborgs. All we knew is that the Hive had control over them still."

"I'm so confused," Janet said.

"It's okay, hon. It just means there are bigger players in the game now. If Gabriel has one, and the Capitol has AI in some of theirs, then we might have a full-on war in the GUC."

"What can we do? Why'd he send us here to you," Janet questioned.

"I have my thoughts, though I'm not sure what the answer may be."

Janet spiraled through her thoughts. "Wait, so you know Gabriel. He has been here before?"

"I know everyone," Mother's eyes lit up. "I run things here in the Deep. The police ask to come and go as I wish them to. My power stretches far, but does not lay over those in the Capitol."

"But, why would they let you?" Janet tried to understand how they would let someone get so much power.

"Creds drive this world, hon. If I funnel shady dealings, I am the government in this sector. I exist out of necessity, and necessity for excess," she laughed.

More crooked dealing in a crooked world.

"You're upset by this."

Janet knew it was written all over her face. "I just don't get it. Corruption on corruption on corruption. It's what Gabriel's fighting to stop."

"Yes. And the only way to stop it is to become it. He does not exist without darkness in him, you know. The people he has killed for the greater good. Some of us just play our part to get through this mad world that we created," Mother smiled a twisted and toothy smile.

"Maybe we were better off Above after all."

"Ahhh, yes. Above. The land of milk and honey. Thrown into chaos. Torched by the great bombs."

"And you know about that too, I assume?"

"I know there was no war that wiped you all out. My guess, it was a warhead exploded in the atmosphere to knock out the grids. Gabriel talked to me about the snow, and that's where my knowledge ends. I'm just an old lady who runs a bar," she cackled.

All rumors and twisted words. I'm tired of this. "Can we get some place to stay, or at least tell us where Jeremiah is?"

"Sure, I won't even charge you this time. But if I have a debt that needs to be paid, you're the first ones I'm calling on," Mother clapped a row of five glasses on the bar top. "We drink to a deal."

"Fine," Janet said as she grabbed a glass.

"All of you," Mother said to Crow, Jamal, and Bernice. She raised her glass and Janet followed. "To a prosperous future," she said as she looked at Janet. "And a crazy world." They all drank, and Janet immediately hated the taste.

"Where?"

"He's up on the roof."

"I need to lay down," Crow said.

Janet looked over her shoulder and saw the tiredness in his eyes. He looked hollow, sunken, a shell of what he used to be when they trekked north from the city.

"We wanna go relax too," Bernice said.

"Okay, I'll meet you guys downstairs," Janet replied.

She walked toward the back of Mother's. Through a metal door she found the staircase, which was hidden by piled boxes and wood. She squeezed through the small gap and went to the roof. *Probably uses all of that to sell to people in the Slums. Plays both sides.*

Jeremiah was sitting on the rooftop when Janet arrived. His jacket clung loosely around him and he did not turn to look at her. The Capitol was still dark, but the flames still coming from it lit up small fractures of glass and metal.

"We failed, you know," Jeremiah said.

"I don't know that we did. Yet, at least."

"I watched him fall. I knew it was him. The moment he crashed to the street below, the Capitol went dark. It was a sign to anyone thinking they could stop them."

"He's alive."

"What?" Jeremiah turned to her. His face held astonishment.

"I don't know how. Acacia was working on him. Then another one of those machines came bursting into the Hub and killed her. Gabriel destroyed it."

"How did it know where to look?"

"I don't know, I was in the other room. Crow saw it all unfold."

"Why didn't you go and look when you heard something then," Jeremiah said accusatorily.

"I'm not one to run towards crashing sounds, especially right now. After running through New York, finding this place, then getting locked in, can you blame me for staying in the kitchen when the entire place shook and the literal ceiling came crashing down?"

"I guess. I'm going to have to talk to Crow to find out more," Jeremiah said as he stood up.

"He's in the basement trying to get some sleep. He doesn't have many vials left that Gabriel gave to him. Let him rest and I'm sure he'll tell you everything. Gabriel is going to meet us, he said." Janet tried to change the subject to allow Crow to get the rest he wanted and needed.

"I hope he knows what he's doing. He's going to need something more to get through this time. They won't let him walk in and do that again," Jeremiah looked back to the Capitol.

"I know."

They stood there in silence for a moment. Janet felt almost awkward for letting the conversation drift to short replies and grunts of affirmation. She turned to go back to Mother's. She was tired and the day had been long. *Maybe Gabriel fixed himself enough to come here,* she thought quietly to herself.

There was a massive clicking noise, like metal fuses tens of feet wide smashing into place. Behind her the Capitol lit up to the brightest white. For the first time in a while, she saw her shadow and turned back to Jeremiah to see the abomination in all of its glory once again. The red and orange flames still whipped from its base.

"When do you think they'll put those fires out?" Janet asked.

"Eventually. They're asserting dominance now."

Janet heard Jeremiah sigh.

"It's eerie with the smoke curling around it. Reminds me of the first fires in New York which burnt down entire blocks."

"Gabriel took me up there, you know," Jeremiah said.

"Wait, really? So you've seen it?" Janet's eyes lit up. *So he knows all about it.*

"Yeah, but it was during the collapse. Not before everything went to shit."

"Where did you guys go?"

"Grand Central. And then he took me to that park in the middle. It was clear that night and I was able to see the stars for the first time in my life," he replied.

"There were very few clear nights after the power went out. I always treasured those moments." Janet reflected on the short nights they could all see the stars, back when Fox was still alive. *Rob, I wish we were able to see the stars during those shitty times.*

"We should get back inside before they send people to put out the fires. There will be people out soon. I expect lockdowns will be swift and invasive."

"You're probably right."

"I know."

Janet followed Jeremiah inside. As they squeezed through the gap and arrived back at the bar, her voice cut through from the back.

"Finally. You two can help me clean now that the Capitol police will be patrolling the streets." She appeared from the back with rags in hand.

I just want to sleep. Janet sighed and walked over to the crone.

CHAPTER FORTY-NINE

CROW SAT ON THE ROOF OF MOTHER'S AND WATCHED AS THE first lights began to come back on over the GUC. First, they started at the UC. The whites and yellows started close to the Capitol then progressed street by street until each one lit up the wall. As he enjoyed the view, he could see people begin to wander out, first cautious, then like nothing had ever happened. He turned to watch the Deep and the Slums. Crow pulled his blanket tighter around him.

The neon lights flickered. Crow watched as they struggled for life underneath their gray film of dust and age. One by one, the streets of the Deep came back to life, and the hustle and bustle of the daily grind started up again. *So different than the UC. They just come out and start pandering.*

He looked up and waited for the few lights of the Slums to click on. They never did. *Odd. Maybe they're doing it on purpose. Keep them down and out, punishment for what Gabriel did.* Crow turned to the Capitol. The fires had been put out late in the day, long after he had gone to bed. Janet had told him in the morning that her and Jeremiah had spoken. There was still no sign or word from Gabriel.

The roof of Mother's was cool. Crow studied the Capitol in the distance. The white lights at the base of it shone brilliantly once again, and for once, Crow felt like he almost admired them. They were a wonder to look at. True human ingenuity. Even though it was oppressive and tumultuous, he knew that he was a part of the same species that had created all of this. *A true marvel. Grand in design. Terrible in practice.*

He sighed and felt almost normal. His thumb ran over the two vials he had left to help him get through the worst of it, but he was jittery. *What if it doesn't work? What then? Do I just go back to the way I was? Do I go back to the drugs? I don't want to. But I know I will.* The cold ache filled his chest. He felt alone and his mouth watered for the cool liquid to flow through him again.

"I'm going to need you to tell me everything," Jeremiah's voice cut in. "And him, too." Crow turned and saw that he was standing with Lew.

"Everything about what?"

"What happened in the Hub." It was a statement rather than a question.

"It was Poin. He came crashing through in one of those cyborg bodies. He said he needed the plan to continue, that they needed it to continue."

"Who is *they*?" Jeremiah asked.

"I don't know. Gabriel got up off the table before Poin fried him. He ripped his head right off. Do you think Poin is dead?"

"Absolutely not. Poin has to be connected to the Hive."

"What's that?"

"It's the entire mainframe of AI, where they come and go, or something like that," Jeremiah said.

"It's more like a central location for them to acquire new

information, a way to transmit knowledge instantaneously. Not so much a place to go, but a place to have always been." Lew spoke up.

"I'm not sure I understand."

"That's alright. It's not important to you, but it has led to interesting thoughts and problems now that we know Poin isn't solely a part of Gabriel's mainframe. With him out in the world, that leaves incredible dilemmas for us. And Gabriel, of course," Lew said.

I wish these two would include me in on what's going on, but I understand why. The thought made Crow irritable, but he knew he didn't have the right to be. He had to earn their trust, because the last time they trusted him, he ruined it, and he knew that it had soured his relationships with everyone.

"Let's go," Jeremiah said to Lew as he turned and walked away. "We have work to be done."

Crow watched as his black jacket swooshed as he walked away. *The more time passes, the more Jeremiah becomes different. More distant.* He shook his head. *No reason to dwell on it. Worry about yourself for now.* Crow looked up to the Capitol once again and wondered what happened to Gabriel inside of it. There were becoming too many questions and not enough answers. He took a deep breath and closed his eyes. *Just sit here in silence for a moment.*

Crow heard footsteps behind him coming up the stairs. *Great.*

"You gotta come with me," Janet's voice disturbed the moment he tried to have.

"Why?"

"Gabriel."

His name made Crow's hair stand up. His eyes darted away

from the building and over to the woman he had shared a few nights with. *Maria, you know it's not personal, right?*

"He came here?"

"No. He routed a message to our bedroom. His new voice came over the speakers and said we needed to head back to the Hub."

"Why?"

"No clue. He said that Mother couldn't trace his voice, that we needed to leave as soon as possible. I came to get you. Jamal and Bernice left already."

"Did you tell Jeremiah and Lou?"

"No. I don't know if Gabriel wanted them to know. If we get there and he needs them, I'll take the blame," Janet said.

Crow stood up and pulled his blanket tight around him. It had become his comfort as of late. The only thing that was normal in his life. It reminded him of home, almost. *That's what life is about now. Small comforts. No more grand events to bring about happiness, only small moments.* He shuffled behind Janet as they walked down the stairs and went through Mother's.

As they reached the door, he heard the old woman clamoring behind them as she entered the main room clinking glasses together.

"Where are you two off to?"

"Don't answer her, just keep going," Janet whispered as she opened the door and walked outside.

"I'll remember that, you hear?"

"What was that about?" Crow asked.

"She had me helping her clean all night. I'm exhausted. We don't have time for her games right now. We have to get to the Hub and see what Gabriel needs."

"I'm still unsure about all of this, you know?"

"Yeah, well you used to tell me how to live, so here I am. Living."

"It was a different time."

"Feels like ages ago now, doesn't it?" Janet turned back to him.

"Yeah. It really does. How long ago has it really been? Only a few months now, right?"

"Something like that. Ever since the power went out and I hooked up with you, I stopped keeping track of the days. It's just a nightmare to try and keep a schedule, you know?"

"Wake up and survive it seems. The new story of our lives." Crow sighed as they trundled through the Deep toward tight alleys and buildings stacked on top of one another.

The cars and scooters were back, this time floating higher than usual. Crow watched as they crossed paths above the lower buildings, maybe fifty feet or so from the ground. *I wonder why they're so high up now? Maybe to let the people roam, since they've been locked inside?* The thoughts wandered through his head as they closed in on an entrance to the Hub. Janet walked up to the door and pushed against it. It did not budge.

"How do we get in without someone's implant?" Crow asked her.

"I don't know. The hole in the roof?" He watched Janet look above the door and wave at the small camera they both knew was there. The door opened.

"Well, I guess he's home," Crow stated as he followed Janet inside. She didn't reply.

The air felt dingy as they walked through the old hallways that they had called home. None of the lights were on yet. Crow could see the glow of the streets above coming from the room down the hall. He knew it was from the hole Poin had made.

Both of them tip-toed closer, and he could have sworn that they held their breath the entire way as they went.

Inside, Acacia's body was still on the floor. The smell had begun to travel to Crow's nostrils before he saw the body. *Why didn't he do anything about her? Give her some respect, at least.*

"Okay, but where is he?" Janet asked aloud.

"No clue. Kitchen?"

They turned and walked back the way they had come, turning left into the kitchen. It was pitch black. Even the faint glow from the neons above couldn't help them. There was a clink, then a rumble as the floor shook. A door opened in the far-right corner where the two walls met. Yellow light poured out.

"Come down here," Gabriel's voice erupted from the corridor.

Crow looked at Janet. They shrugged together, not knowing that there was a deeper corridor to this ant colony.

The room was small and spartan. It had one holoscreen, and old tech that Crow recognized. There were gray computer monitors from the eighties and movable LED ring-lights. Around the room, multiple corkboards had papers thumb-tacked to them.

"What's with all of this?" Crow asked as he spun in a circle, taking in the new atmosphere.

"This is my passion," Gabriel replied. He was standing over a wooden table. Sparks flew from his hand. "My little comforts. Babyle enjoyed his books; Acacia liked the chaos of her holo-screens—made her feel like she was in a simulation. I like the old world you used to live in, way before everything happened for you. Fell in love with those old movies and commercials of kids sitting in front of the wooden televisions with their old games."

"So, you kept it a secret for yourself amongst all of this," Crow waved his hand around.

"Yes. Better to not be personal with anyone so I can focus on my work and the job to be done." Gabriel's new head looked up from his hand and back to Crow.

"I think I get it," Crow said.

"It's just to protect himself from anyone and anything. A false sense of security by playing the mysterious man," Janet interjected.

"You're right. And now look where it has gotten me. My only friends are dead, and I am a living failure. Stuck in a body not my own. Piecing together old parts until I find new ones so I can continue the mission."

"Are you a failure, then, if the mission can continue?" Crow asked.

"Yes. Because I did not complete it the first time," Gabriel turned away and went back to work on his hand.

"Then why did you call us here? Why not get Lew, or Jeremiah? Also, where are Jamal and Bernice?"

"I sent them away. They'll be in the safe in the Slums for a while. I don't know if I can trust Jeremiah, and Lew is too green, too inquisitive for my own liking. You two will be needed."

"For what?"

"You'll burn this place down when I'm done."

"What do you mean?" Janet shot back.

"No hidden meaning. You will burn down this entire place when I walk out. Then you will help me."

"With what?"

"Setting up a new Hub. A new haven for us to work out of."

Crow heard Janet sigh. She was clearly becoming frustrated with the back and forth.

"But then what, Gabriel? How do you stop all of this?"

"I don't know yet. I relied too much on Poin, and he is working for Astar. This entire place is run by the Hive."

"Who is Astar?" Crow asked.

"He's either a cyborg or a robot. I do not know which yet. I saw the metal underneath his skin before he flung me from his suite. He knew everything, knew who I was, what I was doing, and he let me get up there. A goddamn pawn," he smashed his fist into the table and shattered it.

Crow and Janet both jumped at the noise and Gabriel's reaction.

"Then we have to figure out how to stop the Hive. Or find more information on Astar," Crow said.

"That's easier said than done," Gabriel walked over to another table and made more sparks fly as he took small moments to lift his arm and examine his hand.

"Well, let's get started," Crow looked to Janet, who nodded in return.

"Find me in the Slums. I'll be near the Furnaces. Look for the building with the red neon for soup. In it you will find an old man. Tell him I sent you. He will take you where you need to go."

Crow watched as Gabriel moved his fingers, then proceeded up the staircase. They both followed him to Acacia's body.

"Click this button, then this button. Leave the way you came," Gabriel handed them a small black device. It was almost rectangular, but its edges were rounded off, like a football that was smushed. Crow handled it while Janet stared.

"Why can't you do this?" She asked.

"I can't bring myself to. I need someone else to burn it all down for me. For her," Gabriel glanced at Acacia's body. "Thank you," he said before he crouched and jumped through the hole

Poin made. His body took off and Crow was astounded by the mobility of it.

"I guess we burn it down for him, then," he said.

"I guess."

"Need anything before we go?"

"No. I don't think so. You?"

"No, but I wish I didn't have to destroy this place. All that stuff downstairs brought back memories. Lots of nostalgia there," Crow said.

"Yeah, I recognized some of it, but it's foggy memories," Janet replied.

Crow punched the two buttons Gabriel had told them about. He felt the device grow warm. Red lights flickered on. It shown two minutes and started counting down.

"Hell, he didn't waste any time," Crow said.

"Did you expect any different?"

"No," he said as he placed it near Acacia's body.

They ran like hell up the stairs and towards the Slums. Before they got three blocks away through the neon glow of the Deep, they felt the blast of the bomb, then heard its cacophonous roar tear through the GUC. Crow turned to take a look at their doing. From the Hub there was a column of reds, oranges, and yellows as they swirled together with the black and gray smoke. Behind it, he could see the Capitol. Two towers stood now in the GUC, one as a symbol or oppression and one as defiance.

I guess that's one way to send her off.

CHAPTER FIFTY

JANET WENT INSIDE AND TOLD THE MAN WAITING FOR THEM THAT Gabriel had told them to come to this place. The man didn't respond, only turned away and opened the door he stood in front of. He waved his arm to allow them in.

She looked at him as they passed. His wrinkles held secrets in the folds of the years that hung below his eyes. Yet, they were still kind.

The hallway was littered with belongings. Clothes, boxes, metal, wood, busted neon signs, pretty much anything that was worn down from the Deep had come to reside in this hallway, Janet assumed.

The room at the end of the hallway had more junk lying about, though it had a homey vibe Janet appreciated. Each wall had neon signs plugged in and lit up. Some were in Chinese, or Japanese, she wasn't really sure which. Others had symbols for food, or medication. In the center of the room was a massive round wooden table which had eight seats around it, and could definitely fit at least four more. There was an old white refrigerator next to a metal sink on the corner. They weren't dirty and rundown like the rest of the stuff in the room. Janet pulled out a chair, and she watched as Crow did the same. She could see the beads of sweat on his forehead now, and how wet his hair had become.

"You should sit down," she said.

"Yeah, I agree." She watched him walk over, pull out a wooden chair and wrap himself in his blanket. *He's lost a lot. I don't know if he's going to make it.*

Janet stood up and wandered around the room, looking at all of the neon and junk lining the countertops. It was like Gabriel's basement room in the Hub, only without the clutter and with more of a design to it. Everything here looked like it had a purpose, that it was placed with meaning to set a mood or a vibe. The neon signs were stacked sometimes three or four to a wall and then continued in a line around most of the room. All of them bounced and complemented each other in ways Janet wasn't entirely sure of, but it was appealing to the eye.

"I'm glad you made it here," she heard Gabriel's voice come from a corner by the refrigerator.

"Hidden door?" Crow asked.

"No, just a trick of the eye. There's a hallway in that corner but the shadows cast make it seem like a corner to the room." Janet heard Gabriel chuckle. It was almost too fake to be real, his robot body trying to mimic human joy and laughter.

"What is this place?" Janet asked.

"Where I started. My first days leaving the Slums started here. I toiled away in this room, working with Poin on a plan, any plan we could come up with to live a better life. Then I decided the only way to live a better life was to make sure everyone else around me did, too."

"But those people you want to live better lives, some have died in the process," Janet shot back.

"Yes, I feel greatly terrible for it. If I could do this without any losses, I would. But no revolution is without casualties. Any history book, or data mined onto a Holopad will show you that. It's best for me to continue on and not labor away wondering how many lives I could have saved, but how many I will save. It's a sacrifice I have to make and choose, otherwise there will forever be a Capitol running the GUC. People too often don't want to make those hard decisions, especially at the expense of themselves or people they love. It's human nature, built into us to not want to die or see others die. They would rather live under the weight of their oppressors until they burst at the seams than stand up. So, I'm doing it for them. I'll stand up and change their world for the better."

"You sound like him," Janet looked over to Crow. "What's the next step? Where do you go from here?"

Janet watched as Gabriel leaned against the countertop and stared into the neon glow of one of the signs.

"I'm still working on it," he said. "Without Poin, there's a limitation on it. All of this. I need someone on the inside."

"Can't you just get another AI to do it? To be a part of the Hive?" Janet asked.

"It's not so easy when I'm not sure I can trust one."

"What if you put my consciousness into it?" Crow's voice clicked through the conversation.

Silence filled the room for a moment.

"That's not possible, is it?" Janet looked over to Gabriel.

"Technically, with the right neural mapping, I could create a mainframe for you to reside in like I've done to myself. Only your consciousness wouldn't have a body to recognize itself.

That might be a problem. You might go insane from not having a body, but I think that's possible."

"You're not doing it," Janet said to Crow.

"Why? I'm already fucking dying here from my own mistakes. I'm going through withdrawal from all the drugs. I can hardly stand. I'm pissing out of my ass every hour. Why can't I do what I want with my body?"

Janet stood in silence for a moment. *It's just not right. To become something like that. But he's right, he's going to die at this rate.*

"Exactly," Crow said. "How do we do this?"

"I have to get some stuff set up, then we can begin the transfer. Start off small, have you black-boxed in a room with a camera and mic separate from the Hive. Make sure you're okay, then we can release you into a different room, then go from there."

"Can you bring him back if something goes wrong?"

"Hypothetically, yes. But his body is going to be braindead. There's a very small window for that. Unless we get another one of these," Gabriel motioned to himself. "I'm going to get started on the process," he said before Janet could say anything.

She watched him leave through the hallway next to the white refrigerator.

"Are you sure you want to be doing this?"

"Absolutely. I don't have anything left. All I am is this failing body."

She watched him shiver as he pulled the blanket closer around him. His sweat had turned it dark gray almost all over.

CHAPTER FIFTY-ONE

CROW LAID DOWN ON A METALLIC TABLE. GABRIEL STOOD BEHIND him and attached wires and little sticky pads to his scalp.

So this is it, huh? This is what I've done with my life? Out of all the good and the bad I say goodbye to this body. Is this dying? Transcending to somewhere else? His thoughts raced as he continued to shiver and shake from the withdrawal. Crow turned his head and saw Janet standing in the corner, her arms folded. She looked worried, and angry all at once.

"Please stare at the ceiling," Gabriel's voice flashed into his head.

"I'm gonna have a voice like Poin's soon," he said, trying to come to terms with what was about to happen. It didn't feel real to him, some surreal moment in his life that couldn't possibly occur.

"Yes. It will be odd but you will find it rather relaxing once you get ahold of it."

"How are you doing, Janet?"

"I have my opinions. But there's no stopping fate, I guess."

"Still trying to decide if the world is governed by a greater existence or just left in the hands of us, huh?" Crow laughed and heard her laugh too.

"Still an asshole through all of this."

"Absolutely," they laughed together.

"Done," Gabriel said. Crow heard his footsteps wander off and knew he was heading to the holoscreen he would work at.

"Where am I gonna go when this happens? What's it like?"

"Think of it as sleeping, except you'll know the entire time. Your eyes will be new, and you'll be looking on as the dreams unfold around you. The cameras will show you us, and you'll see the world as something different. If we get another robotic body, it will be much easier to transfer to after all of this is said and done."

"I'm scared, you know that?" Crow felt tears run down his face.

"As with all things that are uncertain in life. You either jump in and live, or stagnate and die."

Crow tried to take a deep breath and felt his body shake from emotions rather than the lack of drugs.

"Ready?" Gabriel asked.

"Ready," he said. Tears began to pour and Crow struggled to breathe.

"Initiating upload."

There was a small static hum as all of the wires attached to Crow began to crackle to life. He felt himself slipping and growing tired. The world around him was foggy. He closed his eyes.

Maria, Lucy, if this is the end, I'm coming. I love you. Crow's last thoughts crackled over the speakers.

THE END OF BOOK TWO

THANK YOU FOR READING

Please consider leaving a review. As an Indie author, they help me greatly with getting exposure.
Book Three (Untitled) coming soon.
You can sign up for my mailing list to stay updated, get a sneak peek, or some other fun stuff. I promise I don't spam.

Instagram: NicholasTurnerAuthor
Twitter: NicholasTrieste
Website: Nicholastrieste.wixsite.com/nicholasturner